{ REBECCA WENTWORTH'S DISTRACTION }

Other Books by Robert J. Begiebing

CRITICISM:

Acts of Regeneration: Allegory and Archetype in the Works of Norman Mailer (1981)

Toward a New Synthesis: John Fowles, John Gardner, and Norman Mailer (1989)

The Literature of Nature: The British and American Traditions (1990) (a critical anthology with V. Owen Grumbling)

FICTION:

The Strange Death of Mistress Coffin (1991)

The Adventures of Allegra Fullerton; Or, A Memoir of Startling and Amusing Episodes from Itinerant Life (1999)

HARDSCRABBLE BOOKS—*Fiction of New England*

Laurie Alberts, *Lost Daughters*

Laurie Alberts, *The Price of Land in Shelby*

Thomas Bailey Aldrich, *The Story of a Bad Boy*

Robert J. Begiebing, *The Adventures of Allegra Fullerton; Or, A Memoir of Startling and Amusing Episodes from Itinerant Life*

Robert J. Begiebing, *Rebecca Wentworth's Distraction*

Anne Bernays, *Professor Romeo*

Chris Bohjalian, *Water Witches*

Dona Brown, ed., *A Tourist's New England: Travel Fiction, 1820–1920*

Joseph Bruchac, *The Waters Between: A Novel of the Dawn Land*

Joseph A. Citro, *The Gore*

Joseph A. Citro, *Guardian Angels*

Joseph A. Citro, *Lake Monsters*

Joseph A. Citro, *Shadow Child*

Sean Connolly, *A Great Place to Die*

J. E. Fender, *The Private Revolution of Geoffrey Frost: Being an Account of the Life and Times of Geoffrey Frost, Mariner, of Portsmouth, in New Hampshire, as Faithfully Translated from the Ming Tsun Chronicles, and Diligently Compared with Other Contemporary Histories*

Dorothy Canfield Fisher (Mark J. Madigan, ed.), *Seasoned Timber*

Dorothy Canfield Fisher, *Understood Betsy*

Joseph Freda, *Suburban Guerrillas*

Castle Freeman, Jr., *Judgment Hill*

Frank Gaspar, *Leaving Pico*

Robert Harnum, *Exile in the Kingdom*

Ernest Hebert, *The Dogs of March*

Ernest Hebert, *Live Free or Die*

Ernest Hebert, *The Old American*

Sarah Orne Jewett (Sarah Way Sherman, ed.), *The Country of the Pointed Firs and Other Stories*

Lisa MacFarlane, ed., *This World Is Not Conclusion: Faith in Nineteenth-Century New England Fiction*

G. F. Michelsen, *Hard Bottom*

Anne Whitney Pierce, *Rain Line*

Kit Reed, *J. Eden*

Rowland E. Robinson (David Budbill, ed.), *Danvis Tales: Selected Stories*

Roxana Robinson, *Summer Light*

Rebecca Rule, *The Best Revenge: Short Stories*

Catharine Maria Sedgwick (Maria Karafilis, ed.), *The Linwoods: or, "Sixty Years Since" in America*

R. D. Skillings, *How Many Die*

R. D. Skillings, *Where the Time Goes*

Lynn Stegner, *Pipers at the Gates of Dawn: A Triptych*

Theodore Weesner, *Novemberfest*

W. D. Wetherell, *The Wisest Man in America*

Edith Wharton (Barbara A. White, ed.), *Wharton's New England: Seven Stories and Ethan Frome*

Thomas Williams, *The Hair of Harold Roux*

Suzi Wizowaty, *The Round Barn*

REBECCA WENTWORTH'S DISTRACTION

A Novel

 Robert J. Begiebing

University Press of New England
HANOVER AND LONDON

Published by University Press of New England, 37 Lafayette St., Lebanon, NH 03766

© 2003 by Robert J. Begiebing

Printed in the United States of America

5 4 3 2 1

LIBRARY OF CONGRESS CATALOGING-IN-PUBLICATION DATA

Begiebing, Robert J., 1946–

Rebecca Wentworth's distraction : a novel / Robert J. Begiebing.

  p.   cm. — (Hardscrabble books)

ISBN 1–58465–284–5 (cloth : alk. paper)

1. New Hampshire—History—Colonial period, ca. 1600–1775—Fiction.

2. Portsmouth (N.H.)—Fiction. I. Title. II. Series.

PS3552.E372R43 2003

813'.54—dc21   2003007372

{ ACKNOWLEDGMENTS }

I want to thank several kind friends and colleagues whose wise advice has saved me from myself during the revisions of this novel and whose support keeps me scribbling: Bob Craven, Merle Drown, Bob Hoddeson, Loftus Jestin, Wesley McNair, Jack Scovil, and Moira Sieker. My wife, Linda, continues to be the first and last of my readers and my most patient supporter. Thank you all.

A number of librarians have helped me, as well, throughout the research process. Such devoted professionals are no doubt the unsung heroes of many a book. Any attempt to name them all would inevitably, I fear, leave out some crucial expert. So, I will say instead that the professional and most courteous staff members at several libraries have willingly lent their intelligence, curiosity, and knowledge to my eccentric needs as a writer of historical fiction. My most sincere thanks to the library and reference staffs at the American Antiquarian Society, the Portsmouth Athenaeum, the Special Collections Department of the University of New Hampshire, and the Thayer Cummings Library and Archives at Strawbery Banke. For many years, moreover, reference and interlibrary loan colleagues at my own institution, Southern New Hampshire University, have been helpful professionals and friends.

Southern New Hampshire University granted me a sabbatical and a summer research grant to work on this book. I am very grateful for that institutional support.

Spring 2002

R.J.B.

This novel represents the third installment of a New England historical series covering two hundred years from 1648 to 1850. *The Strange Death of Mistress Coffin,* set in the seventeenth century, and *The Adventures of Allegra Fullerton,* set in the nineteenth, are the two previously published installments. Since this novel, *Rebecca Wentworth's Distraction,* is set in the eighteenth century, it is of course the middle narrative of a trilogy. For reasons that I myself don't entirely understand, I had to write about (which is to say "live in") the seventeenth and nineteenth centuries before I could turn to the eighteenth. Anyone who has read the previous two novels will recognize some continuity of themes and characters—family and economic lineage, especially—but such recognition is, I hope, not necessary to enjoying the story told here.

This book is dedicated to

my most enduring reader:

Patricia Begiebing

{ REBECCA WENTWORTH'S DISTRACTION }

1741

Old Portsmouth was crowded between what is now Pleasant Street and the river; it is easy to imagine the waterside streets and alleys frequented by sailors in pigtails and petticoats; the mighty carousals and roaring choruses; the dingy, well-smoked dram shops; the stews and slums of back streets, and the jolly larks and affrays with the night watch.

— Samuel Adams Drake,
   Nooks and Corners of the New England Coast

Yet even there (without nobility, or orders of gentry) you might see proof how necessarily some difference in rank, some inequality must and ought to grow up in every society and how Eutopian and ridiculous the contrary idea and attempt is. The inhabitants of the town by more information, better polish and greater intercourse with strangers, insensibly acquired an ascendancy over the farmer of the country; the richer merchants of these towns, together with the clergy, lawyers, physicians and officers of the English navy who had occasionally settled there, were considered as gentry; even a member of the Church of England gave a kind of distinctive fashion.

— Arthur Browne, Anglican minister to Portsmouth, 1736–1773

Chapter 1

DANIEL SANBORN THOUGHT he had good reason to feel pleased with himself. He had, six months ago, survived a harrowing Atlantic crossing from Bristol, England, and then endured the exceptionally deep snows of his first January and February in Boston. He had staked his future as a young portrait painter on the prospect of patrons in New England, and despite the presence of Joseph Badger, Robert Feke, and above all John Smibert, he had indeed found several patrons. He had managed to slip into Boston during yet another cessation of hostilities between the French and English. He had arrived in New England sufficiently after the epidemic of throat distemper to avoid that plague. And now, several years following the great earthquake as well, at the age of twenty-two, he found himself for a second day aboard a coastal sloop with gaily painted topsides and bright trim sailing in sunny weather from Boston to Portsmouth. In his portmanteau was a letter of commission from one of the most prominent families in the seaport, indeed in the colonies. He had every reason to believe that any association with the Brownes and Wentworths, yoked by marriage, was cause for unbridled hope.

That afternoon, upon disembarking and finding his way by hired chaise to the Browne manse, he was not disappointed. The fine brick house, three-storied with a gambrel roof and dormers, sat above the waterfront where Squire William Browne might keep an eye on his ships or cargoes at the docks and riding at anchor in the Pool. Two young black men wearing gardener's livery were attending the shrubbery. As he walked toward the front door, Sanborn admired a large, polished brass door handle and escutcheon plate. At the top doorstep he reached for the heavy brass knocker, perfectly centered in the paneling and in the shape of a dolphin, and knocked.

When the front door opened, Sanborn faced a haughty, well-spoken, old white man wearing a crisp Saxon blue frieze jacket with small metal buttons and slash sleeves lined with white bays—no doubt a family retainer from a previous generation. His scarlet breeches topped snow-white stockings. He ordered a black child to take Sanborn's baggage and showed Sanborn through a long stair hall and into an ample, high-ceilinged parlor lighted by substantial windows. He was left alone to admire the rich, well-molded paneling of the fireplace surround, the cupboard built into the chimney splays (replete with china plate, pudding dishes, wine glasses, and punch bowls), the oval tea table, and shapely chairs. After he dawdled in these pleasant circumstances for perhaps a quarter hour, Madam Browne herself came to greet him.

"Ah, Mr. Sanborn!" she said, entering sideways gracefully to manipulate her hoop-petticoat through the doorway. "You have arrived safe and, to all appearances, quite sound."

"Indeed, Madam Browne." He bowed.

They exchanged pleasantries over his means of finding them, the beautiful weather, and the peace and prosperity enjoyed in Portsmouth and abroad. She ordered tea, without asking whether he might prefer coffee or cider. She was an ebullient woman in, perhaps, her late thirties, well dressed, but not given to fashionable excess.

"Mr. Smibert highly recommends you," she said.

"He's very kind, madam."

"Nonetheless, he would not send to us some unpolished dauber, I'm certain."

As she took her first sip of tea, she peered at him over her china dish.

He recalled his efforts of self-restraint with Mr. Smibert. He had not wished to appear arrogant, though barring Smibert he believed himself to be the most accomplished and best-trained portraitist in New England. He knew he needed Smibert's support, and hiding his pride in his own accomplishment had paid off.

"My old friend Mrs. Apthorp wrote also to speak well of you," she continued.

"I shall do my best to give satisfaction, madam."

"I don't doubt it, Mr. Sanborn. Mr. Smibert is well?"

"Well enough, yes, but he no longer travels to paint."

"So I understand," she said. "The terms in his letter meet our requirements, as you know."

He bowed slightly from his chair.

"That you are to have comfortable quarters here and ten guineas for a single portrait. Whole length."

"That is my understanding, indeed, Mrs. Browne."

"Half payable upon acceptance of the commission," she continued.

"Such is the usual practice, madam."

"Good," she said. "It is agreed then."

"I am pleased to be of service."

She nodded and took another sip of tea.

"I have but one question remaining," he said.

"By all means, Mr. Sanborn."

"Of whom is the portrait to be? Which member of the family, I mean to say."

"Oh, of course," she said. "It is to be of our daughter, Rebecca."

"Of the child alone?"

Madam Browne nodded again, her body remaining perfectly erect. "Indeed, particularly as she is our only child."

"It's a blessing she survived the distemper, Madam Browne. There were fearful stories about as soon as I reached Boston. God willing, we have passed this scourge."

"God willing, Mr. Sanborn."

He dared not ask whether they had lost any children in the plague that had appeared intermittently over a period of years. He wondered whether there were any other children in the household, but of course he could not make any such inquiries.

"She is even now in the back garden," Mrs. Browne said. "Would you like to meet her?"

"By all means," he said. He liked to see his subjects first comfortable in their own surroundings.

"It is such a perfect summer's afternoon."

They rose together. She led him into the large back garden, along a path of small stones between planting beds, to where a child of about twelve years sat under a bower of white blossoms. The girl was dressed all in white, to the point, he thought, of affectation. She was reading from a book richly bound in deep maroon leather and did not notice their entrance. The mother and Mr. Sanborn stood by a moment and watched the child, as if arrested by their view of a garden creature of fantastical charm.

But the child rose quickly to be introduced, curtsied, and looked directly, even boldly he thought, into Daniel Sanborn's eyes.

"Mother says you are to paint me," she said after being introduced. She smiled and continued to search his face.

"Quite so, miss," he said. "We can start our first sitting at your convenience."

"Tomorrow morning, I should think," Madam Browne said. She looked at both of them in turn as if for acceptance of the idea.

"Oh yes, Mother, please," Rebecca said. "As soon as you wish, Mr. Sanborn."

Mrs. Browne suggested a few of Rebecca's other obligations that afternoon, "while Mr. Sanborn settles in," as she put it. So they promised to meet in the parlor at ten o'clock in the morning.

When the girl left, Mrs. Browne turned to him. "Just the usual pillar or whatnot, Mr. Sanborn, will prove adequate. Or some pastoral portal or other. But we'd prefer her true dress and likeness otherwise."

"You can rely on me, madam."

THE NEXT MORNING Sanborn had set up his easel and paint box. He had stretched a particularly fine-woven canvas. After a five-minute wait the child came in, dressed just as she had been upon their first meeting. They chose a comfortable spot for her to sit and he arranged her posture to suit his craft.

"How many sittings do you expect, Mr. Sanborn?" Rebecca asked after he had begun.

"I'm not sure. Perhaps four?"

"May I see the canvas as you progress?"

"It might unsettle me to have the object of my study comment on her own developing aspect." He smiled.

"I promise not to comment." She was once again looking into his eyes. It seemed an innocent boldness, however.

"You promise," he stated flatly while he concentrated on some preliminary sketching. The surface of the canvas felt pleasurably smooth.

"Indeed, Mr. Sanborn."

"Indeed? Why such interest in the emerging object? Because it is yourself appearing ever more boldly upon the canvas?"

"No, sir, but because I myself daub a paper or board now and then."

"Is that so? I see. Well, you're hoping for some free lessons then." He chuckled, trying to put her at ease. Yet he suddenly recognized that she was already completely at her ease. She might have been a belle in her twenties, he thought, as he continued his preliminary sketches.

He ignored her request for the moment and concentrated on his work. He felt strangely dull, as if his journey, or perhaps her comeliness, had disoriented him. She would be a challenge to any painter, certainly. Yet this was a very important commission to him, and he thought of himself as an excellent draftsman. With one exception, his few patrons in Boston had been of a lesser sort. As might be expected. He knew from the start of his career that he would not be hired, particularly by the fashionable set, in London and the English countryside. Too much competition and secured patronage about for that. Not only the old British masters still in practice, but a gaggle of foreigners—Moses, Rusca, Soldi, Vandermyn, Vanloo. Even a man of Smibert's capability, whom George Vertue once ranked above Hogarth, had been wise in his time to escape these crowded fields for the gaping boroughs of America.

This commission seemed auspicious to him, as if his life was about to turn.

"Oh, I've never had any real lessons, only a little help from my tutor," she was saying. "Nor do I think I'd like any lessons, Mr.

Sanborn. But I'm very interested in how a painter such as yourself accomplishes his work."

Saucy little thing, he thought. He did not respond right away, and she remained quiet.

Perhaps two or three minutes passed before he said, "Is that so?"

"Yes, Mr. Sanborn."

"Well, if you promise to say nothing, I suppose there's no harm in it. If you're so keen on seeing my artifice."

"Oh, thank you, sir!" she blurted, more like the girl she was now.

He always engaged his sitters in conversation, but he found this child unsettling—whether she saw his depiction of her or not. He shook off his feelings as foolish.

"Do you always dress in white, Rebecca?"

"Spring and summer."

"And what about fall and winter?"

"Oh, then I dress in colors. But Mother allows only the deeper hues, nothing so bright as I might wish."

A garden fairy. The idea amused him. Perhaps he should paint her in a garden instead of conventional interiors. But he recalled his patron's request and gave up the idea. She would look like a flower within doors nonetheless. And a rare flower to boot, rather exotic, by the look and sound of her.

He began to apply his brush to the canvas and the conversation went on in a somewhat more aimless fashion. She loved to read. She loved to arrange flowers. She loved to paint. Then finally more questions: Did he like New England? With whom had he studied in London? What was his source of this pigment or that? What was his first impression of Portsmouth? And so on. She rambled without the decorous reticence more typical of well-bred children, but her queries seemed pointed and purposeful. He didn't know what to make of her.

She had, as promised, said not a word upon looking over his work for that day. But her quiet study of his technique, even his fumbling here and there, disarmed him nonetheless. Before he realized what he had said, he asked whether she might in turn show him something of her own. She was delighted. She bid him sit in a chair while she fetched two specimens for him.

He sat down, tired from his labors. Within several minutes she returned bearing two canvasses. They were conventional subjects— flowers in urns (almost Italianate in spirit) and two small dogs lying upon a floral-patterned rug. But they were so strikingly executed, even in their untutored way, that he could not believe she had done them herself.

"These are quite extraordinary," he said as he held the canvasses up one at a time. "And you say you've never had lessons?"

"Not proper lessons or study, Mr. Sanborn. You like them?"

"Well, I don't know if 'like' is the right word, but they are extraordinary. Let's say I appreciate them."

He was being honest now, but there was something more about the paintings he could not yet understand. Some energy expressed in them: the flowers and the little dogs presenting an unusual animation and verve. They were more like the work of previous centuries or distant lands. There was nothing of the painting master in them, nor the schoolmaster. They were proudly independent, but true and powerful in a completely unfamiliar way for all that. Most of his own masters would not approve. He did not allow himself to believe she had done them herself. Still, she was his sitter and he was being well paid. They would have to get along for several days. As for his misgivings, he kept his mouth shut. But whoever had painted these two was alarmingly gifted in some incomprehensible way.

He painted into the afternoon, when they stopped for dinner. Sanborn cleaned up and walked out into the sunshine. He squinted into the streets, trying to get his bearings. Above the roofs, ship masts swayed and flashed and flickered like silver in the golden light of early afternoon. Would it be possible to paint just what he saw, he wondered, as his eyes began to adjust. He did not allow his mind to think about how it might be done. He was hungry. Moreover, people would not pay for paintings of town or harbor before they would pay for portraits. He had better heed his own true interests; he had better garner more portrait commissions soon if he wished to survive here. He wandered down to the waterfront where he found a huckster selling quick meals of sausage and bread out of his cookshop.

When he returned to the manse, he tinkered with the portrait for an hour more and then quit out of fatigue. His long journey and his careful painting had left him exhausted still. Yet after a few hours of sleep that night he awoke fretful. He kept seeing the paintings behind his closed eyes. As he dozed he dreamed of them. At times he grew angry for her apparent lying to him. A certain trust must be established between the painter and the sitter. If she was a sweet little flower, might there be some bitterness to be discovered behind the floriferousness as well?

Chapter 2

REBECCA, IN A NEW WHITE DRESS, sat for Sanborn the following morning. He had prepared his canvas and carefully arranged his smudgepan, pencils, and maulstick. On his palette were vermilion, burnt ocher, Indian red, pink, umber, black, and, finally, a stiff lake and, closest to his thumb, white.

He tried to make pleasing conversation with her. The painting went very well, he thought, during the first hour or so. Despite his lack of sufficient sleep, he found he had energy and attention. They began to relax in one another's company. Still, somewhere during the second hour the constraints of posture and labor began to wear on them and his mind turned to what he suspected were her betrayals. In the third hour both of them were feeling impatient. He decided to give up for the day.

She looked at the painting, as they had agreed she might. She said, "Oh, yes. Now I see," but made no other comment upon her face and form as it more clearly emerged from the canvas.

"By next sitting this should be quite recognizable," he said. "I've little more than dead colored the face."

"Oh, yes," she repeated. But she kept her promise to make no comment or judgment. She seemed to wait for him to speak.

"May I see more of yours?" he said as he cleaned up.

"Perhaps tomorrow," she said. "I have sundry responsibilities this afternoon."

He found her way of speaking odd, too—not like a child's speech, even a well-bred child. Maybe it was all that reading she spoke of. What he really wished to see was how she painted, or, more accurately, whether she herself actually painted such things. He would devise some ploy.

THE NEXT DAY, he finally finished the portrait. Perhaps it was not his very best portrait to date, but certainly respectable and rather accomplished. Even his own mentors—Highmore, Hudson, Kent, and other masters of the Academy of St. Martin's Lane— might have to agree. The Brownes would not be disappointed, surely. He might well garner other commissions hereabouts. He no longer felt tired or anxious.

"What do you think, Rebecca?" He had to ask, finally.

"What do I think, sir?"

"Yes, how does it seem to you, now it's finished?"

"I promised not to comment, Mr. Sanborn."

He laughed. "That's all right. I've completed my work, so it will not matter, to this painting, if you express your response to it."

"If it won't matter, I should remain silent in any case."

"I don't mean it that way. I mean it won't distract me from the work. Not now." He gave her his best avuncular smile. "Well?"

She turned her full attention to the painting. "I think that it is quite good, Mr. Sanborn. I especially like the dress. The folds and color—your drapery is accomplished." She seemed satisfied with that pronouncement.

"And? What of yourself then?"

"The face, you mean?"

"And the form."

"Well, sir, the face is a good likeness, but I appear a little dull, unfeeling, perhaps a little drowned in cloth. I suppose it is the tedium of my sitting." She looked at him, smiled, and then turned back to the picture. "And the hands, were they a little stiff, rather like a doll's?" She held up her hands and inspected them. "Now I see that even my pose, precisely as I sat, is rather . . ." — she searched a moment for the best word — "derived."

He was taken aback. "I'm not sure what you mean, Rebecca. I paint according to the best principles, and within the tradition of my masters, and theirs before them."

"Oh yes, I see that." She smiled pleasantly. "And I know that people of fashion wouldn't hear of anything else. That they by nature chiefly consider the drapery of others, so that it is a necessary imitation of the best models."

"It is rather a kind of *quotation*," he said, emphasizing the last word. "Each artist brings himself to the task, but mindful of his masters and the great tradition of his predecessors." He looked to see if she attended to his words. "Correctness and order must take precedence over a sitter's personal characteristics. Or eccentricities." Perhaps he was being a little stern, he thought, or foolishly impatient with a child.

"Of course," she said, looking at the painting. "The hands are beautifully colored, that tone of the flesh, I mean. And I'm thankful you allowed my own costume. I think it is very good, sir, and that mother will be pleased."

"Thank you," he said. Was that final compliment enough? Or had the child pointed out precisely his weakness: He had never quite learned to bring hands and faces to life. Mr. Highmore had said as much. But few patrons had expected him to vivify faces and hands individually. Some modest degree of characterization, particularly among the male sitters, was sufficient.

"You paint well yourself," he said, "for someone of your age and without training, who has not closely studied preceding artists." He was cleaning up and being as matter-of-fact as he knew how to be.

"I'm curious as to how you learned to do it. Perhaps you could show me?"

"I taught myself, and Miss Norris, my tutor, has given me diverse instruction manuals. And I do observe, when opportunity arises, the work of others. But ever since I could walk, Mother tells me, I was known for standing before papers and boards applying crayon and paint. It has always been the most interesting thing for me to do, for some reason."

"May I see then?"

"I had better consult with Miss Norris," she said and left the room.

She returned in a few minutes and directed him toward an odd little chamber on the first floor behind the kitchen where she and her tutor had rigged a classroom-studio for her lessons. As they passed through the kitchen, they offered their good-days to the cook and her assistant, and Rebecca introduced him to the governess, one Miss Norris, a small but not unappealing woman, who sat at a long table meditatively sipping her tea. Clearly, Rebecca had already explained their mission. She left the door wide, so that the tutor could look in on them from her seat. In the instruction room there were a number of paintings and drawings about, on walls, on tables and desks, on the floor. He hardly noticed them, however, in his desire to see her perform. Again, he asked her to show him how she painted. She went to a trunk and took out some of her implements and colors. She set a board on an easel, prepared herself and her colors, and then looked up at Sanborn.

"Well, Mr. Sanborn," she said. "What shall it be, then?"

"Oh, whatever you like, surely."

"You're not particular?"

"Not at all, Rebecca. Please, suit yourself."

She began immediately with paint, not sketching anything out or experimenting in any way. She worked from the right side of the board toward the left, finishing as she went. It was very odd to watch. Another dog was taking shape, sitting in a garden surrounded by blossoms. Right to left, almost as if someone were slowly unveiling a completed painting. Almost as if she had seen it whole before her brush touched board.

"What would happen if you had started from the left, and moved to the right?" he found himself asking before he had even thought to speak.

"Happen, sir?" she asked, looking directly at him now.

"Could you have done it that way, I mean?"

"Oh." She continued to paint now. "Well, yes, of course."

She put down the more than half completed board and picked up another.

"Like this you mean?" She was painting from the left side now; a still life was being uncovered left to right. Brilliant oranges and deep yellow pears. Other fruit, grapes, beginning to appear. He couldn't speak, even though Miss Norris walked in just then to observe Rebecca's demonstration. He and the governess merely exchanged glances.

It was the same untutored style, full of force—a dog, quick with canine life; fruit, full of succulence. Almost like unearthly objects, yet at the same time utterly recognizable for what they were. He could not imagine how she managed it. For all his living among painters and academies in England, no, he had never seen anything like this, in method or result. He found it a little frightening, but also wonderfully curious. It was as if between Rebecca and whatever she wanted to paint there were no difficult barriers of execution to be scaled. The heavy gates of perspicacity and technique had been thrown wide for her. It was as if she had penetrated the weight of the mundane world and a strange unnatural intensity were pouring onto her painted boards.

He could not speak to her about it. What, after all, could he possibly say? She continued her still life while he stood there incapacitated. When she put down her brush and palette, he still could not speak.

"Shall I finish the dog, sir?"

"No," he managed to say. "No. We're both tired. Thank you. I'll say good-bye to you tomorrow, after I present the portrait to your mother and father." He gave a little bow toward Miss Norris and started to leave. Then he remembered himself. "Rebecca."

"Yes, Mr. Sanborn?"

"Those are quite remarkable." He gestured toward the paintings, one little better than half completed.

"They are indeed," Miss Norris said.

"Thank you, sir. I'm honored by compliments from so accomplished a painter."

He turned again and walked out of the instruction room, offering a brisk good-day to the governess.

 *Chapter 3*

REBECCA, WEARING A FRESH WHITE GOWN, came into the parlor the following morning before her parents arrived. Sanborn was delicately testing the slow progress of the drying oils with his brush on the completed portrait. Her father and mother had not seen it yet, but Sanborn was confident they would be pleased.

She looked at the portrait and answered his query about her parents—yes, indeed, Mr. Sanborn, they were sure to approve the portrait.

"Do you suppose they might like one of themselves, or of one another as well?" he asked.

"It's quite possible, I think. They perhaps first use my portrait to discover the suitability of your brush, Mr. Sanborn. Portsmouth has never had adequate limners."

He paused to consider her audacity. "I would be delighted to do them, but Madam Browne spoke only of yours."

"I suppose that may be because I'm going away soon, and it's possible they want one to remember me by while I'm away."

"Away," he said. It was a flat statement, almost as if he had not understood that she had spoken first.

"To England. Or such is their misguided plan for me."

"Oh? For how long?"

"I don't know, sir. But for a proper schooling, it is. I think they are a little exasperated with me." She giggled quietly.

"Exasperated? Even your tutor?" She nodded. "How can you be exasperating to them?"

"I don't know. But from what they say, I believe that is the reason. A proper training is in order, however, all the same." Her voice had changed as if she were, but just barely, imitating her mother.

"Goodness," he said. "I can't think why. I can't imagine such a thing, having met you and spoken to you myself."

"Still," she said and smiled. "There it is."

He ran out of words again, but soon Madam Browne and her husband, William, walked in. Just behind them came the governess.

Sanborn put down his brush immediately and made a bow. "Sir," he said, "Madam." He invited them by gesture to look at the portrait. Squire William, a man of sixty, made an imposing figure. Much older than his second wife, he was tall and without the portliness of age. Sanborn had heard that he had once been a hero in certain campaigns against "the heathen and their Jesuitical brethren," and as a result of his exploits he held the title of colonel. He was a man of grave dignity and rectitude.

The mother and father were pleased. They had wanted a conventional portrait and he had given them a fine one. He had learned that he always gave satisfaction, after the proper English manner, here in New England. This was something he could do. Something he relished doing. Although he had enjoyed meeting Robert Feke, through Smibert in Boston, for his useful information and anecdotes of New England, he had judged him a self-taught dauber with none of the requisite polish of London society and academy. Now he happily assured himself that Mr. Feke would hardly have pleased a man of Colonel Browne's urbanity and address. It suddenly occurred to him for the first time, however, that these people might have found Rebecca's paintings troubling in some way.

After light conversation expressing his approval, Colonel Browne paid Sanborn the remainder of the agreed-upon sum. They went so far as to suggest there would be others in the port who might require his services. Sanborn beamed. He forgot about Rebecca and her paintings. He imagined himself growing intimate with captains and owners, with weighty bewigged merchants and assemblymen. He would be toasted. He would accrue wealth and respect over the years. He would settle here after all. Why not? The Brownes would provide him entrée.

Of course, he said nothing of all this. He prepared to leave. He went to his room to gather his things after giving the Brownes his card. He said that he would alert them to his new address as soon as he was in lodgings, in the event they should require his services in any way or have any further requests or queries regarding his portrait of Rebecca. He thanked them profusely for the commission, for their faith in him, and promised to return later next week to apply a coat of varnish.

As he was preparing his gear and clothing to leave, there was knock on his door. Rebecca came in at the sound of his voice.

"Sir," she said, "I have another effort of my own that you may be interested to see. And I'd like your opinion of it."

"Certainly, Rebecca." He turned enthusiastically toward her. She unveiled yet another painting, a portrait.

It was a portrait of herself, painted in a pose similar to his own portrait. But the face occupied much more of the canvas, as if to reverse the English tradition displaying chiefly garment or drapery and setting. The portrait showed none of that common ambition to look, in pose and the latest emblems of gentility, like one's aristocratic betters. Nor had the girl produced a literal transposition of herself, or of his painting of her; nor was there any familiar formality—the etiquette and posture of polite society—about the demeanor. The portrait, the face in particular, was alive with the energy he had come to expect, as if her very soul suffused the girlish figure on the canvas. It was so superior to his own (yet so much more strange) that he had to check his rage. His perfect day was to be ruined. His success was to be undercut.

Not that he believed the Brownes would prefer her painting to his. No, but she had affronted his painterly vanity. She had captured an antic vivacity. She had evoked . . . he could think of no other word in the heat of the moment . . . an "otherworldliness."

"Why have you done this?" he said. His voice sounded desperate even to himself.

"Sir?" she said, looking wounded. "I thought you would approve. I thought you found me, my paintings . . . remarkable."

He didn't speak. Was she mocking him? He suppressed a sudden urge to strike her. The Brownes were sending her away. Perhaps there was reason. But he would do nothing to put the family off him.

"Sir?" she finally repeated.

"I must leave," he said, trying to contain himself. "Immediately. I have rooms to get, and my dinner. I have other work to do." This latter was of course a lie; he had no other commissions in Portsmouth. He picked up his bags and walked past her. "Good day, Miss Browne."

When he glanced back, she was standing in the doorway to his room with an utterly confused look on her face, and more than a trace of sorrow.

Chapter 4

AS HE WAS LEAVING, he encountered the governess Miss Norris, who approached him in a kindly, interested manner. He asked whether she could recommend an inexpensive private room. She was pleased to suggest one Widow McCullough, so he was in luck. A small room on the top floor, its single window facing the wharves over sunlit rooftops.

He unpacked his bags and sat looking out his window, getting his bearings and wondering about this child he had painted. He saw now that he had not captured a shred of her strangeness in his portrait. Would he paint a different portrait of her, given another opportunity? Who was she, really? The family was sending her away, yet they were fond enough of her to go to some expense to arrange for her portrait. Where, how, had she acquired her eccentric yet undeniable gifts? And why had she mocked him with a portrait of her own?

As he sat facing his window he grew more convinced that she had intended to show him just how dull he was. She *had* mocked him! Of course she had. But why should he care about a mere child's opinion? He was an academy-trained artist. His portraits were perfectly acceptable to responsible well-bred adults, not merely to men and women in the middle stations of life, as might be pleased by some raw dauber, but to men and women of figure. Why this silly anger at the child then? In fact, the more he thought it over, he found his anger at her effrontery diminishing. It was good to be out of her house. And he was growing hungry for his dinner. He would need to be busy garnering new commissions or return soon to Boston.

He changed into a clean Holland shirt and neck cloth and put on his coat. He looked in the small glass he carried and retied his hair. It was a matter of pride to him that he wore his own abundant brown hair. And why should he—a young man of accomplishment—not be allowed a minor eccentricity? Moreover, he had learned gradually that top people seem to appreciate a plainness of presentation in clothing and hair, a simple elegance unlike their own operatic display. And then, too, they preferred a degree of cultivation. In short, a modest personal presentability seemed to earn their trust, assure their own sense of position, and smooth their delicacies of taste as to the acceptability of associates beneath them. He was, after all, to be entering their homes and spending hours in their company.

Once upon the street he entered the first respectable-looking tavern he came to. He took a seat and began to feel pleased with himself again. Cod and potatoes, and plenty of cider. He would have to advertise, he was thinking. And he would send the Brownes his card with his new address written in, as he had promised. If he could find work within the week, or at most a fortnight, he could stay on. He might well continue the good fortune that had brought him here. And why not?

The afternoon crowd was arriving in small groups; from his corner seat he enjoyed watching and speculating about these people in his newfound home. He was already beginning to think of Portsmouth that way. A good sign, he told himself. He finished his dinner, paid his bill, and went back out into the street bathed in afternoon sunshine. He decided to explore a bit. He would start with the port itself, the wharves and docks—the source of all this wealth. He would see just how it was being done here.

Walking along the water on busy Dock Lane he crossed the swing bridge over the mill creek, noted well the gravid ships at anchor and others upon stocks, met the road from town entering Pickering's Neck, and returned north on that highway past the pound and gallows toward the Parade and market. When he reached the main highway, Graffort's Lane, he followed it back to the waterfront. He thereby discovered that the town's four main streets met in a perfect cross. And that the town itself, situated on a rise of ground overlooking the great tidal river and harbor, afforded a prospect of the surrounding country on all sides. Radiating from these main roads of about thirty feet in width were many irregular and crooked byways, perhaps ten feet wide, with dwellings and with vacant lots used as gardens. He found shops and taverns and many large houses, well sashed and glazed, often of three stories— comforting signs of the wealth he hoped would support him. He had passed two independent meetinghouses and, finally, upon heading north along the waterfront, the Established Church. All these were built of wood and well spired, which spires he recalled observing as he had approached from the sea.

Within an hour he found himself in a tavern again, but this one in a more shabby side street of slop shops and tippling houses. It was filled with seamen, common laborers, and, he suspected, jump-ship sailors and troopers—and even a servant or apprentice enjoying his illegal grog. But he had always been able to travel in all company, so the clientele didn't trouble him. He took a seat at a table where a mild-looking older man nursed his mug of toddy, his dinner dish pushed aside. A pretty yet unkempt serving woman asked whether Sanborn would like dinner, but he asked only for a pitcher of flip, indicating he wished to share it with his table mate. She removed the man's empty dishes.

The man nodded to him when she left.

"Good-day to you, sir," Sanborn said. He smiled. "And a fine day it truly is," he added. The man nodded again in agreement.

They looked about the establishment for a moment without further exchange, as if they were friendly acquaintances assessing the comforts and possibilities of their circumstances. There was a considerable hubbub of laughter and coarse talk and gesture. He rather liked the feeling of the place.

The serving woman arrived, placed a mug before Sanborn and a full pitcher between the men, took his coin, and left behind a scent of stale perspiration and something else. Sour bed linen? He couldn't quite identify it. He looked after the woman as she left, and his table companion snickered in a knowing manner.

"Not as sweet as some, mind you," he said, "but a good rough go for all that."

They laughed companionably.

"Daniel Sanborn, sir, and happy to make your acquaintance." He stuck out his hand.

"Jeremy Weeks," his companion said. "A pleasure, Mr. Sanborn. New to the port?"

"Indeed, Mr. Weeks. Is it so plain?" They smiled at one another. "I've been here but four days and have taken a room at Mrs. McCullough's. I toured the wharves just now. Boston does not put you to shame."

"You're from Boston then?"

"Yes, recently. From London just several months now."

"In the shipping trade?"

"No. I'm a traveler, sir. Looking to settle. I'm a painter of portraits."

"Portraits is it? Well that's a scheme."

"And yourself, sir?"

"I keep certain of the account books for the customs house, trying to keep my betters honest." He grinned. "Before that, many years as a third mate. West Indies trade." He grew wistful. "I've spent my life in the middle."

Sanborn raised his mug. "To the eternal middle," he said. "It cannot be an easy task, that."

"Scrutinizing my betters?" He laughed. "Not so easy, sir. But I know most of the tricks, have helped more than one ship's master in my former years 'exercise his prerogative,' as we used to say. But now I keep an eye after the king's business. There's no respite for such as me, what with illegal timber operations and dodging customs' duties the most common paths to quick wealth hereabouts."

"Perhaps the new governor will put an end to it once he returns from London."

"Perhaps." Weeks considered and took a long tug on his pipe. "He's an eye for quick wealth himself, I'd say. But he'll never be the prey of such as Jeremy Weeks. I fish a smaller pool."

For whatever reason the crowd was beginning to thin out. Weeks and Sanborn enjoyed another mug each. Sanborn asked any number of questions about the town and Weeks obliged him. Would he still have to advertise in the Boston newspapers? (He would.) The best cheap eating establishments. The scuttlebutt and reputations among the town folk of certain families and officials. The presence, or lack, of other limners. If Weeks were to be believed, Sanborn would not have much competition. There were few limners who passed through, and none to match his training and skill. He would succeed here; he felt more confident than ever.

A woman came in from another room, an obvious jade. She looked about and finally caught Sanborn's eye. Black haired, brightly dressed, and full-fleshed yet hard-looking, she smiled knowingly at him just as another man stepped to her side and began to speak to her as if he were an old friend.

"That's Gingher," Weeks said and laughed. "Not named for her hair, as you can see. But plenty of spice there, if you've a taste for it."

Sanborn had looked away so as not to appear overly interested in her, but she had indeed caught his eye. Young, vigorous, unmarried, he had known his share of jades.

"And do you recommend her spice trade, Mr. Weeks?"

Weeks laughed. "I can't say, but there's others who would. I don't think she'll disappoint." He puffed his pipe. "But you'll need plenty of specie to bustle in her corner."

Sanborn glanced back at the woman, who was now moving to another man of her acquaintance, a rough-looking tar who, cleaned up, would probably have been handsome. "No, she has not the appearance of one who would disappoint."

It was still early, and no one was prepared, apparently, to enlist her services. Moreover, the room was continuing to empty out. One might wonder why she had chosen this time to ply her trade, if that was what she was doing. Before long, she took a seat and was soon attended by the serving woman.

"I'll be missed back at customs," Weeks said. Finishing his flip, banging his mug down on the tabletop, he extended his hand and excused himself. He gave his head a slight nod toward Gingher and winked at Sanborn, but he said nothing more about her. Sanborn stood up and said good-bye to his new acquaintance. Since Weeks had told him he often came here for his refreshment, Sanborn knew where he would find him again, if he wished to. He sat down to finish his flip after his companion left. He took out a notebook he carried with him and began to sketch a few ideas of how he might present Madam Browne upon a canvas. She was a prepossessing woman, to be sure. Should a commission for her ever come his way, he would have to be very careful about her intriguing face. Faces required more attention, perhaps, than he had given in his usual trade. Perhaps that was one thing Rebecca's self-portrait was telling him. It was more than simply a proper modeling technique, it was a matter of character, revealing the sitter's character. He was full of youthful confidence in his own capability. He sketched some thoughts about her face from different angles. When the serving woman passed by again, he shook his head to refuse a refill. He found in his sketching the pleasure of solving a problem or a puzzle.

"Seat no longer taken, sir?"

He looked up in confusion, like a man coming out of a daydream or a light sleep. It was Gingher herself. He was speechless for a moment, coming back into the world from the reveries of his craft.

"It is no longer taken, but I was just preparing to leave," he managed to say. He looked at his sketch.

"What be ye drawing?" she asked, ignoring his lie.

"Faces. Just faces."

"A limner then?"

"If you wish." Why was he indulging her?

"Clever sod."

He looked up again. "Clever enough," he said. He began to put his sketch things away, noticing as he did that there were only two patrons left, besides himself and Gingher. She stood there watching him as if he amused her. She was wearing some strong sweet scent that was rather overwhelming. He thought that perhaps such was her trademark. Her fan lightly tapped his cheek. He stood up and began to leave the table.

"Good day, then," he said, for some reason not wishing to be rude. The two other patrons in the tavern were paying them no attention.

"I'm just up the way, there. Out the door, turn right, and right again at the first lane uphill. Third building, one flight up."

He turned to look at her, a bit astonished because he thought he had successfully brushed her off. It was not that she didn't interest him, and he was no hypocrite about his need for women, even a woman such as Gingher. His mind and aspirations simply were, had been, elsewhere. But she had his attention now. He looked about them again. They might have been alone for all anyone cared. She smiled at him. Surprisingly good teeth, gray-green eyes. Luscious breasts. She did not have the exteriors of a bawd given to drink. In proper dress she might have passed at a distance for a lady. She was a remarkable temptress. Gingher. He began to leave again.

She let him walk through the door where, once on the street in the afternoon sunlight, he felt dazed, and stopped to get his bearings. The flip was buzzing in his head. He had just begun to walk up the hill when he suddenly smelled her scent and then felt her arm in his. She was walking him up the street as if they were belle and beau. At the third building she gently guided him in and up the stairs. He let himself be swept up by her like a man helpless in dreamland, until they were in her room and he came to his senses.

"I have no money," he said.

"That's not what I saw."

"I mean I have very little to get me through till my next commission. I'm just in town."

"Let's adjust the service to the purse, then," she said, smiling slyly.

"I really must go."

"Nonsense," she insisted. She closed with him and put an arm over his shoulder. Her perfume overwhelmed him again, as if she were some enormous narcotic orchid the size of a full-fleshed woman. Against him, her body felt soft and his throat began to thicken. She reached for his pocketbook but he managed to arrest her hand.

"'Tis only ten shillings. We'll see what'ee can afford then," she said. She looked down and her abundant hair, dark-odored, brushed his face. He replaced her hand with his and took out two one-shilling notes and a few pence, counting them in his fingers still like a man in a dream. He burped and kept his breath in. He held out the notes.

"Well, sir, I can lend ye a hand, for that." She smiled at him.

He knew it was a mistake but he was in her control now. "A hand," he repeated, as she removed his coat. She slipped the notes into a pocket carried on the front of her dress. She caressed his groin and he felt himself tighten immediately, despite the excess of flip. She began to maneuver him backward toward the bed and he allowed himself to be maneuvered, fairly tripping on the bedstead and into a reclining position while she stood over him. With professional efficiency she lowered his breeches below his knees, threw up his shirt, and ran a teasing finger around his equipment.

When he shuddered, she laughed. "Now, now," she whispered. "Not so soon as to miss your money's worth."

She was gripping him firmly now, with a practiced, relentless stroking and squeezing. A sickening ache flashed through his body and then the familiar innermost tugs and twinges. She began to laugh softly, devilishly, as if she knew he would be off, and then suddenly he roared like a silly beaten mule and disgorged all over her vigorously working fingers, which were now directing him away from her clothes.

"My my my, sir," she said in a false sweet voice, and laughed again. "But it's been much too long for ye!" She continued to work him, gently now, as he moaned and diminished in her hand. Then she removed his neck cloth and wiped his abdomen.

When she was done she stood up straight over him and said only, "There, now!" She patted her pocket with his shilling notes and smiled at him—almost, he thought incongruously, like a mother over a child she had been nursing back to health. He was unable to move for some moments. She straightened herself up, opened the door an inch, and turned to him. "No need to hurry yourself," she said. She went over to her dresser and began to wash her hands and wrists in a basin.

As he was returning to himself, he noticed a single board about four feet long and twelve inches deep running shelf-wise along the wall where she stood with her back to him. At opposite ends of the shelf were two candles, and between the candles stood a half-dozen books and a stack of used newspapers. He couldn't see what the books were, and felt unable to ask, but it increased his sense of unreality as he lay defeated on a harlot's bed.

Sanborn stood, pulled up his breeches, tossed his neck cloth aside, adjusted himself, and left without a word. In the doorway below, before entering the street, he looked to see that no one was nearby and then counted his money. A door opened in the hallway and a black navvy with a grin on his face came toward him in the doorway. Sanborn immediately stepped out into the late sunlight, a hint of evening in it, and continued walking up the hill toward his new room high above the city streets.

 *Chapter 5*

THE FOLLOWING MORNING he drew up a notice for the Boston papers, which everyone in Portsmouth seemed to read. While in Boston, he had learned the necessity of presenting oneself as having recently arrived after success in London. To be out of fashion in the home country would be the first sin among the New England gentry. The notice included a brief reference to "Mr. Sanborn's evening school for the instruction of Polite Youth in the branches of Drawing." He also sent his card, with his new address inked in, to the Brownes. Yet when no work came his way for a week, he began to make inquiries of the next ship to Boston. He was optimistic by nature, however, and he still had the feeling of something fortuitous about his first commission in Portsmouth.

While he was on the street in the market district the first Saturday, he thought he spotted Rebecca's tutor. He followed the woman to be sure and then spoke to her casually. She recognized him immediately. He thanked her for the advice of a lodging and asked how her charge fared.

"Very well, sir," she said. She smiled at him. As before, she was brightly but properly clothed and very tight-waisted. He felt himself towering above her. He did not want to appear too imposing, so he slouched and spoke quietly.

"And what of your master and mistress? Do you believe they are completely satisfied with the likeness?"

"Quite, sir. The portrait hangs now in the dining room."

"Indeed! And are they well?"

"Very well."

"Do you suppose they might consider a further commission still? Of Colonel and Madam Browne? I would be most honored."

"I'm sure it is possible, sir, though they've not spoken of it in my presence."

"I'll be returning for the varnish, of course, and I've sent them my card."

"I'm sure they are pleased, sir."

He didn't want to appear anxious or importunate. More commissions were lost than gained over how one appeared. "And Rebecca is well, you say. I'm delighted to hear it. She is a most unusual child, do you not agree, Miss Norris?"

"Who would not agree?"

"Yet she said something to me about removing, or rather being sent away. I assume you will be traveling with her?"

"I think not. Or I should say I have no plans to travel. On the contrary, my understanding is that I may well be looking for a position elsewhere. But I have no doubt that Squire Browne will provide me great aid in the matter."

"The girl is leaving then?"

"I believe so."

"To London?"

"I would not expect so, not anymore, but I am not informed as to the family's plans in any regard."

"Even where you are the one to be so affected?"

"Even so." Her light, curious eyes seemed to change before him, as if she was preparing to turn away and about her business. He wanted to delay her if he could, but gently.

"I admire her most unusual paintings." It was all he could think to say at the moment.

She looked up, studying him before speaking. Had she seen the mocking portrait? Had she seen whatever pictures the girl had made over the years? Had she even offered instruction?

"Her childish pictures have caused some . . . discomfiture, sir."

He waited for her to go on, but she was disinclined. Her face flushed as if she had embarrassed herself speaking out of turn.

"Whom have they disconcerted?" he asked.

She hesitated again. It was becoming ever more obvious that she wished to be away.

"Her guardians," she finally said. "And other relations." He said nothing; he was struck suddenly as by a revelation of familial difficulties, of a family as uncertain of an enigmatic yet charming child as he himself, a stranger, had been.

Miss Norris turned. She glanced back to say only "Good-day to you, sir." He was left standing stupidly in the street contemplating what he had been told. The look of discomfort on the governess's face made it clear that she regretted saying as much as she had, as if a family confidence had been breached. Yet they all knew he had spent considerable time with the child. He felt certain they must know that he had even seen several of Rebecca's paintings. Why this need for circumspection about the child herself in his presence?

Chapter 6

JUST AS SANBORN had booked passage to return to Boston while he still had the price of his fare, another commission arrived.

It was to be a portrait of Mr. Alexander Hart, a business associate of Squire Browne's, who had seen the portrait of Rebecca on some occasion at the manse.

This portly gentleman had arranged to meet Sanborn at his very place of traffic upon the wharves. He had pointed to his ships laden with masts and planking, and to the coast of Maine across the bright wide river.

"There's the background I wish to see, sir," he had said. "It can be done?"

"Of course, Mr. Hart," Sanborn said. "Most impressive ships!" He began making some sketch notations.

"That they are, Mr. Sanborn. A long way to wealth, though, I can assure you." He shook his head and looked wistful, as if recalling how he had risen in the world. "That I was educated only to trade, and in the very school of trade, has not kept me back. Over the years it has been my good fortune to supplant men of substance and accomplishment, more than a few of which have long since returned to the motherland, broken or discouraged."

Sanborn looked up at him from his sketchpad. "There are many, no doubt, who made obeisance to the king's timber surveyors and tree markers, rather than to their own best interests."

Hart winked at him. "Aha," he said. "You've ferreted out something of the matter there, Mr. Sanborn." He laughed. "Neither simpletons nor nincompoops"—he gave his stomach three hearty pats—"but somewhat unclear as to just where their true interests lay." He had watched as Sanborn continued his quick sketches of ships and shoreline.

Within three days more, Mr. Hart sat before Sanborn at home, in his costly wig, his broadcloth coat lined in bright silk, his satin waistcoat half unbuttoned in calculated negligence. He seemed uncomfortable, however, sitting for his portrait, so Sanborn began to regale him with tales of his own success as a tradesman in portraiture. These anecdotes had the desired effect, and they began to enjoy many a gentleman's tale and laugh together.

The real significance of the Hart commission was manyfold: It initiated a series of commissions, and Mr. Hart sent his granddaughter to Sanborn for drawing lessons. And thereby Sanborn entered into firmer relations with one of the premier commercial families of the province. In fact, within a month of entering Portsmouth, Sanborn was able to leave his small room and take two ample rooms with a private entrance nearer the market district.

He now recognized men about town and they him. He began to receive occasional invitations, if not to the residences of the more highly placed, at least to those whose names were recognized for respectability and substance. He no longer doubted his ability to stay on if he wished.

He also began to pay discreet weekly visits to Gingher, and at times he himself appointed. He ate and drank well. Eventually, several persons of means approached him about employment as drawing master to their daughters or sons. Those few he deemed of the higher caliber, he took on in his weekly lessons, which gave him entrée to several grand houses and presences. He even began to toy with the idea of investing in the shipping end of the timber trade. All his sunny hopes and aspirations that had brought him to Portsmouth seemed to be materializing before his eyes. Within three months of entering the town, he felt a buoyant complacency about his prospects.

It was in such circumstances that he ran into Miss Norris once again. She was in the very process of removing herself and her baggage to her new position. They tarried before her new residence one afternoon after having met within. She was returning to the Browne manse to close out a few remaining matters, she said, and hoped to be fully installed in her new position within the week. She seemed more deferential to him now, as if she were aware of his rise in the world. And how could she not be? His new clothes—still dark and plain but of very fine cloth—would have suggested as much. He had thought she regarded him with curiosity, as one might a foreigner. But now there was something more—perhaps a flash of admiration? He found his interest in her growing as well.

"And Miss Rebecca, has she by now gone on her journey?" he asked.

"Yes, Mr. Sanborn, indeed she has."

"Not to London then?" He smiled charmingly.

"Not to my understanding." She looked at him as if deciding whether she should entrust him with all she knew. "I was not privy to their plans for her, but I believe it is to be a town on the frontier where the colonel has family relations, a fellow proprietor, who looks after his interests there."

"In the name of goodness, Miss Norris, what on earth could induce them to do so?" He was no longer smiling. "There must be some explanation."

"As I say, Mr. Sanborn, I'm not privy to their decisions. I can tell you only this: The child refused to go to London, had even ceased eating to make her wishes keenly apparent, and had settled for some such alternative scheme as this 'woodland retreat.' She said, 'I am more a child of the forest in my heart. It is to the forest I shall go, then.'"

"What a strange child," he said. How could she say such a thing, born and bred, so far as he knew, in this bustling port on the golden rim of the Atlantic trade? Did the child aspire to the renunciations of some popish saint lost in the dim centuries? Or had she truly some imagined taste or fascination for woodlands and for the coarse manners and employments of the people who dwelt on the margins of the wilderness?

He sensed that Miss Norris had much to tell him but was holding back.

"And what of her pictures, which you mentioned they found so unsettling? It is painting and drawing that she most loves."

She looked down. "They are to be destroyed, sir. Or, most of them." She hesitated and looked up at him a moment. "I think she will be much employed otherwise." Her voice indicated regret.

"Destroyed?" He couldn't speak further. He realized his face must have looked foolishly startled. He tried to compose himself, regain his dignity. "Who is to destroy them?"

"The gardeners are to burn them, I believe. The Brownes have chosen the ones." She made to turn aside, as if she were deeply troubled, or perhaps about to weep. "I myself had to go through many, and gather together all the possibly offensive ones. The colonel . . ." She could go no further.

"Many hours of her work and delight."

She nodded in agreement, her eyes closed.

"It seems monstrous to me, Miss Norris."

"It's a parent's prerogative, sir."

"Still . . . ," he said.

"Indeed, sir."

"Yet, they have not been delivered into the gardeners' hands, you say?"

"No. Soon, I expect."

"Ah." He thought a moment. She seemed sympathetic to him now. He believed she agreed with his assessment of the actions of the parents, or nearly so, whatever she could openly admit. He had no doubt that she, too, found the paintings disturbing, some of them anyway, but nonetheless valued them as the product of her little prodigy's labors and gifts. She had displayed affection for the child when he had seen them together. Still, he knew she was withholding information now, information that might help to explain the parents' excessive response.

"Would it not be possible to salvage some of them?" he asked.

"Against my master's wishes? Certainly not, Mr. Sanborn."

"Don't misunderstand me. Of course not, Miss Norris. I mean

only to do so with his consent. I have a professional interest in the extraordinary execution of one or two I had seen, and there are perhaps others."

"I see, but, no, please believe me, sir, he would not hear of it. I can assure you."

"May I at least view them, Miss Norris. Surely that can hurt no one, before they are, in fact, destroyed forever."

"You ask me to jeopardize my good relations and understanding with the Brownes, sir."

"Not at all, Miss Norris. I ask only to view a few specimens out of painterly interest and respect for Miss Rebecca and her gifts. I think she is misunderstood, but I would not interfere with anyone's wishes or good relations. Nor with her parents' considered decision."

"Misunderstood, sir?"

"One gentleman, whom I'd prefer not to name, referred in my hearing once to Miss Rebecca Browne as 'that little witch.'" Sanborn looked into her startled eyes. He was sure she herself had heard of this attitude, but was merely surprised to hear him voice it. "He was speaking light-heartedly, perhaps as a figure of speech, but I've asked one or two others about word of her, and there seems to be some uneasiness abroad over her unnatural gifts and precocious demeanor. I know it's all nonsense, but there it is nevertheless. It is a narrow prejudice against the child, I fear, for her mere eccentricity and learning."

"There is enough of that abroad, sir, as you say." She looked him in the eye, almost defiantly. "Remember that you are in New England, not England, Mr. Sanborn."

He thought a moment. "You have the advantage of me, Miss Norris." He smiled.

"And of course there is also this new contagion of enthusiasm that feeds the flames of intolerance," she added and returned his smile. She was not, he now believed, immune to his charm. "Squire and Madam Browne, as many other families of Queen's Chapel, count it a great misfortune to New England that Mr. Whitefield and others have initiated this prodigy of New Light. This excess of superstition."

"I quite agree, Miss Norris." He smiled again. "Perhaps the child is somewhat nervous, vaporish. She would not be extraordinary in that. I found the child a bit taunting in one instance, but she was delightful and remarkable in everything else. I value her gift as much as you do, who know her so well. But I also have a professional curiosity concerning her paintings and drawings. Do you not suppose I might see these briefly in some open and agreeable fashion, before they're destroyed? I assure you I'll make every effort to be of service to you in return."

She did not speak. He felt certain she wished to comply, out of their mutual sympathy as much as for anything else. And she must, by now, have found tempting his blandishments as a potential benefactor. How could she not recognize him as a man of growing reputation who might some day turn a matter, here or there, to her advantage?

"Come tomorrow after three o'clock," she said. "But please go to the back entrance."

"I shall, Miss Norris." He took her hand and made a bow. "I'm at your service, and in your debt."

She said good-bye and turned away. A light chaise, the Brownes', no doubt, awaited her but ten steps farther along the street.

He walked toward his lodgings after her chair drove away, pleased with himself for having persuaded Miss Norris. But he was troubled nonetheless: his fear for the girl's well-being, her separation from the family circle she had known, the impending loss of so much of her labor on paper, board, and canvas. And then there was her presumptuous mockery of him beneath it all. Still, he would see the renderings of her mind and soul and that was enough for the present. He would try not to torment himself.

But the child—in her tribulation, as he imagined it—that night haunted his dreams.

Chapter 7

IN A STATE OF PLEASING ANTICIPATION, yet still troubled in spirit, Sanborn stood at the appointed hour before the rear entrance of the Browne manse the next afternoon. He was disinclined to the subterfuge, especially as he expected that the Brownes would be out at the hour Miss Norris had named. But he saw no alternative. She confirmed his expectations when she let him in promptly, so he humored her precautions. He needed her trust and compliance. He turned deferential, if not too overtly so. He felt like a man who of necessity had to balance a jug of water on his head.

The house was quiet. They saw no other servants as she conducted him directly into the child's lesson room, a chamber on the first floor. She was clothed in a fetching purple mantua that accentuated her shape and bounce. The room was nearly empty of furniture and belongings but filled with neat piles of drawings, sketchbooks, and boards and canvasses. On the one little table that remained were a number of loose prints, bound books of prints, and a few instruction booklets. He picked up one of these books and saw prints of the work of Michelangelo, Giulio Romano, and Martin Heemskereck, among others. In the front of the book was an inscription from Colonel Browne: "To Rebecca, upon the eleventh year of her birth, I give these wonders of the masters of whom you speak."

Miss Norris watched Sanborn, transfixed by the book and its inscription. "He had hoped that these beloved masters would turn her out of her preoccupations," she offered in a low voice.

"I see," he said, leafing through the bound prints.

He went over to canvasses neatly stacked on their sides and began to flip slowly through them. He pulled one out and held it up for Miss Norris and himself to consider. It was a view of a bedchamber corner, the foot of the bedstead facing a window in gray dawn. The terrible, powerful face of a bearded old man leaned against the window, as if looking in at the occupant of the bed. The face was pale, almost ghostly, with a ring of seven mystic eyes, like planets, in halo about the hoary head.

"*God at My Window,*" Miss Norris said flatly, announcing the title.

He looked at it carefully, put it aside, and pulled out another. Here, too, was a bearded man, this one rising naked out of a wide river, palms upward, looking worshipfully toward birds circling and roosting by hundreds in the foreground trees.

"*The Prophet Amos Contemplates Creation,*" Miss Norris announced.

He said nothing to these verbal renditions but put this one aside, also, and pulled out still another: Two young men, apparently corpses, lay on their deathbeds, their souls rising out of their bodies and singing as they ascend heavenward in an attitude of prayer. The faces of the souls were joyful and quite particular, as if Rebecca had known them in life. He looked at Miss Norris and raised an eyebrow.

"This one caused particular discomfort to Colonel and Madam Browne," she said, instead of announcing a title. "These are Rebecca's two . . ."—she seemed to search for a word—"brothers, who died in the recent throat distemper."

"I see," he said. He returned to the painting. "But is it not a happy issue of these tragic deaths? Surely they are bent heavenward."

"Still, sir, the parents found it frightful, so soon following their demise. The wounds of mother and father were still open." She looked to see if he followed her. "That she should *see* them ascend, was perhaps a part of the trouble as well. I think it is not so difficult to understand their reaction."

"But is not this canvas a glorious rendition of what she hoped or surmised of her brothers' last hour?"

"She always insists 'I paint precisely what I see.' You must understand: To her these paintings and drawings are all no mere transmogrifying to canvas by way of technique or simple fancy. Such visions she always maintained are as real to her as I am to you, standing here in this moment."

"How can that be so, Miss Norris?"

"Whether it is so is not the question. Why, sir, she is a dear little visionary. Is that not clear?"

He considered her words a moment, wondering if the child might be mad. "And these perceptions, her beatifications? Rendered as an afterthought, so to speak, upon board and canvas?"

"And as many on drawing paper. And why not? Would she be the first to see such things in this world?"

He laughed quietly. "Not the first, surely." But what he had seen unsettled him, too. He understood the parents' trepidation, even if he did not condone their response.

"How else to explain what you have held in your own hands, sir?"

"Indeed, Miss Norris."

"Did not our Savior Himself teach that we should come to see as a child?"

He said nothing. He turned to continue his search through the stack of canvas and board. He imagined them all going up in flames, their destiny now. Many were of a lighter heart—lambs, children playing, flowers yearning toward the sun, beasts of the field and wood dancing in attitudes of homage and ritual. But the darker ones haunted him already, and he knew they would haunt him for some time: a charcoal sketch of lowering skies beneath which a colossal winged figure flew among children playing in a ring. The giant's great saber flashed, like a well-oiled scythe above a field of ripened grain. A crowd of adults looked on in helpless horror.

Another drawing: monstrous dragonlike forms rising out of the earth and belching malignant flame and smoke over sun-struck forest and sea.

"Such visions in a child of . . . what? Twelve years?" he said, as if musing to himself in a quiet voice. "In a child of such beauty and apparent innocence."

"Yet she paints what she sees," Miss Norris repeated. "Surely these are not studies from some master."

"That would seem plain enough, Miss Norris. But why destroy even these jubilant ones?"

"These darker visions are the more recent, but Madam Browne said only that the colonel's orders were to destroy all these."

"All," he said.

"Quite, Mr. Sanborn."

"And these expensive books and prints?"

"To be locked in Squire William's library, a chamber over the back parlor. A harmful influence, it is now believed. Inexplicably so, yet harmful nevertheless."

He had heard that Squire Browne's library was one of the most impressive in the province: arising from a legacy of books passed down through his father, Aaron Browne, from his grandfather, Richard, one of the first-generation "merchant-princes" of the Piscataqua. And to his grandfather's collection of authors from classical times through the previous century, Colonel Browne had acquired, in addition to sermons and other works of Anglican respectability, a fine inventory of contemporary English authors: Swift, Pope, Shaftesbury, Addison, and Steele, among others. It was a matter of some pride with the colonel to say that if Colonel Pepperrell's library was the only one on the Piscataqua to rival his own, his, Browne's, nonetheless, exceeded that of his august competitor on the north bank of the great river.

Sanborn learned that as a young man William Browne had been sent to Harvard where, Miss Norris assured him, he had graduated high in his class in recognition of his social position among the colonies. He was not an ignorant tradesman who had somehow managed to rise in the world, though his father had also sent him to Boston to be trained in a counting house before he became a partner in the family's business.

Sanborn silently and quickly passed through a number of other illustrations. He came upon the canvas of her self-portrait.

He held up the painting and looked at it for some time, turning it this way and that. The face and hands were everything, as if the very opposite of his own rendering. He held the painful thought only a moment, as if she were instructing him by example.

Yet even in her self-portrait was another vision, if clearly the girl's own face. Here, too, some fanciful power was being expressed, rather than a conventional or literal rendering. Here again the face and limbs, the whole body, were merely the material vessel of some other energy, an energy that seemed to arise out of her deeper, more vital character. Once again the artist had focused—he could think of no other way to express it—on a reality behind the physical reality. Not Amos, this time. Not God. Not demons or dragons, but just the girl herself, beautifully, strangely, vibrantly animated with inanimate pigment on inanimate canvas.

Such mystic musings were not natural to him, or easy for him by education or training. But the girl's pictures forced the viewer's mind to dwell on these, as he now put it to himself, "other matters." He knew, of course, that artists in other epochs had painted work that might be considered in "the mystic line"; he knew of, even if he hadn't read, the mystics of the Word as well. All these were not unheard of, but rather simply beyond his ken.

"It is Rebecca herself, is it not, Mr. Sanborn?" Miss Norris asked, disturbing his ruminations.

She startled him back into awareness of her and of the great silent house around them. He looked about the room, as if for a last time. "It is she, Miss Norris, but something more as well, wouldn't you say?"

"Something more? Some grace beyond the reach of art?" She offered a complacent smile. "Well, yes, Mr. Sanborn, I think you are correct on that point. And perhaps that's where the trouble lies."

"Perhaps," he agreed. "But I would have said something beyond grace, too, some amazement in the soul." He looked at her and she stared back as if untouched by his extravagance. "Of course it is a commonplace as well, is it not, that those having the most delicate sensation and taste, whose faculties are the brightest, the most keen and penetrating, nay, even the most spiritual, are most given to nervous disorders." He held up Rebecca's own portrait to better light.

"May I keep this one alone, Miss Norris?" She did not answer.

"For a brief time at least," he went on. "I'll make you a personal deposit for security, to assure you nothing will befall the portrait until I have finished my considerations of it and return it to you for disposal."

"I can't take such a chance," she finally said, "circumventing my employer's wishes."

He decided not to argue or insist. He could see that would lead nowhere at the moment, except to make her more adamant on principle. He knew that she had already given in to his pleadings more than she thought appropriate.

"Would it not be possible to discover the whereabouts of the child, in some town on the frontier, as you said?"

"I don't think so," she said with a grave face, "as it is not my place to make inquiries, and as doing so would only raise suspicions and even firmer secrecy."

"But if you should come into such information, would you share it with me, Miss Norris? I would be most grateful."

She looked at him directly. He was sure, again, that she knew more than she spoke. But he detected a sympathetic attitude, despite her reticence and the formality of their relations. "To what purpose, Mr. Sanborn?"

"I believe this child, whom I came to understand in some small capacity through our sittings, must suffer in her removal, whatever its nature. I have seen enough to know that. Moreover, I believe you share my sentiments concerning your former charge, Miss Norris. May we not inquire into her welfare on our own, out of compassion?"

"Her parents feel compassion. And love."

"Yet they are unsettled by her, they have removed her, and they have denied her exercise of her powers and her deepest delight."

"They believe some discipline is called for, and that is their prerogative, as I have said. Perhaps she need spend more time in this world, rather than some other."

"You are right, of course, in regard to the parents." He believed she was merely mouthing her master's argument, not her feelings. "Yet the heart speaks otherwise, to one outside the family. And as you have said yourself, she draws and paints only what she sees in this world. It is not some other, if you report her words correctly. Her sight will remain unchanged under any discipline. It is her seeing, and there is nothing to be done about it, is there?"

"I cannot say, sir." She made a motion to suggest it was time to leave.

"Think on it, Miss Norris. I beg you." He handed her his new card, in case her mind took a more agreeable turn.

 *Chapter 8*

REBECCA HAD MADE HER MARK on Daniel Sanborn, portrait painter. Perhaps because of his anger at her effrontery, he renewed his efforts to learn the mysteries of painting faces and hands. He had seen what an Old World master could do; now he had seen what a gifted child could do as well.

He found that he continually studied Rebecca's painting of herself, as if by study he might unlock its secret. And how he came to be in possession of it was one of the most unexpected, yet straightforward, incidents of his early months in Portsmouth. He had been sitting in his painting room after a day of good work, enjoying his pipe and a glass of Madeira, looking out his window into the ruddy haze settling over the city of a September evening. There was a knock on his door; he rose at his leisure. Two more knocks before he reached the door suggested to him some urgency about the person who sought his attention.

He was pleased to find Miss Norris wrapped in a hooded cape. Her eyes were fixed on the card he had attached to his door:

She held in her hands a large object, well covered. Upon entering his rooms and exchanging greetings, she immediately uncovered it to reveal Rebecca's self-portrait.

"They have burned the others," she said. "I saved this one out. Surreptitiously, of course. I thought one product of her childhood should be salvaged. And seeing your particular interest in this one, your admiration, as well as my own, I chose it."

"How'd you manage it, Miss Norris?" he said with a great encouraging smile, lit by tobacco and wine.

"I placed it, well disguised, with some other last things as I was removing to my new residence and position." She looked grave, as if the memory of the risk she had run was a sobering reflection. "You may borrow it if you like, for a time."

"Thank you, Miss Norris. You must know how grateful and pleased I am. I stand by my offer to leave you payment in surety."

"That won't be necessary; I know you value it and will take every appropriate care."

He offered her a congratulatory glass of wine, and to his surprise she accepted. She was an energetic little woman who stepped about like some uncaged bird admiring his rooms and views. His painting room was of particular interest to her. And she was taken by a portrait in progress of a young woman.

"Who is she, sir?" Miss Norris said.

"Is she familiar?"

"Oddly so, yes, as if I know her without having seen her."

"Then you've read Mr. Richardson's novel?"

"Who has not? It's all the talk." She looked at the portrait curiously. "My goodness, it is she!"

"Pamela Andrews," he said proudly. "A mere fancy on my part, of course, but perhaps available as a striking specimen. And something of a conversation piece as well." People would visit his rooms expecting specimens, prints, and models, and lessons.

"Indeed. She is very well done, and very amusing, sir."

He had painted Pamela in profile, her dark hair partly covered by a white cap with two little upright points above the forehead. Her bodice and gown he rendered in brown with white trim and white ruffles about the neck. He had gloved her arms and hands.

Miss Norris was completely taken with his Pamela and spent some time before it. Sanborn took her interest as a good sign for the response of future patrons.

He did not pursue the topic of finding the child, for he did not wish to unsettle her, but rather congratulated her on her forethought and temerity and allowed her to savor their mutual pleasure over what she had accomplished for them.

IN THE MONTHS that followed, he made many a study of the painting's confident magic. It was, he often admitted to himself, a little like having the living child staring back out at him from a looking glass. But he grew familiar with the prepossessing face and found that he began to welcome it; he no longer felt the strange apprehension and outrage he had experienced upon first viewing it. In fact, he was reminded of something Smibert had told him when Sanborn called upon the old master in his Queen Street rooms in Boston during Sanborn's early months in the city. He had felt emboldened to call upon Smibert—by that time the dean of American portrait painters—because both of them had mutual acquaintances from Hogarth and Ellis's academy in London.

"I very much enjoyed teaching Anna Berkeley while on shipboard, sailing for Newport, in Rhode Island," the older painter had said. "I now have the pleasure, in addition, to believe that she may not only be the first woman to paint portraits in America, but may well be one of the finest limners to have once practiced the trade on these shores."

"Is that so?" Sanborn replied, hoping the master would ask to see a sample or two of his own work. Smibert seemed charmed by the thought of a female pupil of talent who might make her mark in the New World. That rather surprised Sanborn at the time. But he himself was hoping for some advice and help with securing commissions, so he did not then give much thought to Madam Berkeley, or her renowned husband, or the college they had all hoped to establish in Bermuda.

Yet now the master's words rang again in his ears. Rebecca surely was another female of talent. But Rebecca's gift, unlike what must have been the decorous aptitude of the bishop's wife, was eccentric and rare—not the primitive talent of some untutored New World limner, say a Robert Feke. No, it was the gift of a powerful, disquieting, and deeply personal vision.

Now in Portsmouth all these months later, however, he found that having Rebecca's self-portrait in his rooms kept his curiosity about the girl's fate foremost in his thoughts. One might say that his curiosity and his compassion grew, were nurtured, by her pictorial presence. Miss Norris was obviously acquainted with many family members and relations, so he began to plan a means of convincing Miss Norris to discover Rebecca's circumstances and whereabouts.

He was not sure just what he would do with such intelligence, but he wanted to know so that he might contemplate her fate more exactly. Just as her troubling perceptions and techniques had come to frequent his mind, so now did her actual presence, or the memory of it, haunt his reveries in moments of leisure. Somewhere in the back of his mind he vaguely fancied that he might strike out to find Rebecca at an undetermined point in the future, perhaps months, or even years, from now. He could understand well enough his fascination with her extraordinary abilities, but he found himself less comfortable with his memories and impressions of the child herself. She had become in his mind like some bewitching creature met in an unforgettable dream.

Chapter 9

A MESSENGER BOY CALLED upon Sanborn in his rooms one day in late autumn with an invitation to wait upon Madam Browne. His services were required once again, this time to execute a portrait of the grande dame herself.

When she came into the familiar parlor, she immediately congratulated him on his ever-growing reputation. "My husband is away, traveling with the surveyor general on matters of timber and the law," she explained. "But he suggested I give you this offer, and that if you find it satisfactory, we may begin at your first convenience." She handed him a folded sheet of paper. On it Squire Browne had written a price, ten guineas, and made suggestions as to positioning and attributes.

> We trust to your experience to present Mrs. Browne in the best practice of English portraiture as to her womanly virtues and the quality of her person to be indicated in the drapery. But I would stipulate, if you would indulge me, Sir, that her lovely face be quite her own, that she wear the pink carnation indicative of marriage, and that rather than a bowl of fruit or blossom she hold a book of her choosing.
>
> Upon my return, I would be pleased to discuss with you my own portrait of the marital pair, assuming satisfaction and agreement to terms, etc. . . .

Ten guineas was as good as anyone, save Smibert himself, painting in America was likely to receive. Sanborn was pleased to express his agreement, and they arranged for sittings to begin within the week.

AT THEIR FIRST SITTING he did not mention Rebecca. Madam Browne remained affable if dignified from the first as she sat in her armless Lady's Chair, accommodating her voluminous skirts. Her demeanor emboldened him by their second day together.

"I have not seen or heard the young lady, Mrs. Browne," he said incidentally as they conversed lightly on several topics. "So vivacious and accomplished a child is an adornment to the household."

Mrs. Browne paused a moment in her idle chatter, smiled at Sanborn politely, and with a movement of her wrist and hand only, so as not to disturb her careful pose, said, "Oh, yes, she's a considerable adornment whom few forget, upon once meeting her."

"She is well, I pray, madam?" He feared she intended to speak no further of Rebecca.

"Very well, Mr. Sanborn. Thank you. Just now she is abroad with relations, so she has, as you suggest, not graced our household. May I place this volume on the table? My arm is quite asleep, I'm afraid. It would not disturb your progress?"

"Madam, it is your comfort and ease that speed my progress."

She placed the book on a nearby oval table after taking up a fan to make room for the book. She twice moved her arms outward not unlike a roosting seabird, to enhance her circulation. Despite the awkward movement, the artifice of her coiffure, costume, and toilette were becoming. She was a woman whose striking presence and dignity he knew he must transfer, well placed, to his canvas. He was plying every effort and care, well within the orthodoxy of Squire Browne's requests, to the task she had set him. He thought his work went very well, thus far, and he was full of confidence as he brought out the pearly tones of her watered silks, the white crispness of her laces, the softness of her velvets. It would be a three-quarter portrait, a dark curl falling over the right shoulder, and the whole set in painted spandrels—quite after the fashion they would emulate.

"Is this correct, Mr. Sanborn?" she asked upon resuming her seat.

He posed her further, if only slightly, to his advantage. He wanted to display fully her white under sleeves, just below the elbows. "Well done, madam. You are an excellent sitter." Though he regretted that note of hireling praise, he hummed a pleasant ditty as he returned to his easel.

"With certain of my Portsmouth patrons of the highest quality, I assure you, it is quite a different matter. Some seem unused to the slightest restraint or inconvenience." He smiled complimentarily before he began again, and she returned his smile. He wondered if there were a bit of the coquette in her still. Her décolletage was fashionably appropriate but daring as well, only the slightest hint of a fichu moderating the temptations of her ample bosom. He imagined how as a young unmarried woman she must have taken the widower Colonel Browne wholly into her powers. Yet such elements of her nature he would of course subdue in his portrait. Even if he had the capacity, he thought, he would never display, as Rebecca surely would, this inmost heart of Madam Browne's character.

"Is she gone to London, then?" he asked idly. "I believe I recall her saying something about the possibility of traveling to London as she sat for me."

"London?" She looked at him without her smile. "Oh, no, Mr. Sanborn. She is visiting relations of Mr. Browne's, of the Wentworth line. She is seeing something of the woodland operations and her cousins, you see. The country air and vigor of climate shall do her good."

He thought of winter coming on and wondered how she could blithely say such a thing. But he himself had not been to the frontier, nor had he an inkling of the timber trade, nor how even the higher families or proprietors might live there. He had heard that the more prosperous proprietorships were quite convenient, having little of the rude frontier settlements of a century ago about them. Still, the whole arrangement sounded now, just as it had on Miss Norris's lips, utterly ill considered.

None of this could he speak to Madam Browne. He had to settle for worrying such thoughts in silence, even as he presented to his patron the most genial appearance.

Yet the lady had confirmed everything Miss Norris had said. He began to wonder again how difficult it would be to travel inland and find the child whose self-portrait arrested and enchanted him more and more the longer he studied it.

He tried one or two further conversational gambits to elicit information, but Madam Browne rather too apparently tired of the subject, so he was pressed to give it over for the remainder of her sittings. She wished to speak, rather, on the talk about town—the role of people of fashion in the great celebrations upon the return of Mr. Wentworth from London and his installation as first provincial governor, the Wentworth's renting of the Macpheadris house, and so on. Sanborn's mind, however, insisted on its wayward pursuit of the absent child.

1742

The end of most immigrants was their own material and social betterment . . . to transplant to America the social pattern of the English country squire.

　　— Byron Fairchild, *Messrs. William Pepperrell: Merchants of the Piscataqua*

There are likewise many who will allow that among the sinful nations of the times, pride and luxury are the great promoters of trade, but they refuse to own the necessity there is, that in a more virtuous age (such as one should be free of pride) trade would in great measure decay.

　　— Bernard Mandeville, *The Fable of the Bees*

Chapter 10

THAT SPRING, when Daniel Sanborn had lived and worked successfully in Portsmouth for nearly a year, he called upon Jeremy Weeks in his room by the customs house to invite him for a bowl of punch.

He had conversed with Weeks two or three times since first meeting him in the waterfront tavern shortly after his arrival in the city. He had come to respect him as a man who was particularly informed about the timber and fish trades, and about the merchants and captains who orchestrated such trade, at times illegally, to their conspicuous advantage. And he indicated now, during convivial conversation, a knowledge of the slave trade as well. He announced rather theatrically behind his hand a current scheme.

"Vinegar, sir," he said with a knowing wink.

"Vinegar?" Sanborn looked at him somewhat amused.

"Better than seawater alone for washing out decks during the passage. Greater cleansing, so fewer deaths. Black ivory."

"I see. Still, speed is the essence, I understand." He tipped the punch bowl, drank, and handed it over to Weeks. "You've shipped yourself then, I take it, Mr. Weeks."

"On diverse occasions. Not anymore. Usually out of Newport or Providence, aboard a forty-tonner built for speed. Rough but profitable duty it was, but such days are behind me."

"So, vinegar it is, now."

"Sell it to the slavers, for the Guinea Coast and the West Indies–New England trade as well."

"I had once thought of shipping for Africa," Sanborn said wistfully. "A country worthy of a painter, to record its strange beauties and barbarisms."

"Aye, but you're better off having not done so. It's a brutal place for a man of your kidney. A sea without harbors, a world of sandbars and shipwrecks and sharks. And murderous climate, sir. Murderous." He shook his head and looked down. "Sudden mists that chill the very center of your bones. And heats that drain men of life or drive them mad. Calabar, Piccaninny, Goree, St. Paul de Loango, The Bight of Benin and of Biafra. A journey to hell, sir, but profitable—more so than any other journey—for those who've the constitution for it. And a good shake of blind luck."

"That's what turned me away—rumors of the coast, the trade. And the much greater market for portraits than for land and seascapes."

"Death rides your shoulder every minute."

The two men were silent for a moment, as if contemplating an alien world, one from rumor, one from experience. Sanborn rose to go to the bar.

"The adventure of your life, sir, nonetheless," Sanborn said upon returning and placing another bowl before them.

"It was always that, aye. It's a world you can't imagine, even for all your tales of voyagers, unless you've seen it, braved the dangers yourself. A whole fever coast dotted with the slave compounds of the English, Spanish, Portuguese, Dutch, and French. All fortified against rival traders and native tribes. They're a bloody lot, the tribesmen. If amidst the slaughter of their enemies, the chieftains spare some few men, women, and children from the hideous tortures and deaths of their wars and raids, they demonstrate their power." He drank of the punch. "But once they saw how profitable in rum and cloth *every* slave could be, they turned their ancient enmities to the production of slaves for the European trade. A hundred gallons of rum—some ten or a dozen pound's worth—for a good Negro, sir."

"But three times that in Barbados or the Indies?" Sanborn asked.

"Yes, and more again in Charleston or Bristol or Boston, or wherever you please. And their own laws, too, are productive for the ships waiting off reef and shore. Thieves are enslaved and sold, lovers of errant wives, defilers of another man's god, even surplus wives and children are sold to a black man's good profit."

Sanborn shook his head in awe. "I begin to understand the minister I once heard thanking Providence for bringing to our land safely another cargo of 'benighted heathen,' as he put it, 'to enjoy the blessings of a gospel dispensation.'"

Weeks snickered. "And why should not the sagacious merchant and the dogmatic priest join in singing the praises of this most profitable of all traffic?"

"Indeed, Mr. Weeks. I'm certain it will continue to prosper."

"I'll make you a prediction, sir." Weeks took a shrewd tug on his tobacco pipe. "Mark my words, Sanborn. The white traders, should the supply ever diminish, will foment renewed warfare among the natives, even deep into the interiors, to insure the unchecked flow of gold."

"And vinegar is the solution, you say, to more Negroes surviving the passage and ensuring the flow of guineas all round?"

"Many's the shipmaster who swears by it." Weeks tapped the side of his nose.

"Every survivor, they've finally come to appreciate, is one or two hundred pounds more toward the profit of their investors, themselves, and their daring crew."

"The secret of the vinegar! Would you be interested yourself, Sanborn—even a modest investment?"

"The trade in vinegar, you mean?"

Weeks nodded. "Ask your captains and masters all, if you like. There's a bright future in it, mark me, Mr. Sanborn. Vinegar will not fail, I'm telling you."

"Let me think it over," Sanborn said. "You have, I admit, led me into temptation."

They both laughed. What troubled Sanborn somewhat about such investment, beyond the need to carefully husband his slowly accumulating resources, was the instability of the trade in other ways. He had heard tales of the folly of trusting many of the captains of the passage, who rendered themselves debilitated by taking below a choice young black woman who, as one informant had phrased it, "kept the good master in a continual stupor of sensuality to the neglect of his duties." But as he thought about it, the mere trade in vinegar seemed protected against individual folly, for there was no denying the enormous general profitability of the trade.

Now Sanborn decided would be a good time to exchange such considerations for the true object of his meeting with Weeks—a growing obsession with Rebecca's welfare on the frontier.

By way of transition, he made a few jokes at the expense of some local dandy and official. Weeks enjoyed this new tack of the conversation. "Fools, fops, and knaves grow as rank as formerly," Weeks said and laughed.

"Mr. Weeks, I thought I might rely on you for some information that could be of help to my own trade in portraits."

Before he could go on, Weeks laughed and said, "You take me for an idle dauber, sir!"

Sanborn laughed at himself. "My good Mr. Weeks," he began again, "I have decided to extend the range of my clients, as you might well understand, and see something more of New England so long as I'm here and seeking my fortune, by traveling from time to time to the towns and settlements this side of the Merrimack. Of course I would search out only the better sort in those regions—the overseers, surveyors, officers of the governor, and the like. But as I'm still comparatively new to this country and have never been west of the great bay, I wonder if you might advise me as to how one might best go about it."

Weeks smiled, showing several missing teeth. "I'd heard you've painted the phiz of every man and woman of substance in the port," he said, and laughed under his breath. "Well, I expected you'd wear them out before you wore out your arm, so there's no reason I suppose not to extend your trade to the west, as indeed everyone has but the fishermen. As the king's men complain, we New Englanders are wont to exhaust the forest bounty hardly sooner than we encounter it." He paused as if for philosophical reflection, yet his face was twisted up almost comically and his cheap wig set slightly askew. "But why not return to Boston to ply your fine trade, Mr. Sanborn? You're more used to the conveniences of the city, are you not? And there's plenty of august folks looking to hang their foresides 'pon a Boston wall, I'll lay me."

Sanborn laughed. "There's little doubt of that, Mr. Weeks. As a matter of course, I do intend to return to Boston before the onset of next winter, but I expect to travel and consider this other trade as well."

"Good then; you'll be looking after your interests better in Boston. But as to the western parts, yes, I think I can put you in touch with one who travels there. He works on occasion for the surveyor's office, and for the governor, and even the competing merchants as they have need of him. I lay he'll know everything you require." He paused and addressed himself to the meal, which Sanborn had ordered and had just been delivered to their table. The two men ate quickly and in silence for a time. The rumble of the afternoon crowd caused enough of a din that neither man took much notice of his companion's eating in silence.

"Mr. Ladd, Joseph Ladd," Weeks said finally, smacking his lips. "A good man with a horse or an ax, or a woman for that matter. Regular Buck." He continued eating.

"I'd be in your debt, Mr. Weeks."

"Not at all. It's only a matter of introduction. You'll have to convince him yourself of your plans and projects." He drank from the second bowl. "But he's a fellow you can talk to, once he takes your measure."

"Thank you, sir. If there is any service I can do for you, at any time, please feel free to call on me."

"Think nothing of it, Mr. Sanborn. This is excellent mutton, and tolerable punch. Well charged with spirits." He finished his meal and stood up, bowing slightly. "Back to my customs labors," he said with a grin as he wiped his face. "Don't want to disappoint Squire Solly!"

In Sanborn's estimation, he had but one more obstacle to surmount—the precise whereabouts of Rebecca. He felt sure Miss

Norris knew more than she had told him, either out of some consideration for her former employers or for some fear of his bungling.

 *Chapter 11*

HE FRETTED FOR SOME TIME over the best approach into Miss Norris's confidence. He knew she felt they shared a mutual sympathy for the child. He believed he had detected some degree of her interest in him as a young man of the world: a man of travels and significant associations, a man of craft and more than a middling education, a man of some intriguing ambiguity concerning his past, family, and London colleagues. Yet he had not seen her in some months. He had made no effort to cultivate her acquaintance. Nor she his. Perhaps, he told himself, there had been on both sides a mere lack of opportunity to do so. And there were always considerations of propriety.

The difficulty was just how to induce her to release her knowledge of Rebecca. Nothing occurred to him, the more he considered the problem, so he finally decided that a meeting between them would reveal in the moment his best approach. He sent her a note with his card. A maid-servant brought a note in return; it suggested that he call upon her at eight-thirty in the evening, with Rebecca's painting, well covered, at her new place of residence, the Abidiah Sherburnes'.

They met alone in the kitchen, sitting at a table after the cook and servants had abandoned the room to other duties or their well-earned rest. Miss Norris's charges had been put to bed. She looked well if rather tired. He solicitously inquired after her health and satisfaction with her new position.

"I had never wanted to leave the Brownes', but once it became necessary, I am most fortunate to have landed here," she said. "The children are good and their parents insist they learn their lessons, which eases my way. Mrs. Sherburne appears to suffer some illness."

"The poor woman. I'm very pleased, however, to hear you confirm your own good fortune, Miss Norris."

"It wouldn't have turned out so well for me but for the generosity of Colonel Browne and his lady."

"That is all the more to their credit," he said.

"You certainly look to be prospering yourself, Mr. Sanborn."

"As much as I could have hoped." He smiled.

"And that is to your credit, Mr. Sanborn."

"And to the great need in these parts for likenesses among the better class of patrons. I was right, I've come to see, to leave Boston when I did, on the speculation of less competition for my portraits. I've just completed a likeness of Madam Browne herself."

"Is that so, sir? And your reputation grows with every season, from what I hear." She looked directly at him.

"I've thought to extend my range, so to speak, Miss Norris. In part because I have so thoroughly covered immediate opportunities for portraiture in town; in part to see something more of this New England whilst I'm here. Who knows but that I may decide to make some investment in the forest trade or lands on my own account."

"You are very comfortable indeed, then, Mr. Sanborn." She arched an eyebrow.

"I am to meet a man, one Joseph Ladd—do you know of him?—who is to advise me on such travels, perhaps with one party or another of surveyors or overseers of the wood."

"I have heard of him, but know nothing directly."

"From what you've heard, he should serve my purpose?"

"From what I've heard."

"I rest more confident for your confirmation then," he said. She looked him in the eye throughout this interchange, as if she had anticipated his intentions to ask something more of her. "I'm not certain where this Ladd will advise me to look for patrons, but I may of course come into the neighborhood of your former charge. It wouldn't be impossible at the least for our paths to cross, if what I understand of her disposition is correct."

"Certainly it's a possibility," she said, and waited for him to go on.

He dared not tell her outright that the true object of his desire was to find the child. It would simply seem too odd in a man of his station and reputation. He was not able to admit fully even to himself the degree of his evolving fascination with this girlish prodigy.

"I should be prepared to report to you her welfare," he finally said, "were I to encounter her on my travels. I imagine the Brownes would appreciate word as well."

"Have you spoken of it to them?" she asked, a slight note of skepticism coming into her voice. "For my own part, that would be a blessing to know how she fares."

"No. I don't wish to intrude on what is perhaps for them a delicate matter. Upon my return, however, I could rather incidentally mention that I'd seen her and leave it to them to ask whatever they wish to know. They do, I expect, have others to report to them, even if rarely."

"That's probable."

"But I'd prefer to have some clue as to her whereabouts, the better to look out for her. As long as I may come into—what?—the vicinity of Miss Rebecca."

"I see." She smiled. "And you've come to me to ask if despite my earlier protestations I know something more of her situation."

"Well, in a sense, yes. As I say, I'm going to the frontier in any event, and I thought we might consider together the well-being of the child." He flashed his brightest smile. "We might, together I had thought, honor our mutual concern." He knew he was stumbling and repeating himself, but he was operating extemporaneously as well as he could.

She looked down, saying nothing at first. He decided not to press her further.

"I would have to think much more on it, Mr. Sanborn." She hesitated, and then, as if correcting herself, said: "I don't know that I can help you."

"Us, rather. Say us, then, Miss Norris, for it's an investigation from which we both might benefit, as well as, perchance, the poor exiled girl." When she looked up he smiled sympathetically. "If she is in comfortable circumstances and well looked after, we need say nothing more, do nothing more. We shall be appeased. If she is not, in any sense, we may offer some small help and comfort to her. Just how we might do so, we could determine only after fully informing ourselves on the matter."

"I agree with you there. Thank you for returning this," she said, touching Rebecca's heavily wrapped portrait.

"Will you let me know your decision, Miss Norris?" he prompted her.

She looked at him with a bold eye. "She is not their daughter, Mr. Sanborn. Not Miss Browne, but strictly speaking Miss Wentworth." He was struck speechless by her sudden turn of conversation.

"She is the issue of the Wentworth line, which likes to trace its noble heritage back to the time of Henry the Third. But cousins to Colonel Browne," she continued. "Not the more august branch of that family, but of a lesser tributary. The parents were devastated in the last distemper. She was brought to Portsmouth by her proper father's cousin, Squire Browne, who was her godfather, you see. As I said on an earlier occasion, but did not explain entirely, the Brownes were then struck during the plague. The death of their two sons left them with no children but their adopted daughter, Rebecca. There was some trouble delivering their second child, and they were strongly advised against having any more children of their own. I had been hired as tutor to their sons, to supplement the town schooling, that is. They were deeply wounded by the death of their sons. I became Rebecca's tutor by default, you might say."

"And your tutorship accounts for her remarkable learning," he said as a statement but meant as a question.

"She reads continually, sir, whenever opportunity is presented. But also, her natural father took deep interest in her, after he understood that she was the quickest to learn, the most clever of his children. He indulged her, perhaps unfortunately so. I believe he once applied to his cousin and old friend from childhood Squire Browne to assist him in sending her to school in Boston, after the manner of the Pepperrells, when the elder Pepperrell bore the cost of an extraordinary granddaughter's schooling in Boston. To no avail, as you see, but her father saw to it that Rebecca partook of certain of her brothers' lessons at home, and at the feet of their minister."

"The basis of her learning and lore."

"Precisely. But in time the Brownes, who had indulged her passion for books as did her father, grew troubled by Rebecca's strange gifts and, well, to put it plainly, her unmanageability. . . ." Miss Norris seemed to wish to go on, but something held her back. She looked down. Neither of them spoke further. He remembered the drawing of the boys' souls released and wondered a moment whether the Brownes somehow might have come to blame the strange girl for the death of their sons.

He reached across the table and placed his hand on hers. She did not look up or move her hand. She did not weep or appear confused, merely silent, as if gathering herself, either to go on or to determine to say nothing further about the Brownes. He believed she might be full of regret for having spoken, but he could not be certain.

After they had been sitting quiet for some time, she spoke. "You understand, then, that the colonel and his wife did not forbid Rebecca further learning out of that prejudice that afflicts many men of position. Such men believe it is in their interest to discourage reading and literature because such learning will expose them to the contempt of those beneath them and detract from their sense of significance, their unassailability. Thus they find satisfaction even in the ignorance of their own sons, let alone their daughters. . . ." She broke off as if she had veered into rant that might expose her. She thought a moment, looked up at Sanborn, her eyes full of a strange pleading he had not seen before, and then began again.

"Colonel Browne fears for her, and even for himself, perhaps. I believe madness in any form is his greatest fear. There's a history of terrible distraction in his family, sir . . . self-murder, the visions of religious frenzy. . . ." She broke off again. And this time she could not continue. She looked down again. Finally, in a barely audible voice she said, "I will need time to consider what you have said, Mr. Sanborn."

"Of course, Miss Norris," he said. "I have not made an appointment yet with Joseph Ladd, nor have I made specific plans for departure. There is time to consider well." He touched her hand gently and then stood up. "I hope I haven't caused you discomfort, Miss Norris. Please believe that was not my intention. I was thinking principally of Rebecca's well-being, and of an opportunity arising for us to discover her circumstances. . . ." He paused, but she said nothing. "I'm in your debt for being so forthright," he continued. She looked up at him but said nothing still. "Should you wish to reach me, you know where I am. And I am always at your service."

She stood up slowly, as if it cost her an effort, still looking at him. He had never seen her so sluggish. "I thank you, Mr. Sanborn, for making the opportunity you speak of known to me. I do not know what I can do, but I will do what I can." She supported herself on the back of her chair. "Good-day, sir."

Once back on the street, Sanborn found he was stunned all over again by her revelations. Everything about the child was thrown into a new light. He found that his determination to find Rebecca grew firmer than ever. But he did not want to examine closely yet these accelerated feelings of precedence toward, as he now thought of it, his mission.

Chapter 12

A WIRY MAN IN HIS THIRTIES wearing a deerskin
jacket, Joseph Ladd was an experienced road scout and an
old hand at forest travels. As he rode beside Sanborn their
first day out that June, he spoke of the changes he had seen
in this part of the forest—the trees cut back from some of
the riverbanks, the developing system of mastways, the appearance of a way station or two, and the new towns being
planted, especially along major rivers. They had left Portsmouth
on a river gundalow on the afternoon tide the previous day for Exeter, fifteen miles distant, and set out at first light from Exeter on
horseback by way of the road to Kingston and Chester. Ladd had
business of his own to conduct, serving on a road-surveying commission for the proprietors of Londonderry and Blackstone, as
Sanborn understood it. Both men had packhorses tethered to their
own mounts.

The road they traveled was still rough, the more so the farther
west. Much of it had been a mere footpath within a decade's memory. Now it was a bridle path improving toward a cart-path, and indeed they had encountered the odd oxcart on their inward trek. It
wound among glacial rocks and over the great stems of blowdowns
and the long, low backs of surly hills; it deposited walkers and rid-
ers at the banks of streams and rivers that had to be forded or, in
one instance, swum on horseback. Sanborn noticed here and there
scouts' and surveyors' ax hashes remaining on a tree to indicate the
intended improvements still to be made in the most narrow reaches
of the way. Ladd told Sanborn that until just a few years ago, one

had to travel up the Merrimack River "and come in the back door" to reach the towns thirty or forty miles inland.

As they approached one nearer settlement, in fact, they heard the clanking of chains, the creaking of great carts, and the shouting of drivers. Soon their way intersected a wide mast road. They saw at a distance of perhaps a half mile, coming toward them some fifty or more yoke of oxen heaving and straining to haul a great pine, propped up on enormous chains between two pairs of wheels of more than fifteen feet in diameter.

"They'll be quitting soon," Ladd said, "as the rivers will recede again with the end of the rains."

Sanborn observed that the entire area around the great felled pines appeared to have been reduced to waste.

"This time of year," Ladd explained, "they have to preserve the big ones by cutting down the smaller trees in the direction of the fall, for bedding, so that after a stand of great pines has been cut, there's little or nothing left erect."

"An amazing sight," Sanborn said. "Yet I suppose the smaller trees and stems may be useful for boarding or bow-sprits and whatnot."

"That's so," Ladd said. "They'll all be twitched down river so long as the water's high enough. As it has been this season. Wood-gold." He laughed. "Spain, Portugal, England—it's all the same, a sale is a sale, friend or foe."

Sanborn had heard a great deal in Portsmouth about how efficient the tree cutters had been, especially in the mast trade. "His majesty's woods," as some said with more than a little irony, were becoming depleted so fast of the best accessible stands that the merchants were turning to Casco Bay and other points east to insure their product.

As they would not reach their destination before nightfall, Ladd recommended they lodge at the mast camp. Their quarters in temporary dwellings were primitive yet dry and not inconvenient. The exhaustion of the mast party put everyone to bed early, on two or three noggins of rum and a heavy venison supper. Sanborn slipped toward unconsciousness hearing the distant calls of wolves, then tumbled into deep, dreamless sleep.

THE CAMP WAS ASTIR at first light. After a breakfast of bacon and porridge, Sanborn and Ladd left before the sun was in the trees. The men traveled in silence for a time, so Sanborn's thoughts turned toward his mission to the child. He felt particular gratitude to Miss Norris for finally informing him of her whereabouts—the very town and family her guardians had sent Rebecca. He had not had to prevail upon Miss Norris more than he already had. She had come to his rooms again, well hooded, with the names written in her neat tutor's hand on a half sheet of paper. She had arrived at the opinion, similar to his, that she could be satisfied only by some direct and independent knowledge of Rebecca's circumstances. She, more than anyone, knew of the child's tendency to darker fancies. These often suddenly overcame Rebecca in the very midst of happiness. Over the course of several years the girl and her tutor had developed, Sanborn by now understood, a strong feeling toward one another, and, on Miss Norris's part, a true solicitude for the welfare of the brilliant but moody child. Such sentiments, he now believed, had led Miss Norris to confide in him, as she had no one else to confide in regarding Rebecca.

As far as Ladd knew, however, he was merely guiding a much-respected portraitist into the farther reaches of the timber plantations of the province, of Portsmouth to be more precise. They were not traveling to grinding, primitive villages of a previous century, but to settlements planned as New England towns for the development and stability of trade and the security of boundaries and land claims. It was unusual, perhaps, but not to Ladd's or townsmen's minds extraordinary, that the better-placed families of these districts should wish portraits of themselves and their loved ones. At first Ladd and Sanborn had traveled along much cut-over forest, and on more than one occasion had to cover their faces against the smoke of fires burning the previous year's slash near a settlement's new planting fields.

The rare taverns were, however, of the most primitive kind. By a river's edge where a rude causeway of felled trees served for crossing, they stopped at an equally rude dwelling with a sign of a fish and a boar hung out. Upon entering, Sanborn was glad they were determined to complete that day's trek without respite again for sleep. It was a two-room garrison log cabin with a lean-to stable semiattached, and any sleepers would be obliged to throw their weary carcasses upon a bearskin before the fire or, in warmer months, on bug-infested hay in the second squalid room behind a flimsy partition.

Ladd and Sanborn each drank a noggin of grog. They managed in their hunger to eat some of the nondescript porridge offered as well. There were two other men in the common room—a couple of taciturn forest roughs who had thrown Ladd and Sanborn a hostile glance as they entered and then, to Sanborn's relief, proceeded to ignore them. As Sanborn and Ladd were eating, another traveler arrived—a captain of the Provincial Guard. The captain's name was Carlyle, a huge man of some six and a half feet with a deep bass voice. The two roughs stopped talking and eyed him quietly.

They must have decided to check their native hostility in his presence, for when the captain came in undoing his great coat and stamping his boots, calling for the care of his dogs and horse, for a loaf and cheese, and for a good dram of molasses and rum, they merely looked away, and shortly thereafter got up to leave. But just as they were going out, the larger and fiercer of the woodsmen stopped short at the opened door and called back to the host as he was heading out the back door to the stable to execute Carlyle's requests.

"McGuire," he called, a malignant grin beginning to spread across his face, "here comes Robie, and I mean to set things right between us, if you'll not interfere."

McGuire took one look back at him and said, "Not in here you don't. Settle it outside."

The big woodsman stepped outside while his smaller mate looked out, as if guarding the open door. Ladd and Sanborn, fascinated by this turn of events, looked toward the doorway where they could see but little of what transpired between the woodsman and Robie. The altercation was audible before it turned physical and they surmised the trouble was over the sale of a horse, by which the woodsman now felt cheated. They were just able to see around the door guard into the tavern yard when the woodsman took his first swing and began to beat Robie with his fists, in favor of the stout crabstick he had taken with him. Robie went down under the assault and, to the jeers and encouragements of the woodsman at the open door, began to receive the more damaging blows of his opponent's booted feet.

Through it all, Captain Carlyle, who had given his good-day to Ladd and Sanborn, ignored the violent scuffle as if he hadn't the least interest in such affairs, and only cared to refresh himself at McGuire's bar. When Ladd got up, finally, as if to demand the woodsman discontinue kicks brutally delivered to the unfortunate Robie, who it appeared had gone into convulsions, Carlyle held his arm calmly and said, "Better not, sir. It'll be on his head and McGuire's. The man is in no mood to brook strangers interfering." He leaned back in his chair and applied a candle to his pipe.

Ladd sat down again. "You're no doubt right, Captain, but he'll kill him sure if no one interferes."

Just then the man in the doorway, laughing now, left his post and went to commend his partner and, fearing perhaps Robie's demise, to warn him off further revenge. The big woodsman did cease, finally, as his partner eased him off, but they were not yet quite through with Robie's punishment. All the while the beating of Robie had proceeded, the poor man's little dog had set itself to a fit of barking and growling and snarling approaches to the woodsman's deadly feet. Now the smaller woodsman picked up his friend's stout walking stick where he had dropped it and proceeded to beat the valiant terrier.

For the first time Captain Carlyle looked up toward the altercation. The sharp anguished cries of the dog penetrated the room, and all three men inside had now an unobstructed view of the proceedings. It was the big woodsman's turn to laugh and cheer on his mate, and soon the scampering little dog went down beneath the merciless blows. But just as the dog was falling, Carlyle leaped up and ran out, grabbed the stick out of the man's hand, lifted the man completely above his head, and tossed him headfirst into the nearby stream.

As Carlyle turned, the big woodsman was making for him with his recovered stick. Carlyle raised himself up to his full height, his face red with outrage now. He dodged the stick aimed at his head and took the blow on the side of his left shoulder. He was incredibly fast for such a large man and managed to grab the stick as it slid down his arm, and then jerked the woodsman toward him. As the astonished assailant jumped helplessly forward, Carlyle sunk his great fist squarely into the man's face and he went down, bleeding from the nose, like a man slowly collapsing in a dream.

Now the captain stood over him, stick at the ready, as the dazed woodsman staggered to his feet and backed away, hand to his face smeared with his own blood.

"If I see you again, I'll kill you outright," Carlyle said, calm now. "Pick up your cowardly mate and get out of my sight. Now!"

As the captain went over to inspect the limp dog, Ladd and Sanborn came out into the tavern yard as if to insure the captain's back would be covered as he bent over the terrier, which was still conscious but in obvious misery from what must have been several broken bones and damaged organs.

The captain knelt over the whimpering, panting cur and gently stroked the fur full length with two big fingers. "Poor old brave heart," he murmured and stood up. Shaking his head, he reached within his open greatcoat and drew forth a pistol, which he cocked and aimed at the dog.

"Sir!" Sanborn called out, unable to help himself, but the pistol discharged, the little body jumped once, the pained eyes closed in peace, and it was over.

McGuire had come running out of the stable and over to them at the sound of pistol shot. They all stood in a circle dazed and looking down at the unconscious Robie and his dead dog.

"This man requires a physician," Carlyle finally said, still calm.

"There's a midwife in Blackstone who can help," McGuire said. He looked at Ladd, "Will you send her back, sir, as soon as you arrive? I'll see to him as best I can in the meantime. Name of Mrs. Worthington."

"I'll send her," Carlyle said. "Worthington. I'll see to it she's warned to bring plenty of camphorated spirits for this man." Carlyle turned to McGuire. "My horse ready?"

"As you ordered, sir," McGuire said, looking now toward the two woodsmen as they limped away down the crude road. "Dogs well fed, too."

"You see these cowards again," Carlyle said to McGuire, "you tell them I mean it. I'll shoot to kill the next time I lay eyes on them." He turned to Ladd. "I'd be obliged, sir, if you'd bury this brave little champion," he said. Ladd nodded in agreement. Carlyle walked toward the stable to get his horse and roust out his two dogs.

Ladd and Sanborn helped McGuire carry Robie into the house and onto the bear rug. Ladd went out, buried the dog, and returned with his and Sanborn's horses to the tavern yard. Sanborn heard him in the yard and left the host to tend to Robie alone. He mounted his horse and the two set off again for Blackstone, unable to speak to one another about the drama they had just witnessed, trying to think instead of the affairs that concerned them.

Having much business of his own upon reaching Blackstone that evening, Ladd directed Sanborn immediately to the house of Tristram Prescott, the Wentworth cousin who had, as he now understood, taken in Rebecca. It was a rather fine two-story house, though modest by Portsmouth standards. The wife came to the door herself in a much-used apron over an entirely presentable gown. Sanborn found that Mr. Prescott was not at home, being at a meeting of the proprietors on some matters of taxation and road building.

Standing in the doorway, Sanborn presented his profession and credentials, and as soon as Mrs. Prescott understood him to be recently in the employ of the Portsmouth Brownes and Wentworths, she became more solicitous and invited him in. She removed her apron and called to a serving girl for cider and cakes "after the gentleman's long journey."

In the parlor room, she offered him a turned chair and seated herself facing him in a chair upholstered in fabric.

"And do I understand you correctly, sir, that you had thought to inquire of our own interest in portraits?" she said.

"Quite so, madam." He offered his most charming smile. He was uncomfortable making an appearance in dirty clothes, but she seemed to take no notice of his traveler's disarray. "I had thought that such respected families as yourselves might be in need of my portraits. Madam Browne had mentioned you in particular."

"Is that so?" she said blushing slightly in pleasure. "Well, that is recommendation enough. Yet my husband has not mentioned any thought of portraits, so you shall have to discuss the matter with him." She smiled. "Or should I say, convince him of the necessity."

"And may I inquire, madam, as to how many family members you have? There is yourself and your husband . . ."

She filled in where he hung fire. "And five children besides."

"Ah, I see. We can't, of course, say whether Mr. Prescott will entertain portraits of each, or a family portrait or a children's group, but I am anxious to be of service, whatever his preferences."

"He should return within the hour, and you may discuss it then." The servant brought a pewter salver of refreshments and laid it on the table. Mrs. Prescott offered him some of the delicacies and poured them both a tumbler of cider. "Would you care for pipe and tobacco, sir?"

"Perhaps after the cider, madam, if you care to join me. Thank you."

She blushed and sipped immediately from her cup and peered at him with a twinkle in her eye. "And how go things in Portsmouth, Mr. Sanborn?"

He grew expansive, taking care to enlighten and entertain her with the doings of the port's best society—their new governor (to whom they were distantly related), Parson Browne (who was, despite the name, no relation to the colonel) and his family, and so on. He continued to intimate his own revolutions in these circles of the well-to-do. And he even piqued her with a tale of his painting the portrait of one of the Wentworth clan's enemies, Richard Waldron.

"A most undesirable interloper," she said. "And much too prideful by half. One of the saving graces of life in these parts, sir, is being free of the immediate presence of our professed opponents. These . . ."—she made a dismissive motion of her hand—

"Waldrons and Vaughans and Gilmans, and the others." Her face wrinkled in distaste.

He laughed and she joined him. "Indeed, madam, they have all been a trial to your family, I understand." He decided to engage in a little scandal to place them on firmer ground together.

"And most unfairly, I assure you, Mr. Sanborn."

"Yet I can't discriminate among my patrons, or I'd soon be out of pocket myself."

"Oh, I understand that, Mr. Sanborn. Commerce is, after all, commerce."

"But Mr. Waldron does harbor a vast cyst of ill will in his breast, I must say." He put an amused look on his face and waited to see if she would take the bait.

"I have no doubt of the lies with which he must have regaled you while at his sitting." She shook her head. "Everything not to his personal and immediate advantage he takes for anathema. Every proposal, every vote, every grant and purchase not devolving honor and profit to him, he claims to be the result of the perfidy of others." She stopped as if getting a little out of breath in her imprecations. "I suppose he was relentless in his disparagements."

"Rather so, I'm afraid, Mrs. Prescott. He made a charge very similar to yours, against our governor! But I learned long ago not to take to heart my sitters' rants against their enemies. It was nothing more, I am sure, than the usual list of complaints of his family and associates against yours." He smiled as if about to impart an amusing confidence. "That Mr. Wentworth was stacking the Assembly with his own men, and the Council with a gaggle of brothers-in-law, nephews, and cousins. That they had monopolized the mast trade by way of underhanded influence with Admiralty. That the governor had received unseemly gifts and bribes from lumbermen and mill owners, and was disbursing land grants, high military and judicial offices, and proprietary rights among friends, family, and supporters. I must say, I felt rather an apostate myself just to hear him refer to, in his words, madam, 'that contemptible simpleton Wentworth.' . . ." Sanborn paused to let the words take effect and watch his hostess grow flushed again.

Then he added the final stroke. "He took great pains to assure me that Mr. Wentworth sits in the governor's chair only because he was, in Mr. Waldron's words again, 'a bankrupt whose London creditors thought they'd never be paid, and so inveigled Newcastle to support him.'"

Her face had been growing red as she listened. He made a mental note that it would be better never to repeat this list of charges in conversation with Mr. Prescott. "As if church and family associations counted for nothing," he hastened to add. Yet Mrs. Prescott, he soon realized, was taking pleasure, as many do, in her dudgeon.

"Of course," she began, "he says nothing of the enormous benefit to the home government and to the colony itself—the merchants, timber men, mill owners, land owners, and every citizen great and small! Never has the province flourished, nor have so many benefited so much, as since Mr. Wentworth's appointment to the royal governorship. On that I'm certain he is quite silent. Surely even such a creature as Mr. Waldron could now benefit from our independence from Massachusetts, if he so chose. But one cannot expect a pompous ingrate to admit it."

He felt that he had her in his confidence now, and that she would speak well of him to her husband. But he was unable to witness that conversation or its result because Mr. Prescott did not return. After they had been sitting for some two hours together, anticipating her husband, it became clear he had been detained by more pressing matters to the proprietors. She asked after his plans to lodge, and he admitted he had none, that even Mr. Ladd had no knowledge of a lodging house.

"There is one being built to attach the tavern, but is unfinished," she admitted. "However, Mrs. Sinclair, a widow, now takes in lodgers." She told him how to find the Sinclair house. He made arrangements to return the next day to speak to Mr. Prescott. He decided to make a final bold inquiry, however, before taking his leave.

"You spoke of five children, Mrs. Prescott, but I have not seen nor heard them about the house or its environs. Are they all abroad today?" He gave her a cheery, light-hearted look.

"They are all engaged, sir, while the final light lasts, in the planting fields. It is, as you see, just Betty, who served us, and myself at home this evening. There is always so much to be done."

"I see," he said and smiled. "Well, five children is a blessing, of course. They must be a great help and comfort to you. After the distemper, as I understand it, there were few families who escaped intact. So, you and your husband are twice blessed, to have five of your own dear children in your home."

"Yes, we are," she said, and then added as if in afterthought, "though one is my brother and sister-in-law's child, Rebecca. The entire rest of her family were wiped out in the sickness."

"Dear me. What a tragedy for your relations, Mrs. Prescott!"

"Indeed, sir. She had lived with my husband's cousin, Colonel William, for a time, but they decided she required the better air and discipline of rural life." She smiled, as if she had been clever.

Sanborn put on a look of some astonishment. "I might have met this young lady, briefly, while at Squire Browne's, madam. She was quite a pretty child and showed me some paintings of her own." He thought better, just yet, of explaining that he had painted the child.

"That is she, but there's no time for painting and reading here; she has a more common round to occupy her now."

She seemed almost curt, so Sanborn did not detain the woman any longer; he took his leave, promising to return at the appointed time.

Chapter 13

HIS HAY-FILLED MATTRESS at Mrs. Sinclair's lay in a small but adequate room, and she was a friendly, bustling old lady. There was only one other lodger, who came to Sinclair's later, to share the room. It was the officer in the provincial guard, Captain Carlyle from Londonderry. Sanborn now discovered he was traveling about the countryside to propose the best ways for roads and to assess the condition of peacetime garrisons, as if peace with the French were not expected to last indefinitely. And if in times of trouble, as he had heard, the men of the province preferred to enlist under a provincial officer rather than under a king's regular, Governor Wentworth and Colonel Blanchard might have been grooming Captain Carlyle for future trust.

Sanborn and Carlyle spoke not a word of what had passed at McGuire's, but grew friendly over their jars of rum and molasses. One peculiarity was that Carlyle's two great dogs went everywhere he did, inside and out, and they now slept wheezing like oversized lapdogs before Mrs. Sinclair's kitchen fire while the men around the table in the fluttering light of candlewood spoke of their own adventures. Sanborn thought the dogs must be some kind of Teutonic war beasts—huge, of middling shagginess, one black and one brown, ever alert and patrolling while out and about with the captain.

One confidence the captain offered was that his wife, Maria, at Londonderry, was the sister of an Indian friend who had been frequently at Portsmouth.

"You might have seen him, Sanborn, name of Christo."

"Oh, yes. Heard of him. Performed services for the provincial government, and the like."

"That's the man. I intend to enlist him in my company if the trouble starts again, and I find myself organizing a troop for the frontier."

"I imagine that would be helpful indeed, if, as you say, he's by blood absolutely trustworthy."

"We have some good trackers among us, but you can't do better than an Indian when it comes to discovering the enemy."

Some years later Sanborn would hear others refer to "Captain Carlyle's squaw," but no one seemed to think the less of him. And no one mentioned what he might have thought to Carlyle's face.

Before too long Sanborn felt fatigued from his journey and excused himself to go to his bed.

The next morning over his breakfast of bacon and cabbage, Mrs. Sinclair informed Sanborn, upon his inquiry, that the officer had ridden off at dawn, "Like some invulnerable hero in a romance, sir," as she put it. Sanborn had heard some stirring in the dark bedroom, but he had immediately fallen back into deep sleep.

After breakfast, he walked about the town, awaiting his appointed hour with Mr. Prescott. He noticed the odd fencing immediately: whole logs piled on one another with short stabilizing blocks between them. Every house had its kitchen garden and cabbage vault, or root cellar. And there were many young orchards planted. Before leaving Portsmouth he had learned something of Blackstone, named for an original grantee of old, reverential Massachusetts lineage. His heirs had sold their interest in the land, including a rather crude settlement, to the current proprietors a few years before the Massachusetts–New Hampshire boundary disputes had been resolved.

His thoughts turned to how he might best manage to see Rebecca again and talk to her directly. He imagined several seemingly incidental conversational ploys to try on Mr. Prescott when they finally met. As he looked about him again, he was impressed by the well-ordered town: its planting fields and kitchen gardens stretching behind neat houses, the busy mills and commons, the lowing of cattle and sheep, the bark of dog and crow of cock. Tradesmen—a blacksmith, a hat maker, a clothier and other retailers, and a tanner—plied their trades, mostly from their households. The town seemed a model of industry and beneficent proprietorship.

And no one was more proud of the town's success than Mr. Prescott, a principal proprietor. He was a man some ten or more years older than his wife, and with a distinctly cosmopolitan appearance about him. His clothes were fashionably cut and comfortably draped over his shoulders and paunch. His flaxen wig was of city quality and fashion, and well powdered. Sanborn could see immediately that, like his ornate snuffbox, he could sidle inconspicuously into the best circles of Portsmouth society upon emerging from forest and field.

"So, you have come to Blackstone to assess our interest in portraits, Mr. Sanborn," he said, after they were properly introduced and seated in the same chairs where Sanborn and Mrs. Prescott had held their conversation.

"That is my intention, sir, after the recommendation of several in Portsmouth whose own portraits I have taken." He dropped a few names of weight, mostly of the Wentworth faction.

"Well, I can't say as I've thought of it until this moment, Mr. Sanborn, but there is a certain appeal in the idea nevertheless."

"I'm delighted that you say so, sir. As I told Mrs. Prescott, I am wholly at your service."

The proprietor seemed to mull the idea a bit before speaking. "Perhaps a portrait of myself and Mrs. Prescott would not be remiss," he finally said, almost as if thinking aloud. "Of course, matters press me here, Mr. Sanborn, as you saw even yesterday. I was not in my own house and bed till midnight. There may be certain difficulties about the arrangements, practical considerations."

"I understand, sir. My time is free, while I am here."

"How many sittings necessary, did you say?"

"That depends on my patron's specifications, finally. But as a general matter, three or four is common."

"I see." He turned it over in his mind some more. "And what is your price at three or four sittings then, Mr. Sanborn?"

"Depending on your wishes for the final portrait, usually it comes to something on the order of ten guineas, sir."

"I see," he repeated. His face had the look of mild surprise. "And you would expect it to be as much for your country clients?"

"Indeed, sir, considering the expense of travel and lodging, and guide fees, and so on. In point of fact, I'll not nearly clear the modest profit I do producing likenesses in my home port." He smiled. "In any case, it comes to considerably less expense than in a city like Boston, for example, where you would expect a Kit-cat to require from twelve to fifteen guineas, a half-portrait, say, sixteen, and a whole length above thirty, sir." He did not say that these would be a Mr. Smibert's prices.

"Aha," Prescott said in a noncommittal voice. "I suppose there is some truth in that." He looked at Sanborn carefully. "Though I expect if, as you say, you've been painting in Portsmouth for a year, there may be some dearth of patrons just now."

"That is true, sir. For now. But I had wanted to see something of the interior, and, as I say, on the recommendation of certain of your associates I thought I might try my hand in these parts. I thought there might be some yearning after my traffic."

Prescott was still looking directly at Sanborn as they spoke. "I imagine there is, Mr. Sanborn, but whether people about here can afford your wares is another matter. Still, I expect you'll find some business of the sort to occupy your hours and reward your travels."

Sanborn wondered whether he had just lost a potential commission, a commission that would surely lead to others. He decided at the moment he had nothing to lose now.

"I also paint children in groups or singly," he suggested. "I painted, in fact, the step-daughter of Colonel Browne." Prescott didn't display any surprise, but Sanborn felt sure he had reached him. "Mrs. Prescott had mentioned in passing that one of the children here was from other cousins, and I happened to see the connection the more she spoke. I imagine she told you I knew of the relation. And I quite believe this is the girl I painted, from what your wife said, sir."

"She may well be, Mr. Sanborn. The girl had lived some years with Squire William, as you say."

"She was a delightful child, I recall, and very talented herself, in the painting way."

"Indeed, sir."

"Have you by chance seen my painting of her, on your own travels back to the port, I mean?"

"No, I have not."

"It was hanging in the squire's dining room."

"Aha," he said. "No, I have not seen it, Mr. Sanborn."

"Pity. It was a good likeness, if I say so myself, and I believe you'd have appreciated it, sir." He offered an ingratiating smile. "I hope in any case you will consider my proposals. I know it's a matter that takes some thought, consideration. Perhaps I could return at a day and hour of your appointment to inquire whether you retain any interest in a portrait, or portraits."

Prescott did not answer immediately, but finally said, "Let me consider what you've said, Mr. Sanborn. Should I find I'm interested in your proposal, I'll send a man round to you. You are lodging at Mrs. Sinclair's? Yes, good. Then I know where to reach you if I find I require your services." He began to rise out of his chair. Sanborn stood up and made a courteous bow with his good-day.

After taking his leave, he returned to his rooms where he began to consider the best way to obtain a commission or two while awaiting word from Mr. Prescott.

Chapter 14

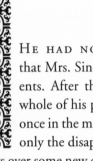 HE HAD NO LUCK from his inquiries of a few families that Mrs. Sinclair had recommended to him as worthy clients. After three days' waiting, he began to look on the whole of his project here as a failure. He saw Mrs. Prescott once in the main street and asked after her husband. She had only the disappointing news that he had been away for two days over some new dispute or uncertainty over the use of 500 acres that had been put aside for the royal governor, his cousin—essential to the agreement for establishing a proprietorship in the first place. Sanborn returned to his room utterly discouraged. His proposals must have seemed but a mere nuisance to Mr. Prescott, whose business, apparently, regularly took him abroad and consumed all his days.

By the end of his first week in the town, he grew desperate indeed. He was convinced he had lost an initiatory commission. But what of Rebecca? Was he to fail in that instance as well? He gave over any hopes of profit by his painting and went to the Prescott house once more.

Again, and as he expected, the proprietor was not in. He told Mrs. Prescott that he had not found commissions and was preparing to leave in a day or two, but he wondered if he might at least pay his respects to Squire William's stepchild before departing.

"She is not in either, sir, at the moment. But since you are on the verge of leaving, let me explain that to Mr. Prescott. He's had no time to think of portraits."

"May I return, then, on the morrow, Mrs. Prescott, to inquire?"

"Yes. Why don't you come tomorrow morning in fact, before the children leave for the fields. And if my husband has no objection, then you may pay Rebecca your respects."

That was all he needed for hope at the moment. Upon leaving the house, he went directly to the town's tavern to pass the time. He looked emptily at a notice of four-pound bounties on wolves and wildcats nailed to the door, and felt vaguely resentful that no one here seemed prepared to spend even that, or little more, on a portrait by a Portsmouth master. As he seated himself at a table, he thought gloomily of how much he missed the companionship of Gingher. But of course, such a well-ordered proprietorship had none of the vices typical of a worldly seaport.

THAT NEXT MORNING, a man called on him at Mrs. Sinclair's to say that the Prescott family was unexpectedly engaged. If, however, he cared to attend them the following morning, they would see him at that time. Sanborn felt deeply frustrated, believing they were putting him off, but he kept a pleasant and expectant countenance while the man relayed the Prescotts' message. What choice did he have? By now he wanted very much to be on his way. He was tired of the town and its insular ways. Its rustic preoccupations. The only light so far in his stay here had been the convivial tavern. But that was hardly enough to keep him occupied.

As another dull day developed, he began to fear that they were removing the girl for some unfathomable reason—anxiety over his own intentions? Biding their time while they effected her "escape," as he began to think of it. He would leave tomorrow, the way he had come, and guide himself along the bridle path if he could hire no other guide for his return. Where was Ladd? He would make inquiries with the time he had left. He found himself calling the Prescotts smug devils and worse. He was convinced they were outmaneuvering him. But he could not say why they wished to.

Feeling he had little choice, he returned to their house the following morning. The entire family, to his surprise, was in residence. They were not disagreeable, as he had half expected by this time, and the parents seemed to be displaying the children as if they were perhaps being considered for portraits after all. At first he was simply confused.

But Rebecca was among the children. She wore homespun now, yet she was still pretty, if less . . . well—he searched for a word— brilliant. In her dull blues and grays she had lost that elegance and radiance of beforetimes, but she looked to be in good health, if a little subdued. There was one concession to her former eccentricity— a white ribbon on her cap tied into something like a blooming flower. She had curtsied to him, with greater politeness than the other girl. The boys bowed like little gentlemen in training. Yet, like Rebecca, they were all dressed for the coarser work of farm and shop. What immediately impressed him, however, was the difference a year had made in Rebecca. She was now, he believed, thirteen, perhaps nearly fourteen, and the child was giving way to the woman. Not conspicuously, and she was not clothed to advantage, but clearly enough for all that. She had every appearance of having grown comfortable with her new family as well.

It was as if Sanborn could feel his fortunes turn even as he spoke to the parents and children, and then, still most unexpectedly, Mr. Prescott proposed an offer. A portrait of the husband and wife together, seated at a large, elegant table pointed out to him for that purpose. He would be paid his ten guineas for the two of them, if that met his satisfaction. He accepted the offer on the spot, inquired as to when they might have a first sitting, and was gratified to understand that they had every intention of beginning the following afternoon. He said nothing about their possible interest in portraits of the children. Taking his leave, he made a special point to speak to Rebecca.

"You're looking well, Rebecca," he told her. "I remember fondly your sitting for a portrait, and I'm very glad to make your acquaintance once again."

"And I yours," she said.

For the first time she turned her attention fully upon him, opening her eyes wide and smiling. Her face seemed to flood with light, a light he recognized from his days of painting the child.

Whatever her domestic circumstances here, he thought, that attentiveness, that brightness, had not been crushed out of her.

"Perhaps before I leave this fine town," he said, "you and I will find a moment for conversation. I come bearing some tales of Portsmouth that might amuse you."

"I'd like that very much indeed, sir."

And that was the sum of his communication with her. The next afternoon he began his connubial portrait, but the children, as usual, were nowhere to be seen or heard. He devoted his conversation with his sitters to petty gossiping. Only once did he insert an incidental reference to Rebecca—how agreeable to see her again, and so well cared for, and how agreeable were he to have a few words with her before he resumed his travels. But they took no direct notice of this reference as the conversation continued to bubble along on this and that.

In the end, the Prescotts were so pleased with their portrait that he began to speculate about their recommending him to others. He was honored and pleased to find that they presented the portrait formally to the children and a few favored acquaintances at an evening gathering. He was invited to look in on them briefly and meet the guests.

From that moment, he found himself in some demand among those townsfolk who could afford portraits of their own. There were two or three weeks of work for him, and he made the most of it. As his acquaintance with Blackstone grew, he seemed to earn the trust of the Prescotts as well. He came, in time, to know those proprietors who lived in town, and families of the first order. And after nearly a month in his temporary residence, he felt ready to renew his request to speak with Rebecca.

He developed, in fact, a somewhat different ploy, however. He would paint the children, a group of three boys and two girls ranging from seven to fifteen years, as a gift to the Prescotts for all the trade that had come his way as a result of their trust. They did not refuse him; indeed, they seem honored by his offer. They agreed the sittings should begin within the week.

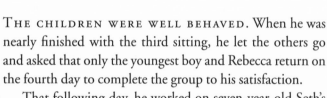

Chapter 15

THE CHILDREN WERE WELL BEHAVED. When he was nearly finished with the third sitting, he let the others go and asked that only the youngest boy and Rebecca return on the fourth day to complete the group to his satisfaction.

That following day, he worked on seven-year-old Seth's likeness for another hour. Then he dismissed him and positioned Rebecca for her last sitting.

He began his conversation with promised tales of Portsmouth.

"You are very amusing, as you promised, sir," she said, laughing now. She did seem, if not happy, quite settled and accepting of her new home and position. Or if there was any unhappiness, she was hiding it skillfully. Recalling what Mrs. Prescott had said in their first meeting, he asked the girl whether she continued her own painting.

"There is little time for the finer arts here," she said. "This is a most industrious family, and we all pull together."

"Do you not miss it, however?" he asked.

"Very much." She looked at him curiously. "As you yourself might expect, Mr. Sanborn." She smiled.

"Oh yes," he said. "I can't imagine giving up my painting. It's all I've ever done, or nearly so. I had my first drawing lessons when I was about your age—when we first met, I should say."

"You studied much?"

"Yes, I continued from there. Three or four masters over the course of nearly ten years, until I turned out as my own master and began to paint portraits and give lessons for my bread and butter."

"And portraits have done very well by you."

"Well enough, and the lessons too." He stopped work on the canvas and looked her in the eye. "Forgive me, but I can't believe you've given over all picture making. You must of an evening or idle moment try your hand."

"I do a little sketching and drawing, but very little. And I have no colors here."

"That's a shame, truly. You could not bring colors with you, or purchase some anywhere?"

"No, sir. I was not allowed to."

Not allowed to? he thought. Had the Prescotts seen her darker productions? Perhaps so, and determined them not suitable or healthy.

"I see," was all he dared say. "I can leave some colors with you, I suppose, when I return to Portsmouth. A few pastels anyway. What sort of drawings?"

"Different things. For a time, Mr. Prescott allowed me to choose some books, under his care, from his small library. But here, beyond school lessons when the town can keep a schoolmaster, the children are only allowed to read the Bible and Dr. Watts's *Divine Songs*. Luke and Joshua, the older boys, are allowed certain readings and sums for trade, for when they grow to manhood. The schoolhouse has been standing for some time, but they have not been able to induce a schoolmaster to stay on. I don't care for the dull illustrations in the *Songs,* so I am making a few of my own, pen-and-ink sketches. On Dr. Watts's themes."

"Is that so? Interesting." He said nothing for a few minutes more while he worked. She was a beautiful child, nay, "young woman," he corrected himself. Character and beauty shone from her face, however dull or common the clothes. It was that vitality she had somehow captured in her old self-portrait.

Finally, he decided to ask. What had he to lose? "May I see a few of those, Rebecca? Your Watts?"

She looked at him curiously again. "If you wish. I suppose there is no harm in it. And if you don't mind my saying so, Mr. Sanborn, it's easy to speak the truth to you as to a young person who is honest and open."

"Even naive," he put in. "Not like other adults." He laughed.

"Most adults are always hiding one thing or another, it's true. They grow afraid to speak their minds."

He laughed again. He thought of Gingher, who always spoke her mind. "So long as you'll allow me to view these new drawings."

"After we finish, then, yes. But I'm wanted in the kitchen garden this afternoon. I mustn't tarry."

When he completed Rebecca in the group portrait, she was very curious to see it. He allowed her to be the first to see the completed painting.

"That is well done, Mr. Sanborn," she said seriously.

"Thank you. Have I improved to your satisfaction?" he said and laughed.

"Please don't mock me, sir. Your portraits please me."

"Well, then, do you suppose you might fetch a few of your drawings while I clean up?"

She agreed and left him. In but a few minutes she returned with the redoubtable Watts in her hands, sheaves of loose paper sticking out of the slim book.

She placed the book on the now clean table he had used for his own materials. She smiled but said nothing as she opened the book to her sketches. They were all in pen on paper, black-and-white only, with something of the quality of wood engravings. The subjects most respectably religious. Nothing offensive or distempered. Yet they were accomplished, larger, and vastly superior to the book's own crude and childish illustrations.

The happier verses were rendered into light pictorials: domestic animals fatted and grazing in fields, while on mountain and in forest birds and deer feasted on fruited trees and bushes. This drawing illustrated the "Song in Praise of Creation and Providence."

> I Sing th' Almighty pow'r of God,
> That made the mountains rise,
> That spread the flowing seas abroad
> And built the lofty skies. . . .

> I Sing the goodness of the Lord,
>> That fill'd the earth with food,
> He form'd the creatures with his word,
>> And then pronounced them good.

Another of the light drawings illustrated "Innocent Play": lambs in meadows sporting by the side of their dams, their fleeces spotless. All the while, on the other side of the picture young doves in a large open cage were playing innocently, "without anger or rage" as the lyric put it, even as good children should play.

But there were darker songs, and to these she had appended darker drawings: a blooming youth "snatch'd away / By death's restless hand." Annanias struck dead for lying and his wife Sapphira dying for confirming his lie. Prideful men and women, looking suspiciously like Dantesque caricatures of Portsmouth merchants, strutting in their opulence, illustrating "Against Pride in Clothes." Beggars, mostly children, in a city street depicting the lines,

> Whene'er I take my walks abroad
>> How many poor I see. . . .
> How many children in the street
>> Half naked I behold
> While I am clothed from head to feet,
>> And covered from the cold.

"These are very well done, Rebecca, I must say."

"You think I improve, sir?"

"Well, these are but drawings only, yet if you do not mock *me*, I think you do."

She smiled, her face glowing. "Thank you, Mr. Sanborn."

"Has anyone seen these? I don't think there could be any offense taken." He held up the drawings, re-examining them one by one. "You are being faithful to Dr. Watts."

"My sister, Sarah. It was she who brought the pen and ink to me." Rebecca smiled, as if remembering the act fondly. "And Mrs.

Prescott has seen only one or two. She found them and saw no harm, finally, such goodly subjects. But she admonished me not to dwell on them or waste precious time."

"Then she agrees with me," he said, still examining each drawing closely, "that there can be no offense in these."

"Oh, do you think so, sir? It gives me pleasure to hear it. I saw no offense, but you see I had been forbidden to make pictures of any sort."

"Forbidden?"

"By Colonel Browne and Mr. Prescott."

"Surely they had nothing such as your Dr. Watts in mind." He laughed to encourage her. "I find these . . . I wonder if we might not encourage such milder productions. Surely Mr. and Mrs. Prescott might be convinced."

"I do not think so, sir."

"Well, perhaps not. But perhaps all the same."

"It would mean a great deal to me if they would allow it."

"I'll see what I can do. It may be that they would allow some . . ."—he searched for a word—"instruction." She looked at him blankly. "Some supervision on my part. It can't hurt to ask."

"If you say so, sir, but take care, please, in how you put the idea to them."

"I shall, I promise you."

She gathered up the illustrations and packed them neatly back into the book. "I must get on with my tasks," she said and left quickly.

Chapter 16

THAT VERY AFTERNOON, once the Prescotts had viewed the still-wet painting of the children with apparent satisfaction, he accepted an offered tumbler of metheglin. While they were enjoying their drinks, he off-handedly broached the question of giving Rebecca occasional drawing lessons.

"She has attempted a few, in pen and ink, which I asked to see," he quickly added, "on divine matters, Dr. Watts to be precise, which she gave me to understand you presented her upon her arrival." He gave Mrs. Prescott a friendly look. "I think such an exercise of her talents would be wholly salubrious. And keep her mind off darker matters."

"Her labors and responsibilities here provide salubrious effects, Mr. Sanborn," Mr. Prescott said. "My wife and I have discussed giving her license to draw, now and then. We are aware of her impulse to improve the rather clumsy little illustrations in Dr. Watts, and in some measure we take your point, sir. However, even if we were to allow her to practice upon such enlightened subjects alone, we would be countering Colonel Browne's will. So, to be brief, we wish to discourage rather than encourage her."

"I see your dilemma." He looked pleasantly at Mr. and Mrs. Prescott in turn. "But if she were closely supervised, if her strong desire to make pictures of any sort were, well, channeled by a guiding hand, a hand such as my very own, it would not only bring the child much delight, but also nourish those very gifts the good Lord Himself provided her."

The Prescotts did not reply immediately, so he continued his case. "These lessons on such pious subjects would, in short, inspire her to her happiest moods, rather than her more melancholic hours. And we would be confirming her Christian duty. Surely Squire and Madam Browne desire only that she be released from her somber moments that her mind and heart may take a brighter turn."

"They had hoped that honest labor in planting field and household would do as much," Mr. Prescott suggested. "And, as I say, we believe it has."

"I agree," Sanborn said. "Yet I, we, would only be continuing her progress, nay, even deepening, quickening it. Perhaps we should ask Squire Browne about my proposal. Put in the right light, the proposal, I have hope, will meet with success."

"There's something in what you say, Mr. Sanborn," Mrs. Prescott put in. "And the Brownes know you and your refined portraits. Perhaps it's not too far-fetched." She looked tentatively at her husband, who returned a more skeptical look.

Sanborn wondered why he had taken Rebecca's cause so vigorously. While he was in this town, her new home, he wished to slake his curiosity about her productions, as much as about her welfare. That much he understood. But he felt a renewed vehemence. An unreasonable desire to see all her drawings—he did not doubt there were more—and probe her state of mind as much as her unsettling gift. Such impulses, he realized now in a bizarre moment of self-reflection, had begun to consume him. He could not explain them yet, even to himself. And he worried that they might distract him from his own more important work.

"We cannot have it until I speak with the Brownes," Mr. Prescott was saying. "I may find I can put the matter to them, but I will not have the opportunity to travel to Portsmouth. Some of our absent, more speculative proprietors have been selling parcels to high bidders from Massachusetts, and they are causing us innumerable difficulties just now."

"I appreciate how business consumes your energies and hours,

Mr. Prescott. You are much needed in Blackstone. However, I wonder if you might write of our proposal in a letter to the colonel?"

"It's not a matter easily presented in a letter. It would require some conversation and due consideration, directly, man-to-man."

"You're perhaps right, after all, Mr. Prescott."

THERE WAS, as a result of all these considerations, a delay in his further contact with Rebecca. Well into his fourth month there, with demand for his services waning, he decided to return to Portsmouth. He had no idea when Mr. Prescott might be able to speak as he had said to Colonel Browne, and soon the season would prevent convenient travel. And the nagging thought returned: Was he spending his own precious time wisely?

Chapter 17

HE FOUND LADD through acquaintances in the town who made inquires abroad for him. It was close to Ladd's intended time of travel, as it turned out, so within three days Sanborn found himself on the path to Portsmouth.

They were nearly halfway in their travels when Ladd stopped and turned in his saddle. "Smell that?"

Sanborn sniffed the air. "Fire?"

"Yes. Listen."

The two men sat their horses in complete silence. Sanborn heard something—a distant angry wind. "Is that the conflagration we hear, then?" he asked Ladd.

"Fire hunt," he said.

"I've never seen one. I thought it was restricted to winter." He had heard of this practice from the painter Robert Feke, after Smibert introduced the two younger portraitists when Feke was visiting Boston. Feke took pleasure in regaling Sanborn, a green Englishman, with tales of the New World.

"Or approaching winter, or in spring," Ladd said, "if the season's wet enough, as our last month has been. Want to join in?"

Sanborn recalled Feke suggesting one of the great dangers of this method—where large companies go up into the woods and set a fire circle of several miles circumference. The danger was that rather than merely contracting inward to trap the animals, the fires sometimes broke outward and burned uncontrollably for several weeks. But it made for very rewarding hunting otherwise, and the original settlers had learned it from the Indians a century ago.

"If you'd like," Sanborn said.

The two men set off in the direction of the sound. Shortly, they came to the burned-over ground, still smoldering in places. The mature trees were all left standing, if severely burned and doubtful of regeneration by the look of them. The huntsmen had already gone well into the ever-contracting burn area and Sanborn and Ladd followed them, yet unseen, inward.

It was not long before they encountered members of the hunting party, one member whom Ladd knew by name. After some talk while they waited for the newly burned ground to cool down enough to proceed, Ladd and Sanborn were invited to join in the sport.

The whole affair cost them a day's delay in their travels, but Ladd seemed especially in his element when the flames finally drew to a small compass and the animals of all kinds began to respond in panic to the full realization of their entrapment. A few of the most desperate, deer in particular, began to break through the smoke and flames to escape the ever-enclosing circle and no sooner staggered in dismay into the smoky daylight than the hunters began to shoot them.

Sanborn took a few musket shots himself, at first, as all the animals began to break out, but it came to seem a very bloody business, this slaying of scorched, dazed, panicking animals of every species, so he refrained from taking further advantage of their plight. He recalled Feke's comment on the practice: "It causes incurable injury and devastation in the woods." Little more than two years later, when the provincial legislature would pass "An Act for the Better Preservation & Increase of Deer," Sanborn immediately would understand the necessity. Now, he assured himself once again that he was never meant for a bloody woodsman, but was bred entirely to a city man of polite taste and urban pleasures.

The butchery in the aftermath was equally repugnant to him. Scores of animals were strung up in a great ring among the trees. What seemed to be tons of offal, steaming and oddly green smelling, fell in piles upon the ground, to be left for scavengers. And then the skinning, the hacking at joints, the cracking of bones. Before dark, Ladd himself had neatly packaged one hundred pounds of prime venison for sale in Portsmouth and a wolf head with both ears for a four-pound bounty. Even the nearby stream could not wash the blood and soot entirely from their hands and faces. Ladd and Sanborn had no choice but to camp with the hunters that night, gorging on wild meats, and resume their journey at first light.

UPON ARRIVING at Portsmouth the following afternoon, Sanborn stood Ladd dinner and a pot of toddy and paid him for his return services. The very next thing he did, after the two men took their leave, and Sanborn returned his hired horses to the livery stable, was to search for Gingher among her haunts.

"Look who's returned from the king's wood," she said, an amused sneer on her face as she left a tippler and came over to Sanborn.

He handed her a pound note and told her to "bathe and purchase a respectable hat and gown," before visiting him in his rooms that evening.

She looked at him, snatched the money, tossed her hair, and turned to go.

"Seven thirty," he said.

She immediately turned back to look at him. "'Ee's been a long time, 'ee 'as." She smiled wickedly.

"And would you mind dropping that ridiculous cockney-talk with me, please. I'm not one of your coarse boys."

He had patronized her enough by now to know that her usual manner of speaking was an affectation, a sort of stage effect, as if she would speak so as to fulfill a sportsman's expectations. She could speak plainly if she wished and, he had confirmed, she could read as well. He suspected that she had had another life, but had somehow fallen into dishonor. And tales of the hanging of two women in Portsmouth for the birth and destruction of their bastard infants kept him from asking about the sources of her disrepute.

"Yet coarse enough for all that!" she jibed him. As she walked away, she laughed, but he knew from past experience, though he had never invited her to his painting rooms, that she would honor his proposal.

His next order of business was to wash any remaining soot and blood from his flesh and send his card around to the Brownes to alert them to his return from, so far as they knew, painting portraits among the settlements. He intended to call on them briefly to report that he had inadvertently come upon Rebecca in his travels, give them innocent but hearty news of her, and suggest to them that her guardian, Mr. Prescott, would be in town for a visit, most likely the following spring. Calling on the Brownes would also help to alert the gentry to his return.

He had many affairs to put in order, and such matters occupied his mind for several hours. Not the least of which was to prepare an offer to speculate in lands as one of the participating proprietors himself through, as Prescott had informed him, a grant of the colonel's. As in England, so in America: A man without property was little more than a vagabond or a servant. Next to his commissions, the slow and careful accumulation of property would become a central concern.

His occupations made the hours fly toward 7:30, when he was surprised in all his plans by a knock on his door. He looked up from his writing table confused at first. Another strong knock, and then he remembered Gingher. He put down everything and hurried to his door. She stood there, well powdered, in a glaring new gown, with an open skirt displaying a silk petticoat, a plunging bodice, and a nearly presentable hat, looking less a common harlot and more a fashionable young widow of flagrant availability. A white mask on a stick dangled from her hand. Her shawl slid from her shoulders and there was no scarf or fichu to subdue her bosom. She smiled but said nothing. He gathered himself and asked her in.

She gave him a rather sly look as she passed him to begin examining his quarters. She bent over his work table, on which he had arranged in "lucky order" his brass crayon holder, his chamois stump, quill drawing pens, pen knife, a compass, brushes, his shell for thinning bister, his water pot, and his ruler. She studied the implements as if they were sacred objects from ancient lands. Finally, she stood straight and glanced at him without a word. She stepped over to his model's rotating stool and sat on it, grinning at him. Suddenly she swiveled to face his artist's layman—a life-size female figure made of wire armature, fabric stuffing, and papier-mâché—and placed her hands on her hips. She looked the figure up and down as if it might be a rival. "God's blood, sir! What the devil do you do with this lot?" She turned to look at him, a taunt in her face.

"It's my artist's model, for heaven's sake, Gingher. It allows a painter to labor longer over the garments and drapery than a sitter can sit. With some patrons it's quite necessary, I assure you."

"I can imagine," she said and turned back to the mannequin. She gave out a little mocking laugh. "Quite convenient."

"Please have a seat, just here. Would you care for a glass of Vidonia?"

She sat down as he indicated, smiled, and held out her hand to accept the glass.

"The governor's health," he said, touching her glass.

"Bugger the gov'ner!"

"Now, Gingher, I thought we were going to avoid the stage antics. Let's talk plainly, if you please."

"You'll see no stage in this town," she said and sipped at her glass. "Too many Congregationalists and hypocrites."

"Be that as it may, I'd prefer to talk plainly, as we have on occasion before."

She drank off her glass and held it out for a refill. "Agreed, sir!" she said with a just audible smack of her lips.

He asked her about her own adventures and the doings about her part of town while he was away, and she inquired a bit about his own travels in turn. With every glass of wine she grew more appeased and friendly, as if suddenly recalling after his long absence what a promising patron he had become for her.

Finally, he stated his secondary purpose. "What would you say if I offered to match your weekly take in the trade?"

She looked at him skeptically and spoke with irony in her voice. "To what purpose, sir, if I may make so bold?"

"To free you from your coarse labors, and the dangers attendant to them. To arrive at an agreement that I shall become, in utter discretion, your sole patron and will provide for you in divers ways." He smiled. "That new gown becomes you, as I imagine you know."

"I liked it from putting it on," she said. "There were very few adjustments required." There was warmth in her voice but she offered no smile. She quietly considered his bold offer, sipping her wine.

He watched her. She was very striking in her clean dress and toilette; he had not yet truly appreciated her . . .—he searched for a word—potentiality. She had gone to some trouble herself.

"How do you know I don't prefer my traffic as it is?"

"I can't believe that. It's serviceable, to be sure, but I can't believe you *enjoy* such . . . attachments."

"And what makes you think I'd enjoy a sole attachment to you the more? It comes to the same thing, don't it?"

She had a point, the darling devil. He held in his laugh. "In a sense, yes, I suppose it does," he said. "But there is a distinction nonetheless."

"Oh, yes," she said. "A distinction." She looked at him as if to see whether he was serious. "To begin, I'd have to leave my quarters. I can't stay there if I'm to be bound to one man in a pretense of respectability. Then there's the matter of your own reputation, should you be seen with me." She held the mask up to her face and began to laugh. "You're proposing 'gainst your own interests, seems to me."

"On the second matter, so long as we are scrupulously discreet, let me worry about that. Would I be the first man to take a mistress? I'm not speaking of traipsing up and down the thoroughfares arm in arm."

"I imagine not, sir." She gave another coarse little laugh.

"As to new rooms, we can arrange something, I'm sure." He held her stare. "I can't believe you'd prefer living in public stews. One might as well live in a bog house."

"Don't you, as everyone, have to pay your visits to the bog house?" She laughed lightly.

"It is one thing to dispense with a necessary office, quite another to take up residence there."

She laughed again, then looked at him without a smile. "That would make for you, all told, substantial expense. Why would you want to do so?" She placed the mask on her lap and smiled. "This proposal of yours seems ill considered to me. How's it in your own interest, truly?"

"It's in my interest because you are in my interest. I propose it so that we may have a more simple, unadulterated connection. An understanding. And, to be honest, I don't like sharing you with others so randomly, so perilously."

Her face lost its smile. "You are not mocking me, then? You are serious after all. A private room." She did not smile or indicate any favor on the proposal.

Instead, she added a stipulation: "I'd like a tutor, sir."

"A tutor," he said, a mere statement.

"To make progress in reading and sums."

"I see." He could not afford the additional expense, not yet.

"Once a week," she went on. "I would, under your proposal, have plenty of leisure now to progress each week between lessons."

"But you already read, Gingher. You are free to continue."

"My skill's not sufficient. And I have no taste."

He saw he could not avoid her final terms. "It will take a little more time for me to arrange for this. Would you allow me to help you in reading and sums for now? We will find you a *proper* tutor as soon as I can manage it."

"Well, then, you can instruct me to draw as well, Mr. Sanborn."

He tried not to hesitate. "If you wish. We'll meet once a week, for an hour or two, devoted to your instruction in sums and letters and drawing. For now. Does that suit you?"

"It does, sir." She flashed a smile. "And we'll begin tomorrow then."

He agreed, and at the time she appointed. She looked at him expectantly, as if it were time to come to the ultimate business of the evening, or to deny it. She put down her glass, half full, and waited for him.

He put down his empty glass, stood, and went over to her. He took her elbows and raised her to her feet and then embraced her, not assertively but firmly. He tasted the wine still on her lips. It struck him that their attitude was a mockery of connubial affections, but she, as if catching his thoughts, slid her hands directly to his waist and then one hand tested his earnestness. He was painfully taut.

He wondered for but a moment what it would be like to have to woo a woman again, rather than this directness between them. He thought another instant that he was glad not to have to woo anybody, to save his strategies and his energies for more important business. This was far more . . .—he searched crazily for a word as her hand boldly stroked him—efficient. Yes, less wasteful.

He began to unfasten her gown as quickly as he could, but it being a new garment, he fumbled, so she helped him. Within minutes they were disrobed. She had held only her mask and a small case with a cupid engraved on it. She placed the mask over her face again, laughing. He picked her up and carried her to his bed, where he flung her down and savored her nakedness an instant more. In a quick movement, she opened the case she had retained in her left hand, took out a small sponge, and inserted it deep into Cupid's grotto. Sanborn fell to his knees in front of her. Her hands grabbed the hair on his head and they began a familiar yet desperate dance together—without connubial tenderness, to be sure, but with a selfish exuberance that, so far as he could tell, enflamed them both.

Chapter 18

FROM THEN ON Gingher became his particular mistress, and he devoted renewed energies to her support as well as to his. Fresh commissions started to come his way following his absence, and he immediately began his own speculations in land, through Colonel Browne and the Wentworth clan's far-flung proprietorships. His investments were, of course, modest at first and worthy of a popular artist's income, purchasing a half-right here and there at about fifty shillings.

But before long he also began to experience success in selling off some properties that rose in value surprisingly quickly, and with his profits, he purchased still more rights in promising towns. With the help of Mr. Hart particularly, the merchant he had once painted, and by cultivating as well other acquaintances, he had kept his finger on the vicissitudes of land values, grants, and proprietors. With some regularity now, he supped with men of substance in the Wentworth Tavern or Colonel Packer's Tavern. A number of these men, and their family members, he had painted. He joined their drinking parties, ever more raucous as they tossed about the bumpers, and their heated political debates, which sometimes devolved into blows. He drank "to the ladies" and "to the governor" and to a host of others as the evening toasts went round. He wandered with them into the streets under the stars, struggling to regain a dignity and propriety they had by tacit agreement cast off within the tippling rooms. And he was all the more pleased to be resettled in the capital during that fall, for the throat distemper had appeared again in Stratham, Hampton, and other towns, carrying away scores of people.

By the spring of 1743, he anticipated, from what he understood of such men, Mr. Prescott was due to return to Portsmouth on business of his own. He, in fact, found Mr. Prescott on a windy May day in Packer's Tavern sitting with a group of notable men. Sanborn was welcomed to join their hearty company, and he then proceeded to outlast several of them at table in hopes of gaining Prescott's ear.

Prescott seemed pleased to learn of Sanborn's success in modest speculations, as if such news placed the two together by some sort of divine justice among men of significance in the very alehouses where provincial business was transacted.

"Have you given any more thought to Rebecca, Mr. Prescott?" he asked, late in their agreeable conversation. "I'm still willing to offer instruction and guidance, from time to time, that might brighten her hours. And concentrate her talents on appropriate matters."

"I'm only just arrived, Mr. Sanborn, and have been conducting other business."

"Of course," he said. "I only meant to ask after your intentions and whether I might be of assistance in any way. You say your wife and children are well, mercifully. But I wonder, how is Rebecca?"

"Very well, if mopish on occasion."

"Indeed, all the more reason to leaven her domestic labors with infrequent drawing lessons and illustrations of Christian themes."

"That may be so, Mr. Sanborn. Mrs. Prescott agrees with you, as you perhaps know. I think I might induce the colonel to agree to these sacred themes, merely. But until we speak to him, and at the right time for so delicate a matter, we had better practice patience."

"I concur, my friend. Allow me to honor you with another."

"No, thank you. I'd better be off. Another appointment with two of our absentee proprietors. Some other time, certainly."

The two men rose and Sanborn made a little bow as Prescott left.

DURING THE MONTHS following his return to Portsmouth, however, it never became clear to Sanborn whether Squire Browne could be persuaded to allow Rebecca liberty either of lessons or drawing and painting on her own. It was disheartening to Sanborn, and to Miss Norris, when he spoke to her. He had put off his conversation with Miss Norris until, as he had hoped, he could report good news. She was not pleased by his delay. Worse, she had found another source of displeasure.

"You should not be seen with that woman," she said.

"Woman?"

"That vile trollop." She looked defiantly into his eyes.

"I am not 'seen' with her, Miss Norris. She is an old acquaintance, who helped me on occasion when I first tried to settle here. I encounter her now and then, as people do in a confined seaport."

"Encounter indeed!"

He knew that he had taken pains to avoid being seen with Gingher. Had Miss Norris heard something? From whom? She looked at him as if he had betrayed her somehow. He believed that he had not been toying with her interest in him as a rising young man of the world, who, he assumed, was roughly her own age. He doubted she saw him as "a match." But they had indulged in a mild, unspoken flirtation while pursuing their mutual concern for Rebecca.

"I'm sorry," he finally said, "that I've somehow not met your expectations. But that failure on my part is relatively unimportant, is it not? There is, Miss Norris, a certain young woman whom we both admire and wish to . . . well, to protect. I think we would do better to combine our energies to help her in any manner we can. The fact of the sorry matter is that Rebecca is to rusticate in her enforced retreat, that she is to be consumed—for some years it seems—by the distraction and rigor of country labors."

She gave him a last angry glance and turned away. "That may be," she said with her back to him. "That may be, Mr. Sanborn. You are, of course, in one sense right. Yet surely you understand that a woman in my position, and who is known to have your acquaintance, cannot continue to associate with one who entertains harlots." She turned to face him, her eyes hardened. "I cannot afford to be dragged into the gutter by association. If I ever see or hear of you in any way entertaining that lewd woman again, I shall be forced to sever our ties." She left immediately, as if to drive her assertions home. He had thought he was being discreet with Gingher, but he saw now the necessity of a more vigilant discretion. In fact, he soon was making inquiries as to the possibility of new quarters for Gingher in the nearby town of Greenland.

1745

Voted that provided fifty good effective soldiers including officers will inlist themselves in his majesties service by ye first Day of June next for five months, under such proper officers as shall be appointed by his Excellency to go in Pursuit of our Indian enemies . . . & for further Incouragement as a Bounty, that they be allow'd for each male Indian they shall kill, . . . upward of twelve year old & scalp produced, ye sum of Seventy Pounds & Captives Seventy eight Pounds, fifteen shillings & for Females & others under ye age of twelve years old killd & scalp produced thirty seven Pounds ten shillings & captives thirty nine Pounds five shills. . . .

    —*Journal* of the House of Representatives, under the
      administration of Governor Benning Wentworth,
      Wednesday, May 7, 1746

I have often lamented . . . that the Art of Painting is made so little use of in the improvement of our manners. When we consider that it places the action of the person represented in the most agreeable aspect imaginable, that it does not only express the passion or concern as it sits upon him who is drawn, but has under those features the height of the painter's imagination. . . . This is a poetry which would be understood with much less capacity and less expense of time, than what is taught by writings; but the use of it is generally perverted and that admirable skill prostituted to the basest and most unworthy ends

    —Richard Steele, *Spectator* #226

Chapter 19

By 1745, however, Sanborn and Miss Norris had other worries. He had grown prosperous, relative to his arrival, and she had long settled into her governess position at Mr. Sherburne's. But throughout the past year, the eternal conflict between the French and English had been heating up again toward, as far as anyone could guess, a major conflagration in America. Towns not far away—Stratham, Newmarket, among others—had been harassed by Indian raiding parties in 1743 and again in 1744. One squire from Stratham had written to the Assembly for aid, complaining of constant alarums and warning horns on either side of the Exeter River. The people were much unsettled by it. And they had had difficulties and suffering enough from the hard winters of 1741 and 1744, from the recent disruptions of religious frenzy in their parishes, and now from the high wartime prices of merchants' goods and basic commodities.

As if the great comet raging in the sky all day—in spite of the very sun—during much of February had foretold some looming cataclysm, all regularities of life and business had been disrupted in the spring of 1744. The home government declared war against France in March and the colonies declared war shortly thereafter. Militia were continually being collected and prepared, many for departures and expeditions, for privateers and cruising service, and ultimately for Louisbourg. Even Sanborn had been called to muster and parade, like everyone else, and he was not amused by the prospect of battle, although he had formerly been amused by the ineptitude and raillery of such harmless peacetime "military" drinking fests. He had no intention of enlisting or being impressed to serve the province at the risk of his life for five pounds per month plus provisions. To encourage men to enlist, pay scales were posted, including potential bounty money, around town. Sanborn began making other plans.

He took some comfort, however, in the long harbor fort, with its great triangle of bastions upon the rock ledge facing the bay, its thirty thirty-two-pound guns, its score of twelve-pounders, its guard of sixty men, its flocks of geese, which the governor touted as a foolproof alarm against nocturnal surprise (after the example of the ancient Roman capitol).

On the eve of the Siege of Louisbourg, the French fortification on Cape Breton Island, Miss Norris and Sanborn's greatest concern was Rebecca's vulnerability to renewed, and more virulent, Indian attacks on settlements to the west. In addition, Sanborn had the harrowing experience of watching his most westward land investments freeze and even decline in value during the new insecurity.

"How can her own kin ignore the danger?" Miss Norris was saying. With considerable effort over time, he had re-established himself in her good graces. Perhaps his most effective ploy was inconspicuously removing Gingher, to her own satisfaction, to a rent (an old two-room dwelling) in Greenland. Through care in her attire and address, he and she had constructed a respectable identity for her—a young widow of some leisure and modest education. The small house with room for a kitchen garden was in a private setting, yet within walking distance from the town center. His weekly tutoring continued, as did his occasional other "visits," as they now referred to them.

Miss Norris seemed wary now, but willing to let him demonstrate his trustworthiness. She had agreed to meet along the Parade, as the most seemly device. "I know that the Prescotts intend to stay on until the signs grow more sure. And they have much faith in their new garrisons. But for the Brownes to leave the child, to whom they had once shown such affection and solicitude, in such a dangerous situation . . ." She paused in her anger to search for words. "I must say, sir, it is utterly beyond my understanding."

"I, too, can't understand it," he said in a calming voice. "My efforts have long fallen on deaf ears. I now believe the squire stands obdurate on principle."

"It's a scandal," she said. She could not speak anything more.

"It may well become so if any harm befalls the child."

They walked for a time in silence, noticing the ladies and gentlemen around them.

"Perhaps I could intervene, in some way, if things turn untenable."

She looked up at him. "How do you mean, sir?"

"I have no idea, at the moment. I'm not fool enough to be taking reckless chances myself. But, I've already made inquiries through Colonel Browne that I might be allowed to look after his interests in Blackstone and its environs, as well as the interests of certain of his associates, and of my own. Were I to visit Blackstone and inquire after her once more, well, I could both better assess the security of their position now and plead with the Prescotts for their own removal, if necessary." He did not add that he would use his official mission to avoid other militia duties he had no heart to perform.

"That would be something," she said. "But there's risk to yourself, and unless they do remove, and soon, it will have done little good."

"You're right, of course." He looked at her. She was not about to be appeased. "What else can I do now, however?"

"I see no alternative. It would be doing something, at the least."

They grew silent again as they walked. Sanborn calculated that Rebecca should be about sixteen years old that year. She was not a helpless child any more, if she ever had been. Still, she was an extraordinary young woman, and a town on the hostile frontier was no place for her.

As they strolled in the May evening, Sanborn recalled earlier that spring attending a sermon—it was more a ceremonial social and military occasion—by Parson Moody in Kittery, seat of William Pepperrell, commander of forces for Louisbourg. It was just prior to the expedition's sailing forth. Several families of stature from Portsmouth were present, largely because of Governor Wentworth's enthusiasm for some ultimate battle with the French papists who would encroach on England's and, more to the point, Wentworth's own royal colony. It was by now widely accepted that the defeat of Louisbourg was essential—as necessary to British interests as the defeat of Carthage appeared to the Romans. (Later, not to be outdone, Parson Arthur Browne would give a similar, Church-of-England version of the sermon in Queen's Chapel calling for the final defeat of the French interlopers.)

"That dearest pastor in Christ, the Reverend Mr. Whitefield himself," old Moody had said, "gave William Pepperrell—justice of the peace, president of Governor Shirley's Council, and now lieutenant general of the combined militias—encouragement to lead and the very motto for our forces: *'Nil desperandum Christo duce.'* And in this crusade, for which I have the honor to serve as senior chaplain, many have joined us with true passion to defeat the French Antichrist. Five thousand militia from New Hampshire and more than thirty-two hundred from Massachusetts and Maine. Thirteen warships from Connecticut, New Hampshire, Rhode Island, and Massachusetts. Can there be any doubt of our Christian resolve? Indeed, there cannot, in the eyes of God!

"Never have greater zeal and purpose shone forth from this New England. The righteous multitudes awaken. Babylon shall be defeated." Here Parson Moody had raised a hatchet off the pulpit and above his head. "I shall be among the first to enter the gates, and with this sword of the Lord and of Gideon I shall rend the church of all vestiges of idolatry." He brandished the hatchet—Nestor in his aged warrior's vigor before Troy. "Thus shall we men of the English colonies, strong and mighty in battle, enlarge the visible kingdom of Christ, even as we diminish the grip of papists, Jesuits, and all anti-Christian powers through the northern regions, from the River of Canada to the ends of America."

By April 29, the forces had embarked on their divine Redeemer's mission. And now Sanborn and Miss Norris, like so many others who stayed behind, awaited news of triumph or, unspoken fear, failure. The waiting caused much anxiety across the province, but the merchants, by withholding goods for war profiteering, had caused further inconvenience and outrage. Finally, even the governor lost patience with his jolly colleagues and confiscated for his troops and the local citizenry all their pork at a fair price.

Chapter 20

BUT THE ENGLISH COLONIAL FORCES did not fail, and in early July of that year there were great celebrations and days of public thanksgiving for the victory of the English against the French at Louisbourg. Speeches and sermons on the "particular providence" abounded throughout the New England colonies, as did bonfires, illuminations, and cannon fire. William Pepperrell, now a general, was given his baronetcy and worshipped as a hero among New England men. He was to return, no less, with the bell of the church at Louisbourg and present it to Curate Browne for Queen's Chapel. Again, Sir William's sumptuous eight-oared barge manned by African slaves soon would be seen upon the river, again his coach drawn by a half-dozen snow-white horses soon upon the street.

But nothing had been settled, really, and Sanborn's worst fears began slowly to materialize. It was not long before the western settlements suffered increased, if sporadic, Indian attacks: Rochester, Contoocook, Pennacook, Suncook. The list grew every week.

That summer and into the fall, Blackstone had been spared. But it was, of course, as vulnerable as any settlement to the west. He called on Miss Norris after hours to say that he had decided to go to the town and, if the Prescotts were not removing for their own safety, he'd rescue Rebecca from danger of death or captivity.

"And how will you do so, Mr. Sanborn?" she asked. "Will you break the law?"

"I do not have a plan as yet. But I take the situation to be desperate, or possibly so. Squire Browne asks that I look after his land interests, but he won't agree to Rebecca's removal. He leaves that to the judgment of Prescott, who, as he says, 'though much occupied in protecting his own interests, is still best suited on the question of removal due to his being on the very site in question.'"

"Scandalous," she said. "In the very teeth of destruction!" She stopped and turned to look up at Sanborn. Her eyes told him she regarded him again as her only ally against the Brownes and Prescotts. "The colonel has, to all purposes, disowned the child."

"Or young lady, rather."

"Yes, young lady, indeed. But, to me, who haven't seen her as you have, she is a child still. Perhaps I will always think of her thus. She was under my tutelage from the age of eight."

"I understand, Miss Norris. I fear Mr. and Mrs. Prescott will place too great a faith in the garrisons. But perhaps they'll relent and return to Portsmouth after all."

"Let us hope they will find their reason."

IN SEPTEMBER, immediately after Governor Wentworth had declared war against the Penobscot, Neridgewock, St. Francis, Wowenock, St. John, and Cape Sable Indians, Sanborn made his final preparations to set out for Blackstone once more.

The day before he left, he paid Gingher a visit in her new rent. She now seemed comfortable in the copsewood privacy of her cottage. He explained that he was leaving for the interior on a potentially dangerous mission. But he assured Gingher that he had arranged for Mr. Hart, who had by now become a trusted business advisor, to manage his investments in his absence. Mr. Hart, Sanborn explained, had also been charged to provide for her rent and sustenance should he, Sanborn, come to a tragic end.

She looked at him. "You are thoughtful, Daniel," she said, "and I am grateful for your thoughtfulness."

She went to a cupboard and drew out a bottle of his favorite sherry. While she poured two thimblefuls, he examined the books and amusing periodicals from the home country she had been using to practice her reading. He explained that his tutoring would have to cease for a time, that he would soon hire her another tutor. He turned over the books to look at them. They were mostly, he gathered, the fashionable romances of her mother's day: *Cassandra, Cleopatra, Astrea, Tryall, The Fifteen Comforts of Matrimony,* and so on. He wondered if she had stolen them.

As she handed him his sherry and looked into his eyes, he felt a strange and desperate curiosity about her former life. Perhaps, he thought, his desperation arose from the danger to which he was about to subject his own life, just as she was becoming more familiar to him. Whatever the source, he just blurted the question.

"Gingher. You once told me you were raised in London. Surely you can tell me now how you came to be here."

Despite their ever-more-comfortable liaison, she had refused to discuss her past whenever he tried to bring it up. Now she shot him a look that said: You believe you own me now?

She had put on a loose silken robe. He went over to her and picked her up, then returned to the single chair. She allowed him to adjust her comfortably on his lap. He lightly kissed her neck and shoulders, breathing her familiar scent, until she began to smile.

"Did you come to Portsmouth directly?" he persisted.

"No."

"New York? Boston? New London? By way of the Indies?"

"Boston."

"Ah," he said. "Boston. Just as I did."

She said nothing.

"As a child with your family?"

She laughed mockingly. "My sister. With my sister. When I was fifteen."

"Oh," he said. "Your parents. They remained behind. Perhaps they had passed away."

"Behind."

"You and your sister were sent out to service?"

She looked away.

"You were running away," he said, a statement, as if he had readily solved a riddle.

She would not speak. He thought that she must already regret this new arrangement, his impertinent intrusions that were never part of their bargain, their understanding. Still, he could not help this new sense of desperation and vulnerability, his own vulnerability to injury or death. But he lost his courage to press her further, and they sat in silence for long minutes.

Suddenly she stood up and turned her back to him. "Running away," she said.

He hesitated. "I see. With your sister."

"My parents disowned my older sister, Jenny. She was thereby forced to leave. She and I were the only surviving children. And we had grown very close. I could never have tolerated her absence in our household."

He said nothing, believing it now better to wait.

"Of course, they were not wealthy people, my parents," she said. "But they were not ignorant people. They ran a Cheapside mercer's shop, a successful one. My sister and I were apprenticed into the family business. Jenny they educated, and she in turn taught me to read, and something of figures as well."

When she paused, still looking away, he remained silent, as if the sound of his voice might stop her. Finally, she turned to look at him. "But she shamed them," she added.

"And they would not have it," he said, a simple statement.

She sat on her bed and looked at the floor. "Yes," she said, nodding her head. But she would speak no more of it, and he thought better of asking further questions.

THE NEXT MORNING he set out with the express rider under guard of two scouts. The scouts were joining one of the several parties of a dozen to a score of men and their dogs whose job was to range continually from garrison to garrison to discourage the enemy from crossing the line of frontier fortifications and to protect townspeople in their outdoor labors. Men had been induced to such hazardous duty by the temptation of high returns for scalps— thirty, forty, fifty pounds and more each that they would divide among the members of the scout.

There were a few way stations along the road now. Sanborn took some minimal painting gear, clothes, and a few rations on a packhorse. Should circumstances require, he was fully prepared to leave everything behind and give the second horse to Rebecca. That was the extent of his "plan." He knew only that he could not settle for Squire Browne's assurances and complacency from his secure position in Portsmouth. The only flaw in Sanborn's plan, a flaw he tried not to contemplate, was that he had no rational explanation as to why he had come to feel so personally responsible for Rebecca that he would place his own life at risk.

The town looked as he remembered it, but now there were men on guard duty and a new blockhouse in addition to the old garrison. There was also a new lodging house, a regular ordinary, to which he was directed upon querying an old peddler.

At the ordinary he saw notices for one of the town's biannual fairs, to be held soon on the parade ground nearby, as if the townsfolk had set themselves an oath not to be distracted by the enemy from common yet essential pursuits. There were to be the usual displays of livestock and produce, the horse races and contests of manly strength and skill, and "live turkeys and geese exposed to marksmen between sunrise and sunset." He found himself anticipating the fair with some pleasure.

The next morning he paid a visit to the Prescott house, but Mr. Prescott, again, was out on business. And because fall chores were well under way, Mrs. Prescott, working beside her servant in the kitchen garden, could spare him little time. He mentioned the uneasiness he felt in the town.

"We are all cautious now," she assured him. "No one ranges into the woods or planting fields alone and without muskets. But perhaps because of our vigilance and care, we have not been attacked or harassed, and we begin to hope we may well not be."

"And you haven't made arrangements to secure your family beyond these wilds, back in Portsmouth?"

"Wilds?" she said. "We have, but only in a general sense. We are, as I say, most vigilant here, everyone sharing the responsibility."

"I see." He marveled at the mechanisms by which people come

to believe whatever suits their immediate convenience. "As you may know, I've come to look after my own investments, and would speak to Mr. Prescott of the matter."

"I'll be sure to tell him so."

He stood there a moment longer, then decided to ask. "This feeling of trouble I sense, is it something more?"

"More?"

"More than the threat of the enemy, I mean, that possibility of imminent attack? Perhaps it is just my imagination, Mrs. Prescott, but I feel something more has caused a lack of spirit and industry I once knew here?"

She put down her implements, stood straight, and looked at him. "Well, it may be understandable that many here believe it is God's judgment on us. You may be feeling something of the sense of hopelessness . . . or not hopelessness, really, but the helplessness of people unwilling to flee to safety and thereby leave all they have built up here, their new lives, behind them."

"Their minds tell them to flee to safety, but their hearts won't allow it."

"Yes. That's what I'm saying."

"And they see God's hand either stayed in some special providence or letting loose destruction upon them."

"Yes, I think that's it. You see, we had a preacher here, one of those New Lighters passing through, and he turned many people's minds. . . ." She stopped to see if he understood the import of what she was telling him. "He put a frightening sense of the wages of sin into them. The other fear, that apprehension about the enemy, was already there."

"But he gave it direction. And they responded with their testimonies and conversions."

"Indeed, Mr. Sanborn, it is something of that. Mr. Prescott was thrown into a rage by it all, but what could he or a few men do? We've had no preacher of our own for some time. No milder influence. And Mr. Prescott had no strength equal to the New Light among those ripening for it."

"So they live in fear yet try to assert their fearlessness and courage."

"I might put it otherwise, but, yes, it is something of that as well."

"No wonder I felt a certain, well, suffocation here, if that's not too strong a word for it. A joyless, spiritless feeling. And false bravado. I hope it has not contaminated you and yours, Mrs. Prescott."

"No, it hasn't. Nor some other families who remain untouched. Mr. Prescott says we should let the frenzy die of its own accord, eventually. In the meantime, we are all the more guarded and vigilant against a real enemy."

"Well, madam, that is a sadder state of affairs than I had hoped to encounter, though I, too, fear the real dangers, of course. One doesn't want to fall asleep only to have some savage knock one's brains out." He looked about the grounds. "And how, then, is Rebecca, if I may ask?"

She looked up and squinted into the sunlight. "She is untouched by the frenzy. It is not her sort of enthusiasm, though I believe her uncle once thought otherwise. And she is quite the young lady now, Mr. Sanborn. We've had suitors at our door."

"Suitors? Well, of course. And why not? Is she about? It would please me to have a word."

"You might try the barn. Or the cabbage vault." She wiped her face with her wrist, then wiped her hand on her apron. It was clear she wanted to get on with her work. "I'll give your regards to my husband, and tell him of your business here. I'm sure he'll be pleased to see you again, Mr. Sanborn."

When he called down into the root cellar Rebecca responded with pleasure in her voice. She came up into the light to greet him. Her hair was in some disarray beneath her neat cap, her clothes were plain, and her face had traces of garden soil on it, but he was utterly taken with her. She was wholly "a womanly creature now," as he put it to himself. He asked after her health and whether she was concerned for living where she did in these times.

She said nothing of herself, but said, "You look well, and prosperous!"

"Thank you. I'm pleased to say I've had good fortune."

"And I'm too busy, Mr. Sanborn, to worry much about the times."

"I see. You are all deferring to Mr. Prescott's judgment."

"That's true, sir."

"I'm sorry that I was unable to prevail upon your guardians to allow for some drawing instruction. That's one reason I had not returned earlier. But I find now I had better begin to look after my own interests here, and some of the colonel's as well."

"Yes. Mr. Prescott told me of your efforts on my behalf. I'm grateful."

"I suppose you managed to continue with the Watts, or some other innocent sketching." He smiled. He lowered his voice conspiratorially. "I can't imagine you don't steal a private moment for yourself."

"Very few."

He wondered if she had not returned a look of conspiratorial impishness. "I'm sure most of your hours are occupied."

"That's so. It's the way of life here."

"Well, I mean to daub a bit while I'm here. Would you not spare me a moment to show some of your own drawings? You've finished Watts? And what else have you turned to at odd moments?"

"I completed my Watts a long time ago, yes. I draw a few pictures that are in my head from time to time, or something of particular interest I've seen."

"A private pastime. And harmless enough."

"Yes, I'm private about it. But I think the Prescotts don't mind how I spend a free hour, now and again. They have business enough of their own."

"I quite imagine they do." He stopped to consider his words. "It's always dangerous to avert the wishes of your elders, but in this instance you are only exercising the gifts God has given you, in rare moments of well-earned leisure." He found he was beginning to enjoy their confidence. Her winsome smile encouraged him. And again he felt astonished by the character of her new womanly beauty.

"I believe the Prescotts see that, given my own rare leisure, as you put it, this scratching on paper is necessary to my composure. They've come to an opinion of raising me in their own way. I've been dutiful since arriving here, and they appreciate my contributions to the household."

"And, thus, do not begrudge you the occasional peccadillo."

"Well, they simply do not ask after it, and I still have no colors, since I've used what you left behind, that is. I ask for nothing, and make use of whatever comes to hand."

"May I see a few then?"

She wiped her soil-darkened hands on her apron. "I suppose we can take a moment. Shall we go in?"

Once inside the empty house, she hurried up to a room under the eaves. In a few moments she had returned, with a sheaf of drawings from Watts and a handful of other sketches.

He looked through the completed Watts. What struck him immediately was her reversal of the typical emblem book, and even of Watts's crude *Divine Songs*. The pictures were no longer dull and subservient to the text. She had shifted the emphasis onto the designs, to which the text now seemed subservient.

"You've done well, as always," he said. "I half wonder if we might not submit the Watts to a Boston printer, perhaps under another name," he added, almost as if musing. "A notice or two in the Boston press, a word here and there, and we might gather some demand for these."

"Do you really think so, sir?"

"And why not? They are well done, and better than what's available. What else have we here?"

"Odd sketches." She handed them over to him. They were all plain and harmlessly lifelike. Trees, birds, forest streams and flowers. And very well executed, intimating some of the energy of her more mystic productions, as he remembered them. Then she uncovered several pen-and-ink portrait sketches.

"Some of the people I know here," she explained.

On each of three sheets were studies of heads and faces, the same face from three or four different angles.

"I see, yes," he said as he held them up and looked them over. "Sitters?"

"No, I sketched these from memory. I see the faces clearly in my mind."

"These are very finely done," he said quietly. "As are all of these you have here." He looked her in the eye. "And the other kind, the more . . . visionary fancies. You have left off those?"

"Yes." She smiled at him. He continued to look directly at her. "For the most part," she added.

"I see. Well, sometime perhaps you will honor me with a few of those, as well."

"If the occasion arises, sir."

"I will be here on business of my own for some days, at least, so perhaps it will."

"Perhaps," she said.

THE NEXT MORNING Mr. Prescott called on him, and after breakfasting at the tavern, they set out together and with two other townsmen, all well armed on horseback, to view some new properties in which Sanborn had an interest. There were no house lots on these yet, nor had the land been broken up and fenced, as the property was more outlying. For some time no one would build, whether they preferred to buy or to rent. He thought that was probably just as well for now. The property might be all the more valuable one day, perhaps not too far off, for never having undergone any destruction in war raids.

During their return, Sanborn took the opportunity to ask whether Mr. Prescott knew of any likely patrons for a portrait or two.

"You might try the Wiggin family," he suggested. "They have labored to prosper. You did not limn them in the past?"

"I did not. Thank you. I'll call on them, tomorrow before the dinner hour."

As they rode on, Sanborn debated to himself whether he should raise the question of Rebecca's drawing. Finally, the two other horsemen a short distance behind them, he decided there was nothing to lose.

"It is a shame Rebecca cannot exercise her talents by painting a portrait now and again," Sanborn said. "It would be a delight to the community and a source of remuneration to your family."

"I had thought of it, but I've wished, in the main, to honor Squire Browne's wishes. When I spoke to him, he did not express complete disapproval of her Watts and sacred drawings, but he doesn't intend to countenance anything more."

"I understand."

"She has no colors, no canvass, no oils of any kind. But I tell you in confidence we don't make a particular point of forbidding her use of pen and paper."

"Yes, that is good of you. Rebecca intimated as much when I spoke to her briefly yesterday."

"She hasn't much leisure, as things are."

"Of course, and in that you fulfill Squire Browne's design."

"My feelings precisely, Mr. Sanborn."

When they rode into the village center in silence and mutual understanding, Sanborn was already thinking up ways to peruse Rebecca's more exotic sketches. And he still had hope that he would be able to talk them into allowing her to take likenesses of Blackstone gentry, a project she seemed to have begun on her own.

Chapter 21

SOON INTO HIS SOJOURN in Blackstone, he was standing before the three Wiggin children, taking their group portrait. The eldest, a girl, was seven; the others, two boys, were five and three. At Sanborn's request, Tristram Prescott had agreed to release Rebecca for a few hours because the Wiggins, associates of Prescott, were concerned over their children's capacity to endure a lengthy sitting. The strategy was working well; Rebecca was good with children and the Wiggins all liked her.

He would not have admitted it to himself, but Sanborn was taking more care than usual, and trying the children's patience. He felt a vague apprehension over Rebecca's eye on his work. But by the end of that long session, he had enough to go on; he could finish the portrait another day. He could return Rebecca to the Prescotts without begging them to release her again. And it was as they walked to her house that he repeated his interest in viewing her other productions.

"If we are alone for a moment, I'll bring down a few sheaves," she finally agreed.

As he awaited her in the parlor, he tried to examine his feelings toward Rebecca. That strange, unpredictable turn of mind that had marked the child seemed to have calmed under the influences, he assumed, of her maturing and rusticating. Yet her mind was as agile and unclouded as ever. And now, more than the appeal of a brilliant, even exotic child, there was the undeniable appeal of the young woman. Suitors indeed! he thought.

She entered the room with a slim bundle of papers tied around with white ribbon.

"Aha," he said.

She placed the bundle on a table before him and untied it carefully. She hung the white ribbon around her shoulders and removed the protective cover. The first drawing had been colored in, from the pastel chalks he had left behind long ago. Perhaps, he thought, these were arranged chronologically.

It was a drawing of lambs gamboling in a spring pasture of an evening. Swallows, like sparks of pure energy, or joy, darted about them. A sort of golden late light suffused the scene. It was meticulously executed yet full of feeling.

"Happy lambs, those!" he said.

"And swallows, too." She laughed a little.

"Indeed they are." He turned the picture over to the next. It was like an opposing vision. A dog before his master's door, in the city. The dog, in a supplicating posture, was obviously underfed. And the artist had somehow depicted the body so as to give the impression of shivering. It was winter, clearly. She had not colored this one. Black on white made it particularly affecting, as if he had received bad news in the midst of a satisfactory day.

The next drawing had been colored, however. It was of a titanic, shapely woman giving birth to a child resplendent in glorious light. The woman's flesh shone as well. To the left of the scene, a dark, rather caterpillarlike figure stood by observing the birth and recoiling in horror. Along the bottom of the drawing were St. Augustine's name and some of his more notorious words: "*Inter faeces et urinam nascimur.*" It was a brilliant—he searched for an appropriate word: speculative? philosophical?—picture, as if executed by a master. In a sense, all her pictures were speculative, but he could discern no systematic philosophy or vision. He began to understand, as by her own testimony, that she did not merely see things differently; rather, she saw different things.

"That must be St. Augustine, then," he said, pointing to the small dark figure.

"I believe it is, yes," she said.

"I can think of a parson or two who would agree with you about him." He smiled.

"It's no doubt all popery to them."

He laughed. "These are extraordinary," he said, for lack of a better word at the moment. "Disturbing, some of them, but extraordinary all."

"You believe so? Thank you, sir."

"Have you kept up your reading?"

"Not as at Squire Browne's, before he forbade me. Much of his library was open to me, for a time. But since coming here, my reading is limited. Mr. Prescott has a small collection, mostly devotional and didactic. I read whatever I can, but I find I have to make words and stories of my own. And pictures."

"And these more ominous fancies. You continue to depict those as well?"

"These are private depictions, or, well, meditations. How can there be light without darkness, Mr. Sanborn?"

"How indeed," he said, turning over the drawings.

"'Must we employ all our faculties merely to humor and please men in their vices and follies?'" she said.

He looked at her, confusion on his face.

She smiled. "Blackmore," she said, "from *Prince Arthur*."

"I see." He turned back to the drawings. One of the darker ones caught his eye particularly. It was a scene of pestilence of some sort. Perhaps inspired by the distemper that had carried away her own family and her brotherly cousins. In a city street among Greco-Roman buildings, children lay dying, while small bodies were being carted off to common graves. In their passion to find hope, parents and citizens dressed in robes were gathering around energetically somber clergymen who held prayer books aloft. The effect was one of timelessness, as if in one such catastrophe lay eons of all such catastrophes. The next scene of devastation looked like something out of Revelations: a decimated forest, cut over, burning in great dragon flames, with scores of God's creatures fleeing like outcast Adams and Eves toward distant, brooding mountains.

Another depicted men aiming muskets in sport at fish teeming and leaping in the river. *Shooting Salmon,* she had labeled it. She had captured, as if sidelong, even in this picture of destruction, something that evoked a powerful memory from his first journey through the woods to Blackstone.

He and Ladd had dismounted to water their horses down a side path in a part of the forest seemingly untouched by Europeans. As he stood beside his drinking horse, he became aware—in his whole body more than in his ears—of the thrumming of insects, the voices and movements of birds, and the mild wind pushing against the high, deep canopies of foliage. It struck him that the whole forest was heaving with some energy not unlike the music of a great organ or the deeper chanting of monkish choristers—subdued yet profound enough to reach into his muscle, sinew, and bone. He had no name for it, or for the resonances in his being. Was it something of God speaking in biblical wildernesses? Or something awakened out of timeless heathen demonologies? He stood there looking into the canopy, ignorant and amazed, listening until Ladd asked him what he heard.

"The forest," was all he could say at the moment.

Now, however, he stood before Rebecca wondering how she had evoked the memory through the picture he had in hand.

"You say you draw these in secret?" he said.

"In private."

"Not in secret, but not openly," he suggested.

"Privately," she insisted.

He could not numb the effect her pictures had upon him—the enduring impression. He recalled one of his masters, a curmudgeon with little patience for fashion, once saying to him in a picture gallery, "Too many of these men know everything of artifice and nothing of art." It was a sentence that had haunted him for years, probably because he could not understand it adequately. But Rebecca's pictures seemed to give him better understanding now. It was as if she avoided all formulas, as if all her heresies were singularly her own, as if she abjured merely describing a thing in favor of seeing it more deeply, penetrating it with a more primordial eye.

Her drawings infatuated him, and humbled him. He felt a

shiver run along his spine, up to his neck and ears. He put down the stack that had accumulated in his hand and looked at her. Finally he found his voice. "Rebecca, I find you amaze me." He arranged the drawings neatly and in the order she had presented them. Without speaking she carefully placed the cover over them, pulled the long white ribbon off her shoulders, and tied it around the bundle again.

"It would cause trouble for you if some of these were to be seen."

"I know that, Mr. Sanborn. Yet I would not destroy them."

"No. You should not. But you had better take care they don't fall into another's hands. Greater care even than you have, I mean to say."

"Perhaps you are right."

"Please don't misunderstand me," he said, "but I wonder if you might like me to care for some of these." She looked up at him. "For you, I mean. To preserve and secrete them, so to speak. You must know I would allow no harm to befall them."

"I believe you would not, but I don't think I want to part with them."

"Nevertheless, I advise you to consider the matter."

She picked up the portfolio and held it to her breast. "I shall. Thank you, Mr. Sanborn. I believed you would understand."

As she was about to turn away, he stopped her. "Rebecca, I wonder if you might do better to turn to plain, simple portraits. Your gifts, properly directed, surely these people would appreciate, and you might thereby contribute further to the income of this household."

"I don't think they would be friendly to the idea. And besides, I have no proper colors and equipment."

"Well, I spoke to Mr. Prescott, and I think he might be persuaded with more effort. And as to colors and equipment, I shall leave you with mine, those I have brought here."

"You're being too generous, Mr. Sanborn. It's too much to ask, and you must attain your own commissions, rather than making of me your competitor."

"Nonsense, Rebecca. In the first place, I'm leaving soon. There is nothing further for me here, unless I can persuade you to accompany me—for your personal security. In the second, it is nothing for me to leave a few items behind, to get you started, until you can command your own materials by virtue of your success." He felt certain that if he could distract her away from these melancholic illustrations and toward portraits, she would discover a proper outlet for her desires, which would be constrained, and at the same time discover an occupation that the Prescotts would soon find remunerative and congenial.

"I'll consider what you have said, Mr. Sanborn."

"Consider it well."

"I shall," she said "I've much work to catch up on now. Many obligations here." When she smiled her whole face brightened; then she turned again and headed for the stairs.

He stood there, as if to leave, yet frozen, looking after her. He recognized the signs. He was smitten. In every way and by everything about her, he was smitten. She had transformed into an appealing, beautiful young woman, and she was undeniably an artist he could not yet understand perhaps, but an artist of great dedication and fearsome originality nonetheless. What might she be capable of producing, he wondered, with proper training and the appropriate restraint of taste?

Moreover, he felt certain that although Rebecca had learned to contain herself under the strictures of her guardians and her service here, a deeper, even more troublesome life stirred within her still. It was just this deeper life, whatever it might be, that was so mysterious and compelling to him.

Chapter 22

WITH SOME DIFFICULTY, Sanborn finally persuaded Mr. Prescottt to join in his "experiment" by allowing Rebecca to paint, in rare leisure hours, a few portraits. She had accepted Sanborn's offer of colors and materials. That would be for him a small sacrifice if the experiment worked. Since she did not require sittings, but only memory and accuracy of vision, the whole portrait project promised to run smoothly without trouble to anyone. From her sketch studies, as if to create her specimens that would arouse wider interest, the first portrait emerged.

As soon as he saw it, however, Sanborn was troubled. But he dared not say anything to discourage her at first. He would now have to steer her toward a different tack: the portraits, too, might remain secret, private. In fact, she had from the first seemed less interested in their vendibility than did the Prescotts. The problem was that she suspected, and he could not disagree, that her continued freedom to paint—the Prescott's indulgence—depended on some financial return and community interest.

He said nothing that day, while he considered carefully how to turn Rebecca away from public portraits. Moreover, other matters weighed his mind. While he closed out his land affairs and prepared to leave, he could not dismiss his fears for the Prescotts and Rebecca. There had been reports of skirmishes in other villages, not only to the north and west on the other side of the Merrimack River, but even to the east of them.

He decided that if he were to follow his considered judgment, he would try once more to persuade the Prescotts to allow Rebecca, at least, to return with him to Portsmouth until the immediate dangers subsided. With the Prescotts' agreement, surely the Brownes would be capable of understanding the danger she was in. He spent another two days arranging his affairs and then went to bed on the eve of his departure making plans and mentally rehearsing over and again his final appeal.

He was awakened just after midnight to a row below his window. He arose and looked out to see people, under the sputtering glare of torchlight, moving in the general direction of the Prescott house. He dressed and ran out into the street. By then there was a crowd milling in front of the Prescotts'. On his doorstep stood Tristram Prescott, in his nightcap, speaking forcefully over the noise of the crowd, which must have made up half the men and women of the village. He heard Rebecca's name. There was some jeering, but Prescott, his voice booming, stood his ground. He agreed to listen to three representatives that night and to hold a proper hearing the next afternoon.

"But only if the rest of you return like Christians to your beds," he insisted.

Prescott stood there facing them without another word. There were mutterings and agitated gestures, but finally, in the face of his resolute silence, three leaders of the mob stepped forward and the others began slowly to disperse.

"What in the name of God is going on?" Sanborn asked a woman he recognized.

"It's that Rebecca," she said, her face angry. "She's finally shown herself for the evil young woman she is." She hurried away down the street with the others.

He was unable to gather any further information and spent a long wakeful night.

The next day, just before noon, Sanborn returned to the Prescott house. He knew he would not by then find Mr. Prescott there; his only plan was that he would be able to induce Mrs. Prescott to speak to him.

No one answered when he knocked on the door, however. He believed she was inside, and he became desperate not to be defeated or excluded so readily. He knocked louder. He called to her repeatedly: "Mrs. Prescott, please. It's Daniel Sanborn!"

Finally, the door opened a crack and the woman peeked out. "It is you," she said.

"Of course, and I want to help. May I come in please?"

She hesitated but the door finally opened just wide enough to let him in.

"I can't think what's happened!" he said as he entered. "My good Mrs. Prescott, they were speaking of Rebecca last night, some horrible, confused accusations."

"It was surely that!" she said. "It is a most horrible mess, Mr. Sanborn."

"May we sit down, then," he said, "and calm ourselves? Pray tell me what happened."

She led him into the parlor and seemed only too willing now, as if she had wanted to unburden herself to someone.

"I'm afraid we've made a terrible mistake, Mr. Sanborn," she began. "It's the portraits, the portraits she did, that caused the trouble."

He feared he understood what she was telling him, but he was relieved to hear that she wasn't blaming him entirely for their decision to allow Rebecca some limited exercise of her gifts. "How is that so, madam?" She did not answer immediately. "I've seen sketches she did of townsfolk," he prompted her. "They were well done."

"The sketch studies must have been incomplete then."

"Incomplete."

"Indeed, let me show you something." She got up out of her chair and went into the next room. She returned with a canvas, sat down, and then turned the face of the canvas to Sanborn. "This is the only one here, for safekeeping. The other three are in Mr. Prescott's possession; he has taken them to the hearing."

He looked at the oil portrait, executed with the very colors he had given to Rebecca. It was a beautiful painting—beautiful but, as he feared it would be, disturbing. Indeed, he understood it all—the mob, the accusations, the hearing. It was foolish and vile and superstitious, but he understood it now. Still he let her talk.

"As you can see, Mr. Sanborn, it is no mere portrait."

"I see, Mrs. Prescott. Neither is it some rude caricature. It is well executed; it is subtle, but unsettling, I expect, to the subject."

"Precisely. And she did four of these. Without our knowledge, she had taken them about town to their subjects—there were no sitters, properly speaking—and as specimens to show others. She saw no harm in it; she expected, God help us, to profit by these paintings."

"I see now," he said. He searched for words. "Do you—how shall I put it?—see any truth in them, Mrs. Prescott?"

"Oh, they are true enough, in a sense," she said, "but that's not the point, is it?"

"No, I suppose not."

He did not know the subject of the painting, just as he had not known the subjects of the sketch studies. He did not doubt the accuracy of the image, but she had expressed what he took to be the character of the person, the deeper character, perhaps the very life the person would have kept hidden. It was not flattering, neither was it degrading; it was neither serious nor comic. It was simply "true" in a sense, most likely in a disturbing sense, as Mrs. Prescott had said. He saw in the proper woman depicted here a sullen selfishness hovering like dark light behind the very flesh of her acceptably pretty face.

"It is not the duty of the portraitist, Mr. Sanborn, to depict what the prospective client would not broadcast to the world," she said. "Is that not so?"

"Of course, Mrs. Prescott. And if she has done the same with the other three—each character's secret life, so to speak, emerging from behind the face—I begin to see what the hubbub was about last night. I imagine those she has painted, and any who have seen the portraits, beyond not wishing to have themselves displayed (whether they believe she has found them out or not) are as greatly troubled by how a young woman such as Rebecca could plumb their secrets."

"Some of these hardly knew her. They knew of her and saw her about, but did not know her very well." She leaned the canvas against a nearby table leg.

"And so they cannot attribute her view of themselves to mere skill, whether she paints lies or truths? They search for something more to explain it?"

"I daresay they attribute some maleficence on her part." She looked at him, her eyes wide with significance. "You saw them all last night. They have no other means of apprehending her powers. I must say I have no means of comprehending her, myself. But I do not attribute her ability, be it truth or falsehood she discovers, to any evil source or intent. The young woman, we now see, is simply too naive to paint, and to paint portraits above all."

"Yes, Mrs. Prescott, for all her youthful wisdom she is, as you say, a sort of naïf."

"Well, she's gotten herself into trouble by it this time."

"Where is this hearing to take place?"

"It's taking place as we speak," she said. "It is closed to all but those whose faces she painted, to Rebecca, Mr. Prescott, and two other proprietors, allies, Mr. Wiggin and Mr. Congreve. We may have to pay recompense, on her behalf, before we're through. I have come to love Rebecca as a daughter, but she does not seem to understand how she has betrayed our trust."

"I expect she will understand better in the aftermath."

"That may do no one any good."

"I suppose the recent enthusiasm has not helped matters," he suggested.

"It may well be the greatest source of our troubles, Mr. Sanborn."

"Many were ripened to attribute what they do not comprehend to God or the devil?" He put it as a question. She did not answer. "And there's little doubt in their minds whose hand is behind this wizardry in the portraits?"

"It is a mystery they cannot otherwise endure," she finally said. "They had, those who followed the New Light, recently come to believe themselves regenerate. It's as if some mocking presence has come to deny them their renewed belief, their turning to accept God's grace. Each of the portraits happened to be among the many who counted themselves among the reborn. I don't think Rebecca intended this. But these people, perhaps a third of the village, had gone so far already as to threaten to establish a new parish."

He looked at the portrait again. It was as if the painting vibrated with the unsettling implications of the woman's physiognomy.

"I will take her back to Portsmouth with me," he said.

"I don't think it will be that easy. And Mr. Prescott, if he can contain them, will have to appease them as well."

He rose to leave. "And this hearing, where is it being held?"

"In the blockhouse," she offered, after hesitating. "But you will not gain admittance."

He took his leave of her and headed for the blockhouse. Not that he expected admittance. He only wanted to be nearby when they finished, when Mr. Prescott came out.

Within an hour everyone but Mr. Prescott and Rebecca had come out, so Sanborn waited still. Finally, Prescott emerged alone.

"Mr. Prescott," Sanborn said, "I've just spoken with your wife. I see what has happened here. I am sorry for anything I might have done to lead to such a misunderstanding."

"It is regrettable, Sanborn. Very regrettable. We all seem to have gone against our better judgment."

"And Rebecca, where is she now?"

"She will remain in the blockhouse. At least as long as is required to settle this matter. She has a comfortable room there."

"Is she . . . indicted then, in some way? Is she to be found guilty of some transgression? I think, rather, sir, she is merely naive."

"That she is, Sanborn. No. She is not being brought to any sort of trial. But let me assure you of something." He looked about inconspicuously, as if to make sure no one was within hearing. "The young woman is not free of danger even yet. If we lock her in the blockhouse, under guard, whose trust I have completely, she will be far safer than if she is allowed anything approaching her former freedom. You can't tell what some people will do once they get worked up like this. And I can't possibly put Mrs. Prescott and my family to the trouble and anxiety it would cause to have her locked away at home."

"For how long is this incarceration to continue?"

"For as long as it takes for people to calm down and come to their senses. I don't expect it will last beyond a week or two. The flame of this frenzy, I trust, will not burn for long."

"That's a long time to be locked in a room."

"It is, but there is nothing to be done. She's fortunate that we were able to calm the waters as much as we have. The general understanding abroad is that she is being punished and interrogated further as to the source of her effrontery. I think in a week or two we shall be able to quietly introduce her back into her home and keep her out of the sight of others."

"Then, sir, you must see that if she were to return with me to Portsmouth, and were introduced back into the Browne manse, she would be better served."

"Would they welcome her after this? It cannot be kept from them forever."

"But if these people were to break in somehow and take her away for their own purposes. . . . Well, there is, as you say, no telling what they might do. Last night I was ready to believe they would have put their torches to her skirts had she come into their hands. As you yourself suggest, they are a superstitious lot, and dangerously superstitious now."

"Believe me, sir, she's safer where she is than anywhere else within miles. I've seen to it. Don't forget that I'm responsible for her."

He was unable to persuade Prescott to allow him to slip away with Rebecca back to Portsmouth. He himself, of course, could not now leave for Portsmouth. He would have to stay on to see this through. But what was he to do? If he could get her to Portsmouth right away and introduce her back into the Browne family under the widely accepted argument of the general insecurity of the frontier, she would be well ensconced there before any word of last night's debacle came to them.

All he could think of was somehow getting Rebecca into his own hands and fleeing with her. The problem was how to get hold of her. He planned incessantly, but Fortune was making her own plans.

· · ·

FORTUNE ARRIVED in the guise of Captain Carlyle, his two great dogs, and a half-dozen men of his scout who came roaring into town the next morning just after dawn, calling the townsfolk to arms. Everyone was suddenly out of doors and armed and scrambling toward the garrison and the blockhouse. Women and children were hauling provisions, while men carried powder, muskets, pistols, swords, and any farm implements that might serve as weapons in a desperate moment.

Sanborn ran back into his room to grab his own pistols and musket. When he emerged again, at least half-dressed now, he looked down the street toward the nearest garrison, the blockhouse. Nearly everyone that side of town must have been within, for there were only two or three people hurrying along the road. The officer of horse troop rode up and down the central street, sword in hand, calling out advice and moving stragglers along.

"Captain Carlyle!" Sanborn called out as he rushed toward the garrison. Carlyle rode up to him. "Daniel Sanborn," Sanborn said and held his hand up to the captain. "We met here a few years ago, at Mrs. Sinclair's, and shared a noggin or two."

Carlyle looked at him as if he were mad. Then a light came into his face. "Oh yes," he said. "How are you, Sanborn?" They shook hands. "Don't dally in the street, man, or you'll be knocked in the head before you're fully awake."

"I know. But tell me, sir, what's the true danger?" He looked around. The town was oddly peaceful now.

"War parties. Four or five. Two other towns west attacked before dawn. Quickly, and then they move on. No idea how many dead or captured."

"And your own men?"

"I've fewer than eight of my own company of horse left. Many were out patrolling yesterday or guarding work and haying parties. They had not yet returned when the attacks began. The savages have skirted the fort, penetrated the scout lines, and gone directly into settlements. Other of my men are sounding the warnings elsewhere, while some remain in garrison."

"No way of knowing where the savages will attack next."

"Of course not, but Blackstone's right in the line of fire."

"I see. Can I help?"

"Just take your place, Sanborn. We're making sure everyone is out of the dwellings. Good day to you. Hurry in. Now's the time for prayer."

He rode off to strike on doors and call out to any laggards. Or anyone fool enough to think it best to fight alone for his property. These alarums of the captain and his men were all that could be heard from within the blockhouse. Everyone inside had taken up a position, either as a musketeer or as a supplier of powder, shot, flints, pipes, tobacco, rum, water, weapons, or medicinal aid. They all had rehearsed this before. Mr. Prescott, who lived in this part of town, took charge within the blockhouse Sanborn had fled to. It was very crowded and still smelled of sleep and unwashed clothing. Rebecca was helping the women with heating water from the well in the cellar and the distribution of dried cornmeal for breakfast. The women who had been making soap yesterday now reheated pots of boiling soft soap to pour down on the enemy. Very few spoke. All were watchful or busy with their tasks.

An hour passed like that. No longer could they hear the captain or his men. No one now knew where the soldiers were. Eventually there was talk of a scouting party. There was talk of returning to their dwellings. There were warnings about savages in hiding until the garrisons emptied once again. A man said he had once seen them hiding by dwellings within bushes they carried before them. But otherwise the waiting endured mostly in silence.

Rebecca, who in this extremity was free to help, brought Sanborn some water and meal.

"Will the Prescotts return to Portsmouth now, if we survive this?" he asked her in a harsh whisper.

"It's impossible to tell," she whispered in turn.

"Then you must plan to return with me. I'm sure your former guardians would take you in against such clear danger."

"I don't think they would."

"Why not? Don't be silly. You can't stay here after all this. And it is only a matter of time before you are attacked again. An hour, a day, a month. It will surely happen."

"It will be up to the Prescotts," she said and turned away to continue her deliveries.

He almost went after her, but thought better of it and maintained his post at a loophole on the second floor. He followed Captain Carlyle's advice and began to say the Lord's Prayer to himself, over and over.

But still nothing happened. By midmorning discipline began to relax. Several men, heavily armed, crept out among the back gardens and fields to have a look around. Then the smell of smoke penetrated the garrison.

When the party of men returned, they reported that one by one the houses and barns were being set on fire. They had not been able to see anyone, savage or soldier. Almost immediately after reporting this, several shots rang out.

"Must be Carlyle and his men," said Prescott, who had been listening to the report.

"That may be," another man Sanborn did not know said. He looked to have authority, the authority of a large man, perhaps a former soldier himself. "But I say we go out and protect our homes. If there were many of them, they would have attacked the garrisons by now."

"We cannot say that for sure," another man said.

Sanborn agreed. The last thing he wanted to do in the face of the fires was to go about the town looking for Indians with torches or fire arrows or cartloads of burning faggots.

There were more sporadic gunshots. Every man with a gun was straining to catch a glimpse of the enemy to shoot at. Desperate to get a shot, two men went up on the roof. The smell of smoke grew stronger.

Finally Prescott gathered a dozen men who volunteered to set out to add their firepower to the captain's, or whomever it was who had been shooting. It was a very dangerous move, and Sanborn did not volunteer. The lands of his chief interest offered no dwellings or barns to burn. If he survived this, he kept telling himself, he would leave Blackstone as soon as it was safe to do so. What in the name of Hades was he doing here in the first place? The town had turned to bedlam.

Everyone inside the garrisons had to wait. There was enough gunfire that people said that the other garrison must have also sent men out. They could see a few houses that had not been set afire yet. Most of everything else in sight was burning, and now the smell of burning animal flesh was in the air.

Within another hour wounded men were being brought in, gunshot mostly. The French had seen to it that the Indians would be well supplied. Outside, the shooting was dying down, returning to sporadic pops and booms again. The prevailing sense was one of helpless confusion.

Captain Carlyle, bleeding from a head wound, was brought in. "They are retreating," he said two or three times, as if that were all he could say. But he might have been reporting accurately after all, rather than in delirium, for soon the gunfire stopped almost completely. More wounded arrived, and the smell of smoke began to give way on a noon breeze to the close smell of blood and sweat and wounds enclosed within the building.

Rebecca and Mrs. Prescott were among the women nursing the wounded men. One of her suitors was among them, Sanborn discovered from Mrs. Prescott. He did not know whether she even liked the young man. She had never said a word of suitors.

It was decided that the rest of the men should go out into the town in parties of five or six, paying special attention to any buildings not yet burning. It was too late to save anything that had already been torched. Sanborn went along with one of the parties. They met no Indians; Captain Carlyle had been right.

But Sanborn's party made a gruesome discovery. Mr. Prescott's mutilated body lying among three of his men, all of them scalped. Only one of the bodies appeared to be alive, but it was doubtful the man would live long. For some reason a strange thought surprised him: How much were the French paying for English scalps? The English were paying fifty pounds for Indian scalps, about ten times the bounty on a wolf. Sanborn now believed that when these men went out to join Captain Carlyle, they were engaging a larger party than Carlyle had anticipated. Had more men left the garrison, more would have been killed and wounded. Why had the savages not attacked the garrisons then? A sufficient number of Indians might have overwhelmed them. They might have had many valuable captives, including women and children.

The devastation to property was massive, and that seemed to be their principal purpose, by the look of it. They simply must have assessed quickly how to do the most damage with fewest casualties of their own. They had succeeded admirably, if, Sanborn thought, one might admire the devil. He was confused to see no bodies of slain Indians as well, given the whole morning of attacks, affrays, and skirmishes. He asked Mr. Congreve, who led his party, why this was the case.

"They conceal their losses," he explained, "by crawling under fire to their slain comrades, fixing a tump line to the body, and cautiously dragging it to the rear."

And what of the Prescotts now? Who would tell Mrs. Prescott? Congreve ordered the men to carry Prescott's body to the burial ground and begin digging a grave. No one wanted his wife or children to see him. They would explain afterward, and beg forgiveness. But it was a necessity, given the circumstances. Other men of stature in the town started coming into the burial ground as the men dug the grave. Congreve explained what had happened, and there was general agreement that this was best, if highly irregular. An elderly man began to read the burial service in a monotone voice.

They would have to tell his widow that he had been disfigured, but without details, and that it was best for no family members to see him. They would assure her, though they were unsure themselves, that the disfigurements had been perpetrated upon a corpse, not a living man. They would tell her that he died quickly from gunshots and that the barbarisms were committed later, after his party had been killed and scattered. And they would hold for him a proper Christian service, Congreve explained, and then added, "In the midst of life we are in death."

It was crazy of Prescott to have endangered himself, Sanborn thought, as they took turns by twos digging the grave. He was no hero, no young blood, but a middle-aged merchant and proprietor. What had compelled him to do such a thing? What askew sense of duty? He should have sent only others, even Sanborn himself. That would have made more sense, he thought. Sanborn had to admit that he was greatly relieved. He was no soldier or fighter, but, yes, even sending one such as himself would have made more sense.

Chapter 23

A DAY LATER Sanborn was ready to leave. The captain, much bandaged about the head, was leaving as well, and one of his men with him. His lieutenant was to gather and take charge of the small scouting company he had raised. Carlyle was heading to Portsmouth to report to the governor on the toll of recent skirmishes and war raids. He was hoping that an army would be raised for several major attacks against the Indians and Canada. It was hopeless, he said, unless they blunted the enemy with a series of offensive strikes. Head wound and all, he would make his case.

That morning before they left, Sanborn went to the Prescotts. By some strange twist of the violence, theirs was one of the few dwellings left unburned. Mrs. Prescott had taken to her bedchamber upon hearing about her husband and had not come out. Her children nursed her. A neighboring woman who had come to help out reported that she was delirious.

Immediately, Sanborn found Rebecca, who had been set free by the rigors and terrors of the attack, and took her aside. He told her he was about to leave for Portsmouth.

"You must come with me," he said firmly. "Get a few things, your portfolio, other necessities. I have a horse for you outside."

"But, Mrs. Prescott—"

"The woman is delirious. Understandably. Her children are here to help her. Other townsfolk. I'm sure she and her children will leave this place once she regains herself. And if you stay here there is no telling when the people might turn on you again, perhaps even extend your blame to this savagery just endured. Their minds were distracted by enthusiasm, and now by destruction and terror. But you and I must go now. The captain is leaving for Portsmouth and we may accompany him." He touched his hand to her back as if to propel her toward her room and things.

She turned against him. "I can't go now—" she started to say.

"Rebecca! You're going with us. If the captain and I have to bind you and throw you over my packhorse. You'll be well looked after in Portsmouth. I'll see to it, I promise. Now get your things."

She looked at him boldly, staring into his eyes. He did not flinch but stared back. He could feel her resistance. He was nearing desperation, ready to throw her to the floor if he had to.

Perhaps she saw or felt his desperate determination. She relaxed her whole frame finally, the rigidity gone out of her. But she did not move.

"I am, I do not doubt, saving your life," he said. "Along with my own. I'll do what I have to in order to see you out of here. Now, please," he repeated each word slowly and firmly, "get . . . your . . . things."

Without another word or a look, she went upstairs. When she returned she wore a dark traveling cloak and carried a bag full of he knew not what—clothing, he expected, and her beloved drawings. She refused to speak to him further. He headed them out the door.

SANBORN, Rebecca, Captain Carlyle, and one Sergeant Grimke rode out of town on horseback. Sanborn looked back at the village. Smoke still rose above the remains of dwellings and barns; planting fields were in ruins. He assured himself that these disheartened and wounded people would care nothing now for the missing Rebecca.

It would be all they could do to rebuild their lives here or flee in desperation.

The men on horseback were heavily armed. Rebecca, hidden in her great hooded cloak, rode like a man astride Sanborn's pack-horse. They rode quickly, the dogs loping ahead of them, every mile east a milestone to safety. They stopped briefly and only to water the horses, dismounting and fanning out in a tight perimeter, dropping on one knee, muskets at the ready, while Rebecca tended the drinking horses. Along their road, the way stations were closed up, empty, against further raids. One station, about halfway to Portsmouth, had been burned to the ground, smoldering, still, like so many buildings at Blackstone.

Stopping to water the horses shortly after the smoldering way station, they formed a perimeter while Rebecca led the horses to the side of the stream. Carlyle's dogs, who were trained to patrol the perimeter about thirty feet in front of the men, stopped their movement and, heads and ears lowered, teeth bared, fur up, began to growl in the direction of a large boulder perhaps another dozen feet beyond the dogs.

"Get down, Rebecca!" Carlyle called to her, "and hold the horses well."

Without a word, Rebecca wrapped the reins doubly about her wrists and, leaving her hooded back to them, crouched low along the bank.

The dogs stood their ground, awaiting Carlyle's orders. The three men turned their muskets in the boulder's direction and Carlyle called out "Choboy!" Both dogs broke into a dash for the boulder, growling and barking furiously. Their fearsomeness flushed out four Indians in ambuscade. All three men in Carlyle's party fired at once and two of the enemy dropped.

The dogs pursued the other two into the immediate woods, but Carlyle soon called them back. On their return, the dogs stopped over the two bodies, as if to test them for life, and then sat beside the slain Indians waiting for Carlyle to come up.

"Stay with Rebecca," Carlyle said to Sanborn, who was recharging his musket. Carlyle and Grimke approached the bodies cautiously.

Sanborn went to Rebecca, who had not moved from her position, and spoke her name. He put his hand on her and she looked up at him from beneath her hood. "It's over," he said.

She stood up slowly and handed his horse to him. "Yours and mine became awfully jumpy," she said. That was all. She tried to get the other three horses to drink, but they were too wary.

Sanborn looked over to Carlyle and Grimke. The sergeant was just finishing with the scalp of the second Indian.

"Don't turn around yet," Sanborn told Rebecca.

The men finished with the bodies and the dogs patrolled until they were appeased that nothing more lurked nearby. Carlyle and Grimke came over to Rebecca and Sanborn.

"Have they watered?" Carlyle asked. His dogs joined them and slurped lustily at the stream. Grimke washed his hands.

"These two just now. Finally," Rebecca said, handing over the two horses.

"Then mount up and we'll be off," Carlyle said.

They did not stop to camp or rest. They pushed the horses without mercy, assuming all their lives—the three men, the woman, the horses, the trusty dogs—depended on relentless flight.

Chapter 24

WHEN THEY ARRIVED in Portsmouth, exhausted and still full of vexation, Captain Carlyle presented himself at Colonel Browne's residence to inform him of the death of his cousin Tristram Prescott in the attack on Blackstone. Sanborn had argued for this strategy along the way as the best means to assure a refuge for Rebecca in her uncle's house. While the captain reported to the squire, the others waited by the carriage shed, baiting their horses with oats and water. News of the recent depredations along the frontier had spread to Portsmouth, but the casualties had been unknown. Within twenty minutes, a serving girl emerged and said that Mrs. Browne requested the presence of Miss Rebecca in the hall. Rebecca removed her portfolio from her bag and handed it to Sanborn. "Keep these for me, sir, if you would please."

"I'm honored," he said. She turned and walked into the house.

Sanborn believed his purposes would be best served if he stayed out of the way. He did not know, therefore, what transpired between Rebecca and her former custodians, but Captain Carlyle finally came out to say everything had been settled—Rebecca would stay with them and they would arrange for the governor to send a well-armed party out for Mrs. Prescott and her children, and anyone else who desired escort to Portsmouth.

"Thank you, Captain Carlyle, for executing the matter so effectually," Sanborn said. "I realize this caused you some delay in making your military reports to the governor. But it was a noble office on behalf of Mr. Prescott's wife and children."

"Don't mention it, Sanborn," he said. "It was a proper enough duty. But now we must be away." The sergeant handed him his reins, he mounted his horse, and they rode off with dispatch.

Alone, Sanborn returned his and Rebecca's horses to the stables where he had procured them, and walked directly to his rooms for a wash and a good sleep.

For some days he went about his business, trying to forget the attack he had endured. But he received a gruesome windfall. Sergeant Grimke had appeared at his rooms one day with a gift of thirty pounds from Captain Carlyle. "Your share of the scalp bounty," he said. He urged the notes toward Sanborn, who stood dumb in his doorway.

"I did nothing to earn this. It's yours and the captain's," he finally said.

"Don't be a fool, Sanborn. It's yours. You fired on the enemy, just as the captain and I did."

Now he had bad dreams and difficult nights of waking. The mutilated body of Tristram Prescott seemed to appear before him continually.

And Rebecca. She seemed to haunt his days as well. He could think of no one else. He was functioning well enough to garner a couple of commissions and renew his acquaintances, a renewal made all the more easy by the fascinating story he had to report. He avoided portraying himself as a hero, but he of course said nothing of his fear and caution throughout the experience either. If he embellished anything, it was perhaps the tale of their mad dash for Portsmouth. All this gave him notoriety about town. Even children in the street had taken him for a trooper on account of his pistols. He was able to use this new reputation in favor of his trade. It was just as well he did not swagger, however, because his courage would soon be tested.

A week after his return, he called upon Madam Browne during her morning levee to inquire of Rebecca's state of health and mind. He was kept waiting some time in the hall while other people of standing paid their respects, but he was pleased to have more time to prepare himself.

"Mr. Sanborn," Mrs. Browne said, as he entered her parlor finally. She did not rise, but indicated a chair nearby among a little cluster of chairs about her tea table. "I understand from Captain Carlyle that we owe you our gratitude for rescuing Rebecca and alerting us immediately upon your return to the dire circumstances of the poor Prescotts."

"I knew them well, Madam Browne. It was little more than an obligatory and humane duty. But I'm delighted to be of service."

"Colonel Browne intends some recompense, for your trouble and loyalty." She held up her hand as he was about to protest politely. "Let me assure you, he insists. Now, as to your calling, let me hazard a guess. You wish to share your concern for the disposition of Mrs. Prescott and her family."

"Indeed, Madam. And Miss Rebecca as well. We suffered a rather harrowing hegira, no one more than she." He smiled and accepted the dish of tea she had poured for him.

"You will be pleased to hear, then, that the Prescotts have arrived, just two days ago. One of their Wentworth cousins has taken them in. Mrs. Prescott slowly improves despite her deep mourning. The children will be sent to school, and Colonel Browne is making arrangements for the sale of property and some of Prescott's proprietor's shares to ensure their maintenance."

"My mind is relieved, madam. The Prescotts were always kind to me, and they did very well by Rebecca."

"She's a striking and appropriate young lady. We have not fully settled on her disposition yet, of course, but something useful is in order now. It might be well to place her in service for a time, in some pedagogical capacity. Or some manner of beneficence to the community."

"She is a most clever young woman, Madam Browne. I should like to think that her gifts would be adequately exercised, as I'm sure the Prescotts hoped for her. They placed great trust in her, many responsibilities."

"She might perform well as a tutor or governess. I agree, Mr. Sanborn."

"In due time," he said and smiled pleasantly. "Any family would be fortunate." He knew Rebecca well enough that she would be disappointed to be placed in service to anyone, especially outside her family relations. His mind raced with alternatives, but he couldn't concentrate at the moment. Madam Browne was not a person to offer your partial attention.

She asked after his commerce and his plans "for the duration of these hostilities." She was glad to hear he intended to ply his trade about the port again. She even suggested a few personages who might be well disposed now to receiving his card. She would make an inquiry or two herself. This turn of generosity toward him emboldened Sanborn to ask more particularly after Rebecca and whether he might speak with her briefly.

Madam Browne was agreeable, and thus he soon found himself in the kitchen where Rebecca was employed on some gustatory project—the addition of garden herbs, it appeared—with the cook, a widow lady of some fifty or more years. Sanborn and Rebecca seated themselves at a worktable at one end of the room, while the cook continued her ministrations to a pan of lamb.

"You are well?" he asked, once they were seated.

"Well enough," she said. "I'm all the better for knowing Mrs. Prescott and the children are here. I hope you understand that I did not wish to leave them in their condition. I thank you, however, for your protection and judgment."

"It was my duty, and my pleasure." He looked at her. There was some discomfiture below her courteous manner.

She glanced at the cook, and he understood that she wished to speak more plainly.

"Perhaps a moment in the back garden," he suggested. She stood up and he followed her out the back door of the kitchen. It was a fine day, the garden full of birds stopping by on their autumn migrations. He remembered meeting her here four years ago under the bower they entered, its white blossoms gone now, and he remembered recognizing her as an exotic little creature from the first. But by now she had grown to a woman, and her character had been tempered in labor and trial.

She seated herself and he remained standing. "They speak of sending me into service, Mr. Sanborn."

"So I understand from Madam Browne," he said. She did not respond. "It's possible they will avoid placing you in an unpleasant situation."

"Anything is possible," she said. "From the least to the finest. That is what troubles me."

"I see. You don't think they will make every reasonable effort for you?"

"I don't know. It seems clear only that they wish to have me out from underfoot."

"Perhaps they are reminded too much of an eccentric child. They may come to see you otherwise in time."

"I don't think I have much time."

"I don't know how I can help, in this instance, Rebecca. What would you have me do?"

"You have my drawings still?"

"Of course."

"Safe keep them, please."

"I never intended differently."

"Thank you, Mr. Sanborn."

"You are not contemplating something foolish, I trust."

"I contemplate many things, foolish and otherwise. Doesn't everyone?"

"I think you understand my meaning, Rebecca. I'm at your service; you know that. But I can't stand by and have you take unnecessary risks."

She looked up at him, directly into his eyes. "You are quite comfortable here, Mr. Sanborn, aren't you?"

He hesitated. "Quite."

"That is your good fortune. I find I am less so. I find I am exposed to chance, to the caprice of others. I am no longer a child, yet I am not a proper woman. How does such a thing come to be? I doubt anyone can provide a satisfactory explanation. Yet here I am nonetheless."

"You are not to be a daughter, you remain merely a charge."

"That is well put, Mr. Sanborn." She looked down. "A charge and an inconvenience."

"I could not presume to tell the squire and his lady their business."

"Of course not."

"It's a sadness, Rebecca. But perhaps you should wait to see what decision they make—before you overly vex yourself, I mean."

"That is little consolation," she said. "I'm not a boy, or a man, so I cannot go to sea, sir. I cannot work on a masting crew. I cannot join a regiment."

"That may be so, but you must exercise every caution nonetheless." He looked her in the eyes to try to discover her secret resolve. "Were I to continue to speak with you, meet with you, we would raise suspicions and doubts. I don't think that would help matters. Why don't we agree to correspond until the decision appears more settled, if there is someone you can trust."

"There is Abigail, the maid. She's but a year older than I; we formed an understanding as children."

"Her discretion is reliable."

"Yes."

"Good. Then we can proceed, quietly. I promise to help by any means within my power."

"You are very kind, Mr. Sanborn."

"Let's not assume the worst. Let's proceed with reason and caution."

"Agreed."

He took heart that for the moment she was following his lead, however desperate she might have felt beneath her appearance of agreeableness.

Chapter 25

ONE EVENING THE FOLLOWING WEEK, Abigail delivered a note from Rebecca to Sanborn's rooms.

"She asked me to wait a reply, sir," the maid said.

Dear Mr. Sanborn,

It has become clear that Colonel Browne has not settled, and may not for some while settle, on my disposition. I am therefore requesting that you return my folio of drawings to me via Abigail that I might resume my private musings. We can count on Abigail's discretion, and despite my responsibilities here, I have more leisure and privacy now than I've had in years. I do not believe my humble collection would be discovered, nor that I would be without resources to continue, in private and rarely enough, further compositions. I know not what the future holds for me, and I wish to improve my time while I can. I know you would not refuse me that which you, above all others, understand provides for my peace of mind.

By the by, sir, so far as I can tell, nothing of the fiasco my paintings caused in Blackstone has reached Portsmouth yet.

Yours faithfully,
Rebecca Wentworth

It occurred to him that perhaps she was the best judge of her opportunities for private work. As for securing her productions, it was a large responsibility to have them in his possession. He felt unburdened, he realized, even as he handed the portfolio, bound with a white ribbon and covered in an old painter's cloth, off to Abigail.

But in a corner of his mind, a corner room to which he closed the door, he wondered if he might by his compliance be exposing her productions to discovery.

"Please wait another moment, Abigail," he said, after handing her the sheaves. "I wish to scribble a note to send along with you." He hurried to his writing table while the servant stood holding her burden patiently. She smiled as she watched Sanborn dash his thoughts on paper. He was indirect in case the note should fall into another's hands. "One must always guard against becoming vulnerable to those who might not comprehend or wish one well," he scribbled. "I recommend watchfulness and offer you my continued desire to aid you in any extremity."

He recalled one drawing in particular he had discovered in her portfolio. It was rather simple: a committee seated in a chapel; before them stood an ambitious man of fashion and his wife in high dress. Behind the committee and two aspirants sat anxious people of figure, with lesser lights on the social ladder—suspicion and envy creasing their faces—properly arranged in the pews receding behind them. *Reassigning the Pews,* Rebecca had written as a caption. She had managed to illuminate the absurdity of establishing in the house of God each man's, and therefore each family's, close degree of social rank and privilege amidst constantly changing fortunes. It was such drawings that most spooked him now with the thought of their discovery.

After he sent the maid away with the note, however, he realized fully, again, how powerless he was to provide Rebecca any proffered aid.

HIS OWN HELPLESSNESS was made clear to him shortly thereafter. A second note from Rebecca said that, encouraged by their care for her and concerned over subterfuge in the very home of her benefactors, she had requested permission to continue her illustrations of Christian subjects, after the matter of Watts. But she had been rebuked. Indeed, she had made a fatal error. Her request had resulted in her being sent for guidance to the Reverend Mr. Arthur Browne, rector of Queen's Chapel, and she had brought her Watts to the interview; she had hoped "to display the innocence and Christian wholesomeness of my illustrations, both accomplished and intended." Now, her note read, "I fear the worst as to my final disposition."

Holding her note in his hand, Sanborn sat in a chair he had placed by his second-floor window. He looked out toward the bustling seaport. Why had he involved himself in Rebecca's troubles for so many years? It was a question he could not adequately answer. His involvement could have no salubrious effect on his own reputation and trade. What was he to do now? He tried to examine his sentiments toward Rebecca but found it difficult to think with honesty about the strength of his affections. His thoughts recoiled from the memory of a dream he had had where the identities of Gingher and Rebecca somehow overlapped. Though it still troubled him, he could not credit the dream by any tortured appeal to reason.

He got up out of his chair in frustration at the muddle of his own thoughts. The only thing he could think to do was to visit Gingher in the rent he now provided her. When, ultimately, they lay unclothed and quiescent on her bed together, the soft afternoon air bathing their slack flesh, their conversation as desultory, intimate, and unguarded as between people paired in a comfortable marriage, he asked again how she and her sister had first come to Boston.

"A ship from Portsmouth, England," she said.

"Directly? From London, I mean."

"No. We lingered there."

"At the port."

"Yes."

"Entered the trade there, or later?"

"There. Finally, yes. There was little enough choice. And by then I was very angry." She sighed deeply at the memory. "So it suited my anger."

"So, how did you ship for Boston?"

"She followed a trooper, and I followed her."

"His Majesty's Service."

"Yes, the colonies." She let out another sigh. "He betrayed her of course. Soon after we arrived."

"Of course."

"We had a falling out, then. I grew ever more angry; now her foolish gullibility infuriated me."

"So, you left her and Boston."

"Yes. And there was too much vice already, besides—a mob of working trollops." She laughed a little. "One of the women suggested I try Portsmouth."

"Ah. I see." He thought a moment, feeling that he understood it all at once, what had been said and what was left unsaid.

"How did your sister shame them, your parents, though?"

"Well, they *believed* it a scandal. A man who owned a tailor's shop not far from ours. He took a fancy to Jenny. He and his wife had hardly spoken for years. He left her as if to prove his devotion to Jenny. She swore that she hadn't encouraged his continual attentions, that he deluded himself. But he wouldn't be defeated in his suit. He got it about town that he and Jenny had sworn secret allegiance. To my parents it all became a public shame. It didn't matter that my sister was innocent."

"Innocent."

"Yes. She had been known as something of a coquette. But that was just in general, her ways. He took her otherwise. He constructed some frenzied drama between them, acting the blade's part, and broadcasting what he trumped up to be her part. . . ." She stopped as if to catch her breath. "It was all so pointless and destructive."

"And preposterous. You believed her. You believe in your sister."

"No reason not to. He'd been an coxcomb all his life."

"Yet you parted, forever. You sisters."

"Nothing has ever hurt me more. No one will ever hurt me again."

He moved two fingers gently against her leg. "I'll never hurt you, Gingher."

"Easily enough said. Now. Here. Like this." She waved her arm above them to indicate the room, their recumbent state in the aftermath.

"I make you that promise."

She took his hand and laid it on her naked abdomen.

"I accept your promise, Daniel, in good faith. Still, no one will hurt me again. That's my promise to myself."

As he lay there absorbing her words, his thoughts by some inexplicable chain of associations turned to Rebecca's plight. What was she suffering now that everything was uncertain again and she was powerless in others' hands? Suddenly an idea came to him: a visit to Parson Browne. It would be the pastor who would report, and most likely recommend, to Squire Browne himself. As he lay in bed, his arm around the dozing Gingher, he recalled his first sight of the parson's Queen's Chapel on a Sunday morning during his early weeks in the city.

He had been exploring his new home afoot when he came to the crest of Church Hill as the gentry were about to emerge from dutiful worship. He stopped to admire the private carriages and costumed footmen waiting for their masters and mistresses. He had arrived just in time, for shortly the doors opened and the gentlemen in great snowy wigs and gold-trimmed coats and embroidered waistcoats and lace ruffles and silk stockings, gold-buckled at knee and shoe, came out into the glowing sunlight—amplified by the adjacent river—and spring air. They wandered down the steps in conversation and consultation—as if in a slow, leisurely dance—toward their impressive chariots. Parson Browne stood on the top step and beamed among his parishioners. Then the ladies emerged in all their own exquisite laces and brocaded dresses and beautiful, exotic mantles. There was a flash of cane and hat trimmed in gold, as if the entire display were designed to enhance the late spring sunshine. Sanborn had stood there stunned by the spectacle, and he knew at that instant, being raised Church of England himself, that it would be of great benefit to make Queen's his own chapel.

Like so many other men of name, he had by now come to know the curate, and he would, he thought as he lay in Gingher's damp bed, send his card around to request an interview.

. . .

THE FOLLOWING WEEK, Parson Browne's black servant Pompey led Sanborn into the front parlor at the appointed time. Sanborn chose one of the many flag-bottom chairs to sit in and observed once again, for he had sat here on several occasions, the modest elegance of the room's appointments. The room spoke of a man who, though he would never achieve wealth himself, would always remain a center for the society—the round of cooperation, connection, and obligation—of wealthy men. When Parson Browne entered, they exchanged warm greetings, the parson indicating that Sanborn resume his seat while he chose his favored Gardner Windsor chair. A glass of sherry, the parson suggested, would be in order.

Sanborn liked the parson. There was little cant about him, normally, and he had been an athlete in his youth and during his Trinity College days, in Dublin. He reportedly had been capable of leaping over a pitchfork balanced upon two others, and his physical presence was still imposing, if now given to the stockiness of a man into his forties. He also had the reputation of a formidable scholar, having once in fact labored as private secretary to Dean Swift in the interim between taking his B.A. and M.A. degrees.

They divagated over the Indian troubles and trade, over an anecdote or two, and then Sanborn turned to the business he had intimated in his note to Parson Browne.

"I spoke to the young woman, yes," the parson confirmed, "and I must say the experience, after we dispensed with introductory courtesies and pleasantries, was disconcerting." He looked at Sanborn in a friendly manner. "I understand you are chiefly responsible for rescuing her from the ravages suffered at Blackstone."

"I, in the company of Captain Carlyle and one of his men, was rather rescuing myself and brought Rebecca along with me," Sanborn offered, "for having known her and even taken her likeness during her residence at Colonel Browne's."

"You're too modest, Daniel. The colonel and his wife speak well of you. Word is that your own heroism in battle did much to disperse the enemy, though no one could have saved poor Mr. Prescott from his fate, as I understand it."

"He was determined to root out the destroyers of his town at all costs, poor man. It's his actions that approached heroism, I assure you, Parson, not mine."

"Nonsense," the parson insisted. "But as to Miss Rebecca, I must say the colonel has difficulty on his hands, there. Do you know the effrontery of that fair creature, Daniel? When I reminded her that, divine subjects or no, the Brownes for very good reasons had their own designs for her, she had the face to quote the Archbishop of Cambray: '*In our daughters we take care of their persons and neglect their minds.*' I said to her, My dear young lady, you dare quote archbishops to me? And, I pursued her effrontery: Do you tell me that you converse with great churchmen now, living and dead?"

Sanborn stifled a laugh. "Forgive me, Parson. I know her ways. She's unsettled me many a time." He held up a finger to detain the parson a moment longer. "But I can assure you she is extraordinarily clever and a gifted draftsman and painter. So I find I indulge her much more than perhaps one should."

"I care little enough for all her cleverness," the parson said.

"Understandable, certainly. How, may I ask, did she respond to your disapprobation?"

"She said that she had conversed with too few churchmen in her time, but that she had only read the archbishop in Essex—John Essex's *The Young Ladies Conduct.*" The parson was growing red in the face.

Sanborn dared not laugh, but found it difficult. It was not the pastor's anger that amused him, nor that the girl would try the parson for a fool, but the simple thought of Rebecca jousting with scholarly divines and besting them now and again on thrust or parry.

"We've had our differences on the technique and purposes of illustration and portraiture, I can tell you, Pastor," he finally said. "She has a way of leading you into readily sprung traps. She's too easily underestimated, from her youth and sex. But I've seen her also dutiful—a model of charity, and familial responsibility and modesty. However, I think that her intelligence overruns her, when she strains after accomplishing what . . .—well, how to put it?— what is in her. Has she shown you her Watts?"

"Indeed she has." The parson seemed to be calming down somewhat. He sipped at his glass before going on. "Impressive, and in their own way appropriately sacred, I must say. I could hardly credit the work to the little saucebox before me. Yet I reminded her of the greater weight of her filial duty."

"I think if she were to find some exercise of her gifts, she would be more compliant and purposeful."

"That may be true, but it is not her decision, as I troubled to remind her. She forgets that, all too conveniently for the moment. But I daresay such forgetfulness will cause her enormous inconvenience in the long run. Do you suppose she continues to produce any of those maniacal illustrations, in secret I mean?"

Sanborn stumbled. "As before? Had you seen them?"

"No, but Madam Browne once described some of them to me in detail."

"It's possible, of course. You saw that she continues her more sacred productions. . . ." He hesitated. "But, really, I don't know enough to report."

"You seem uncertain, Daniel." The parson looked narrowly at him. "She perhaps confides in you, as a fellow dauber."

"She has, to some extent. I had offered to provide her proper training, once. Her guardians wouldn't hear of it."

"And you have no reason to suspect her return to this pictorial . . . melancholy?"

"I have nothing to go on, as I say, beyond her occasional spleenishness, as I believe Madam Browne reports."

"Yes. She does indeed." The minister still fixed him with his penetrating gaze, as if he wished to ferret out some unspoken truth.

Finally, the silence grew uncomfortable for both of them, so the parson continued. "She had better marry, I told the colonel, and provide for herself some more appropriate line of endeavor."

"You may be right there, Parson." He laughed congenially. "She had suitors in Blackstone."

"I don't doubt it for a minute. Though I expect they knew little enough of her outlandish ambitions. She's a little upstart Camilla."

"Camilla?" Sanborn said.

"One who has shaken off all female folly save dress and show. Virgil."

Sanborn laughed. "I assure you, Parson, she has never even learned the language of looks and glances, of the blow of a fan. What may appear as renunciation is mere innocence, and a passion for quite other things."

Sanborn thought it was very lucky Reverend Browne had never actually seen, apparently, the more fantastical productions of Rebecca's pen, pencil, and pigment. Moderate though he was compared to the local Congregational divines, the curate of Queen's might well have condemned her for such visions so powerfully expressed.

"All passions in excess are un-Christian," Parson Browne said. "This is what these itinerant Enthusiasts misunderstand. As you well know, I'm not a man of intolerance or narrow principles, Sanborn. I'm speaking of her familial and her civil duties. However, even love, if it does not first serve our duty, is certain to make us fail in that duty."

"She is fortunate, then, all the more, to have a man of your moderation as her counselor, Parson." The parson nodded in agreement and refilled their glasses. "There was some trouble in Blackstone, following a visitation and much preaching by one such Enthusiast."

"Indeed?"

He first assured himself of the pastor's strict confidence, and then he explained what had happened, the frenzy of some of the populace and their turning on Rebecca for "a portrait or two she had done," as he put it. The curate shook his head knowingly. Then Sanborn repeated that it was her good fortune to have a true Christian leader of his temper as her spiritual advisor.

He was betting on Browne's distaste for the New Lighters, aware as he was of Browne's sermon "Against the Pernicious Doctrine of Enthusiasm." He had a printed edition of it, and a passage came to mind as they spoke:

By the lights of these Enthusiasts, these Illuminati, he is the best and most edifying preacher who is most presumptuous and unintelligible and can boldly anathematize all that dissent from him. Visions, Dreams, Trances are as frequent in our day as they were in those of Fox and Nayler. People making all manner of mouths, turning out their lips as if convulsed, straining eyeballs and twisting their bodies into unseemly postures. Nothing but Scotch Cameronian Divinity will go down with them, and thereby do they disturb our peace and promote division. These itinerants pour in from all parts to pelt us with their sermons and lectures, sometimes four in a day and into the night in a most disorderly manner. It is a specie of madness and frenzy.

The pastor's voice returned Sanborn to the moment. "She shows little recognition of her good fortune, Daniel," he was saying. "I spoke to her of the necessity of humility before God, of the struggle against crippling ambition all men and women must wage, and do you know what she said to me?"

"I dare not ask, Parson. Really, I can't imagine. She always surprises." He prepared to contain himself again.

"'So much religiosity about us, sir. Yet so little Christian charity.' I'm not exaggerating, Daniel, I assure you. Her very words. Followed by the most complacent smile. It chilled me. It chilled my heart."

Sanborn could see that what remained with the good reverend were her quips and challenges. He had no doubt that Rebecca was, otherwise, the model of courtesy, as he had seen she could be. Might she have been referring to the Episcopalians as much as to the dissenters and Enthusiasts? Her words reminded him again of her forbidden drawings and paintings. Her thoughts and her pictures, he realized now, were of a piece. She could at times act like some ancient sophistic gadfly. Was that her ambition? Were her darker paintings above all criticisms? None of this could he consider with the good parson, so he kept his thoughts to himself.

"Perhaps she was thinking only of this infection of Enthusiasts, Arthur, which you've spoken against so often yourself," Sanborn said, trying to mollify him. "I've never taken her for an Enthusiast, nor any of her disorders of intellect and fancy for sectarian distempers. I take them to be more mundane distempers of the brain. I trust you've spoken to Colonel Browne since her visit."

"Yes, immediately," the pastor said, "as it was he who sent her to me. They have been thinking of service, but I advised them to consider matrimony, provided they had someone in mind to protect and tame her."

"I see," Sanborn said. "He would first have to appreciate her delicacy of mind and sensibility. My own feeling has been all along, if I may speak frankly and confidentially again, that she would be more malleable if they were to find some appropriate channel for her talents and energies. But they've insisted on restraining her from a more acceptable exercise of her powers."

"That is their prerogative. I trust they have good reason."

"I wouldn't presume to inflict my views on them. Perhaps you are right."

"Matrimony would not be an unusual palliative in a case of such extremity," the parson said. "I'm put in mind of another instance, some few years ago, over Durham way. Perhaps you've heard of it? An Enthusiast by the name of Mary Reed—one of Mr. Gilman's, the most fanatical of New Lighters? One among those true Aeolists, as my good Doctor Swift used to call them."

"Not of Miss Reed particularly," Sanborn said. "Mr. Gilman is rather infamous among Church of England people, however, as he must be among his own clan. I'm given to understand he'd preach some eight hours running, only to be taken outside by a church elder to be walked up and down until the screaming from his congregation drew him back into meeting."

"Precisely. However, I'm not suggesting Miss Rebecca's an Enthusiast, but there is a certain visionary similarity leading to what Madam Browne has described as bizarre flights of fancy and intervals of unmanageability."

"I take your point, sir."

"Oh, Nicholas Gilman had a veritable apoplectic entourage—Hannah Huckins, Mary Reed, others. But my point is that these fits of vision, these hysteric disorders, this fantasticalness and co-quetry, indicate some want of a more legitimate manly presence, some connubial balance, in the young woman's life. In Miss Reed's case, her behavior provoked a scandal and anticipated the minister's final undoing."

"Scandal, sir? From what cause?"

"When Mr. Gilman had just moved to his Durham parsonage, his wife and family still at Exeter preparing to join him, Miss Reed presented herself at the minister's door in a state of 'exceeding joy' that she proclaimed had possessed her all day. She was invited in, innocently enough one supposes, but soon fell into a trance and ended up spending four days in a parsonage bed—envisioning, by Mr. Gilman's own defensive account, her soul in heaven the whole time."

Sanborn suppressed a laugh; he looked down and shook his head.

"A great upheaval ensued," the prelate went on, "but such was the state of the enthusiasm at that time the people were finally induced to exonerate their new minister and the prostrate seer herself."

"A scandal indeed," Sanborn said, allowing himself a small laugh finally. "But I take your point, sir. And I find myself of your mind as well. Perhaps marriage is the best physic in such instances—and in this instance of the fair Rebecca."

Chapter 26

SANBORN DID NOT TRY to communicate with Rebecca. He would see her at Queen's Chapel of a Sunday, but they did not speak. Abigail delivered him no further missives, so there was scant opportunity to send or respond to private messages. He believed that calling upon Rebecca again, or even speaking of her to her guardians, would have had too much the appearance of intrusiveness. And he had no wish to confirm further his unreasonable preoccupation with Rebecca and her affairs. He went about his business for some months, right through the terrible news of the destruction of Saratoga and other settlements deep in the western frontier, thinking about her but without speaking his thoughts to anyone.

This strategy of aloofness and self-interest began to unravel, however, when Rebecca finally renewed their correspondence after the Christmas season.

Saturday, January 4, 1746
Dear Mr. Sanborn,

I hope you will forgive me the impertinence of this epistle after so long a silence between us, but I have no one else to whom I can unburden my thoughts and fears. Aside from court paid by two suitors chosen by my guardians, my life in the Browne manse has been severely restricted. I am limited for the most part to my chamber, as if association with the staff and visitors would somehow taint or endanger them. (I am allowed out only for the medicinal powers of Reverend Mr. Browne's sermons and for the amusement of my suitors.) The colonel and Mrs. Browne are convinced my picture making is at the core of my "nervous distempers." So I dare not continue to follow my heart.

My suitors are one Mr. Buckminster, a merchant of perhaps forty-two or forty-three who might stand for a model to Mr. Hogarth, and the impetuous Mr. Paine Wentworth, one of the scores of young cousins, who seems to believe the Lord's creation was laid before us for his personal self-indulgence and the aggrandizement of our multitudinous clan. He attended Harvard College but is a gentleman of superficial learning and flashy parts. Mr. Wentworth is inordinately handsome, and though my guardians do not favor him so much as they do Mr. Buckminster, they believe me deranged for not displaying a proper enthusiasm over the blandishments of so charming a rival.

But lately there has been one thing more. Parson Browne, with whom I am given to believe you are well acquainted, had advised my superiors to search out any such illustrations as those I had shown him and any such as I had executed aforetimes in my "more melancholic moods," which he somehow came to suspect I had turned to once again. Without my knowledge, several of the house servants were charged with this quest, the result being that I am paying now for my own impetuosity, when I should have left my pictures under your beneficent care.

In short, the choice my benefactors seem to be contemplating for me is either to marry me to one of the aforementioned gentlemen or remove me to a private madhouse in Boston. Much as I would prefer the dreariness of the former to the horrors of the latter, I live as if in a state of perpetual darkness while others consider my fate. I wonder if you might, as a last resort, so to speak, intervene on my behalf. Might there be some means for a gentleman as yourself, whom they respect and whose pictorial judgment they honor, to shepherd them toward a more sensible accommodation?

Respectfully yours,
Rebecca Wentworth

Had he said something that sent the good parson on such researches into Rebecca's private quarters? Sanborn tried to recall their conversation precisely. Or perhaps it was something he did *not* say? How could he be certain? He was certain, only, that the

Brownes would hear nothing more of his proposed lessons or his pleas to indulge her a little in her passion to draw and paint. He might be somehow implicated in the strictures of her present condition, but there was little he could do about it now. Moreover, he had come to the opinion with so many others that perhaps marriage was her best recourse. If only the alternatives in that line were not so "dreary," as she had put it. He did not really wish to see her married to another, especially to one who would make her unhappy. Nor did he allow himself to contemplate the pangs of jealousy he could not entirely deny. But the fact remained that, married, she would be protected from the intrusions, even the vagaries, of guardians and ministers. Whether she would be allowed to continue her drawing was another matter. If she were, a husband surely would countenance only the sweeter delineations. That was quite understandable, he thought. One couldn't expect a husband to revel in her more antic figurations. But at least she would be exercising, rather than suppressing, her talents, however narrowly to her mind.

He began to wonder if there were not some way to make the young Wentworth more pleasing to her. He knew who the proud young man was, however, so that line of thought ran out quickly. Or perhaps another suitor, one more tolerable to her, yet equally acceptable to the Brownes. But how would he initiate such a scheme of matchmaking? Moreover, would the Brownes ever countenance his own suit? Not for a moment, he assured himself. He was no longer poor, but he was irrevocably beyond their marriageable, clannish circles.

He couldn't trust any of his female acquaintances of standing; they would be too loyal to the Brownes to join in his scheming. And his closest associates who were women, Gingher and Miss Norris, were outside the sphere of proper husband-hunting. Nevertheless, he called on Miss Norris for advice.

"She will be ruined," Miss Norris said after he detailed Rebecca's own description of her narrowing circumstances. "Not only are such men unworthy of her, they will never understand her and therefore soon tire of her. She will live abandoned in her marriage."

"I suppose ultimately she will be marooned," he finally admitted.

"To put it bluntly," she said.

"Yet the alternative is even more frightful."

"A certainty, Mr. Sanborn."

"Is there nothing to be done?"

"It would take some drastic measure on our part, or *your* part, Mr. Sanborn. Something daring and audacious."

"What do you mean?"

"I'm not at all certain myself, yet. I think she will refuse these chosen suitors, as you intimated." She got up from her chair and began to pace about. "And when she does, the Brownes, I now believe, will complete their threat. They'll not be crossed or blocked."

"It's vexing to think it may be so. They believe she is, in some degree, mad. They seem to believe that as separation and domestic labors were the curative for the child, so now marriage would be for the woman." He got up and began to pace about, too. "Perhaps you should talk to her of your conviction, as you have to me, and at the least enjoin her to marry, for her own security."

"You may be right," she said. "I don't know that she'll listen to me, but marriage, even such marriage, is preferable to destruction."

That evening they discovered no other way to proceed, so Miss Norris prepared to call on Rebecca.

UPON CALLING, however, Miss Norris understood that it was too late. Rebecca had refused both suitors and she believed the Brownes in the process of making good their threat. Whether they saw this as a punishment to bring her "to her senses," or as a more permanent means of disposing of their recalcitrant ward, Miss Norris could not yet fathom. But Rebecca was in a terrible state of mind herself, Miss Norris reported. One might be convinced she *was* mad.

"She somehow keeps stealing paper and pen and making her secretive and ever more bizarre illustrations," she said, reporting to Sanborn on her visit. "They've had to lock her in her room for long periods to keep her from it. But the very drawings now incriminate her. As they did at Blackstone, I now understand."

"You heard of that mess?"

"Miss Rebecca told me. And Mrs. Prescott, still in mourning but come to her own senses, has told the Brownes of the incident. You'd have done better to tell me of that yourself, sir."

"I intended to, and soon would have, but had remained silent out of my fear for her."

Miss Norris was now beside herself, and she and Sanborn fell into a chaos of helplessness, and, in Sanborn's case, self-recrimination. He, after all, had returned her to her guardians-turned-persecutors, he told himself.

"I don't understand how they can contemplate such a course of action," he said. "This trade in lunacy. They baffle and anger me."

"They will brook no rebellion," she said. "And they believe her lucid intervals grow more infrequent by the month."

"But this?"

"As I mentioned before, there is a history of madness of some sort—religious melancholia, hypochondria, suicide, and the like—in Squire Browne's lineage. His people have always feared it greatly, all the more so for occasional manifestations through the generations."

"But Rebecca comes by way of the other side of the family—the Wentworths."

"That doesn't matter, or lessen the fear of it, the repugnance, the shame of it, in the squire's eyes. Her grandmother Mehitabel, on the Browne-Cutts side, married a Wentworth. And Mehitabel's grandmother in turn, Elizabeth Browne, drowned herself in the river on her birthday. That woman is none other than the Squire's own grandmother, on his father's side! There were, I believe, others. Of this only you can be certain, Mr. Sanborn—he'll have no mad woman, by his lights, under his roof."

Sanborn looked at her without speaking.

"We must get her away from there," Miss Norris finally said. "We simply can't let such a thing happen."

"But how?" he asked. "Shall we ruin ourselves into the bargain?"

"Could you not return to Boston, or some farther center, Mr. Sanborn, to ply your lucrative trade, and take her with you? For a time only, of course. Provide for her safety and work, without any-

one knowing who she is or how she helps you, painting drapery—
or whatever you wish. She might well be a younger sister after
all. . . ." She ran out of speech as if she had run out of silly ideas and
explanations. She stood before him desperate and empty.

He could not make an answer. He knew that he most certainly
could do no such thing. And he knew that she was equally certain
of the impossibility of it. Every instinct told him it would be his
ruin as well as Rebecca's. A thought returned to his mind: He might
marry her himself and indeed take her away. But it was a useless
thought. The Brownes would never hear of it—a painter of portraits, a man of social servility when all was said and done, marrying
into the Browne and Wentworth families.

Chapter 27

YET WHEN HE NEXT SAW Rebecca he knew he had to
do something. She appeared not well, as if surely she were
becoming what they had already determined her to be: recalcitrant and mad. She no longer paid attention to her appearance; she cared little for manners and conventions,
even outwardly now. Her frowsy back chamber overlooked
the gardens, and he noticed a chair by her window, as if she spent
much of her time gazing at the dead, snow-covered planting beds
below. Perhaps the sun brought needed heat through the window,
too. He felt a chill and stepped over to the fire to stir the smoldering wood.

"How did they allow you in to see me?" she asked immediately
after speaking his name in surprise.

"I asked if I might reason with you, and they saw no harm I
could do."

"The Master of Reason has a forked tail, has he not?" She smiled. It was not her old smile.

"If so, his underlings, such as I, are granted no such distinguishing demarcation."

She laughed. "It's pleasing to see you, Mr. Sanborn. It's pleasing to see anyone who speaks plainly to me."

"Miss Norris?"

"Yes."

"Parson Browne?"

"Less so."

"Your guardians?"

"They speak only out of fear of reproach, of dishonor, to the family."

"Miss Norris thought so too."

"She is a kind, knowing woman."

"Indeed." He knew that Miss Norris had sneaked a few books in to Rebecca. He couldn't stop noticing the disarray of her hair, the soiled clothing. "She wishes to help you. We both do."

"You are kind. But it's futile now. What could you do?" She didn't expect an answer. She looked around the room. "I'm hardly ever let out of this chamber now."

"No suitors," he said flatly.

"No more." She looked around the room again. "They don't allow suitors to see me like this."

"That is a relief to you."

"A blessing."

"You have been drawing and painting on the sly."

"Yes, I *had* been."

"The colonel showed me a few."

"Did he?" Her face revealed nothing. "He constructs his proposition, his plea against me." There was a taint of amusement in her voice.

"Perhaps. You've been a willing accomplice, I daresay."

"I interfered with no one. I was a model of propriety, otherwise."

"You disobeyed their explicit instructions. Your actions have caused more than a little disorder. They were bound not to take kindly to that. And then you rejected the suitors they took pains to send your way. What, they kept wondering, are they to do with you?"

"If you are here to reason with me, then you know they have been unreasonable."

"You've misunderstood them. In time you would have found a suitable match and perhaps even found a way to pursue your drawing."

"Do you understand so little the ways of the world, Mr. Sanborn?"

"Is it I who have denied this world for some other? I've seen your recent drawings. They are extraordinary, as ever. But they are not of this world."

"So sayeth Parson Browne." There was a measure of sarcasm in her voice now. "He held two of my specimens before me and said, 'Miss Rebecca, it appears you much desire to deny this world, even while you are living in it, in favor of some other. Would you not do better to follow the nature of it, the world we must live in?'"

"And did you answer him?"

"How could I not? 'Would not such an attitude separate your doctrines,' I said to him, 'from those of our Savior?'"

Sanborn hung fire. He was aghast at her courage and effrontery. "And how did he find your speculations?" he asked finally.

"He left this room without a word, Mr. Sanborn."

"You endanger yourself. You do harm to yourself. You challenge your betters and they will not abide it, Rebecca. You're bringing destruction upon your own head when you confront those whom you should, rather, respect."

"I don't say that you are wrong, Mr. Sanborn."

"But you don't admit that you are wrong. You don't admit that your temper, your speculations as to the shortcomings of others and of this world, and your more melancholic productions, are wrong."

"I am perhaps too impetuous and strong-headed for my own good. But if I am wrong essentially, I am in good company."

He wanted to slap her to her senses, to a degree of more becoming humility for a girl of . . . what? Seventeen? Instead he raised his voice. "You will be in good company indeed in the madhouse!"

She looked at him. Her eyes began to glisten, softening for the first time since he had entered her chamber. He had not come here to wound her. He recalled one of her drawings the colonel had just, that day, held up to him as if to demonstrate his view of her. In the foreground a gigantic androgynous figure knelt in prayerful attitude over an abyss, an abyss like a great smoking crater formed by war or disaster. "Nature contemplates man's destruction," the colonel had said in disbelief. "That's what she says of this one, sir. It is the work of one who is deranged. Clearly. How can there be any other explanation?"

Now Sanborn looked into Rebecca's eyes again. They were moist, and they told him that she no longer cared to speak to him. She must view him, he thought, as an old friend who would now, at this terrible pass, forsake her.

He left her room and went downstairs. Colonel and Madam Browne awaited him in the parlor. They had a sheaf of papers, drawings he was sure, to show him.

"And how do you find her, Mr. Sanborn?" Squire Brown asked. "Atrabilious of countenance?"

Sanborn looked at them calmly but he had no sympathy for them. "Troubled. Confused. In need of understanding; in need of our prayers and our Christian charity, perhaps."

They both looked at him skeptically. Madam Browne showed him to the table where the Squire placed the bundle of drawings and paintings.

"Against our expressed admonitions," he said, as he untied the white ribbon around the bundle. "What, Mr. Sanborn, would you, an accomplished painter, make of these?"

Sanborn looked at the one placed on top of the pile. A woman with long unruly tresses forlornly looked out her moonstruck window, from what could be a castle or a manor house. A great dark bird—a raven?—with its back to the viewer seemed to return the woman's stare. Sanborn peered at the tiny inscription near the bottom. *Night Thoughts.*

"Does she title all these?" he asked.

"Many," Colonel Browne said.

Sanborn turned the first sheaf over to expose another illustration. A naked woman slouched sensually on a couch of woodland moss. From the other side of the couch, near the woman's left thigh, a huge serpent's head and neck (large enough to devour the woman) crept toward her. The serpent held a golden apple in his jaws. There was no title. "Eve and the Serpent," Sanborn said. He turned the sheet to another. Fires raged in distant forests. In the foreground ships plied turbulent seas, and in the middle ground milldams, log drives, and heaps of sawdust blocked rivers where fish leaped and churned, as if in agony. *Never Does Nature Say One Thing and Wisdom Another,* the tiny inscription read.

"Juvenal. I am not unread, Mr. Sanborn," the colonel said. "Imagination is essential to original expression in the fine arts. But Reason must ever hold the reins, for without it, one descends to chaos, to the chimeras of unbridled fancy, to loss of judgment, to the tyranny of the imagination. Here we can plainly see a capital disturbance of the Reason."

"We have tried, Mr. Sanborn, believe me," Madam Browne said. "We have tried."

"Is none of these in a more rejoicing mood, as before?" he asked.

"None of these," the colonel replied, tapping his hand on the small stack of illustrations before them. "There are some others of a lighter mood, but fewer, collected in a separate folio." He indicated a smaller pile on the sideboard.

"I see," Sanborn said. "She appears to be more changed than I had hoped. What a sadness!"

The colonel insisted on turning over several others. One in particular, another Hogarthian pen sketch, depicted corpulent merchants (some with strangely familiar faces) dancing with audacious bawds. The figures were done in just enough caricature to suggest, beyond moral wickedness and corruption, the corruption of their brains in lunacy. In the spirit of her inspirational master, she had managed to depict not "all Britain is Bedlam" so much as "the New World is Bedlam."

"What is this?" Sanborn asked, squinting at the tiny scrawl at the bottom center of the drawing. "*Semel—insanivimus—omnes,*" he spoke each word singly. "We're all mad"?

"Precisely, Sanborn. Burton, I believe. But now you see the uses to which she puts her reading and study."

Who was it, Sanborn tried to recall, that called our times the Age of Satire?

The colonel fumbled through the pile again, barely containing his rising anger, and pulled out two sheaves sewn together. "A diptych, Mr. Sanborn!" He held opened both sides and held it before Sanborn's face like a minister bearing witness to devils' work. "*Black Ivory,* she writes on this one."

On one sheaf was an ink and watercolored sloop of perhaps some forty or fifty tons. The ship flew under moonlight while phosphorescent sea creatures danced in the bow-wake. Two figures only were on deck, drenched in moonlight—a steersman on watch and a Negro tied to a whipping post, unconscious or asleep. On the other sheaf attached were ladies and gentlemen riding out into the New England countryside—the ladies in chaises driven by black servants, the gentlemen on horseback with black lackeys in attendance.

At the moment Sanborn didn't have the heart to continue through the pile before him. The Brownes' point was taken.

He moved over to the more joyous pile and opened the covers. The first was a still life: a prayer book, silver communion and christening vessels emblazoned with the royal coat of arms. "Are these not of Queen's Chapel?" he asked.

"Quite right, Mr. Sanborn," the colonel said.

"To demonstrate the ecclesiastical ties between us and King George and Queen Caroline?" Sanborn asked.

"So it would seem, if there were not some irony intended."

Sanborn mused over the painting a moment. "It appears straightforward enough to me."

"Well, she says it is nothing more than a gift to our dear curate," Madam Browne said, "but we doubt her."

He looked at them. "A peace offering, perhaps," he said. "And a way of letting the curate know she has a mind capable of lucid practical work."

"Is not the perfect mimicry of sanity itself a sign of madness?" she said. "She takes him for a modern-day Pharisee. We have not offered it to him."

"I understand." He turned to go. "I thank you for allowing me to see her. I'm afraid I haven't been of much help." He dared not speak his mind and felt like a coward. "I have an appointment to keep with a patron, if you'll excuse me, sir. Madam."

As he entered the wintry streets again he blew out a great sigh of relief. The manse itself had come to feel like a prison to him. He felt confused about what he had witnessed inside, upstairs and down. What could he alone do? Or even he and Miss Norris? They both seemed to be as helpless as Rebecca herself to change the direction of her life.

 *Chapter 28*

SANBORN, IN DESPERATION, paid another visit to Parson Browne.

"As you may know," Sanborn said once they were seated, "Squire Browne has made discreet inquiries of one Reverend Mr. Oldmixon, of Boston, who boards the distracted at his parsonage."

"It is good of him not to inflict upon her the fate of a pauper," the minister said. "Or an unmanageable wife or relations: the almshouse, workhouse, or jailhouse that serve our Bedlams." He crossed his legs comfortably and waited for Sanborn to come to the point.

"Yes, but I have not been able to learn anything of this

Oldmixon, and I wondered if you might enlighten me. I would not burden the Brownes further with my curiosity or concern."

"I see." The minister appeared to search his thoughts a moment. "Well, from my discussions with Squire Browne and from what I know in the first place, I can tell you that he is a godly man, and for some reason known only to himself, he and his good wife had boarded distracted persons at their parsonage just outside London. He's a physician as well, you see, and he seems to have taken a physic's interest in such matters—at least among his parishioners, as I understand it."

"A private madhouse keeper, then?"

"In effect, yes."

"That's not unusual in England, but I hadn't, until now, heard of it in New England. How did he come here and establish this house?"

"For over a decade the selectmen in Boston have complained of the number of distracted persons in the almshouse at public expense. But Oldmixon came to be here, to my knowledge, not entirely of his own volition. There was some scandal, and it appears he fled."

"Scandal? As to the nature of his private house?"

"That is rather uncertain."

"Is he some mere mendicant or mountebank then?"

"No. A proper practitioner of physic—"

"Perhaps a latitudinarian," Sanborn interrupted.

"I think not quite. He's solid Established Church. Which is of course sufficiently tolerant in these times to encompass many. Nor was it narrow enthusiasm undid him."

The minister stood up and walked to a front window, his back to Sanborn now as he spoke. "It was doubtless the usual thing, or so I believe from my imperfect knowledge of the affair. His churchly labors had always been in order, remarkably so, and his piety unquestioned. But there are, as you know, Sanborn, always factions and professional jealousies—the host of political pettiness to which the flesh is heir.

"Some who opposed him," he went on, "called his practice into question—the manner of his madhouse keeping, I mean—and joining with a cabal of disaffected parishioners created a hubbub sufficient to raise an inquiry, which in turn the anti-Oldmixon faction blew into an utter scandal. In defiance, and to protect his good name, he quietly resigned his pastorate, and not long thereafter, I believe, removed to Boston."

"He was called to Boston?"

"I'm not certain of that. It's quite possible. It was some five years ago now."

"And he brought with him his practice of keeping a madhouse."

"That would seem to be clear. Though I don't believe he would have begun his curacy as a keeper of lunatics. At some point, he simply reintroduced his practice and treatments, as a physician, you see."

"Do you know anything of these treatments?"

"No. I do not."

"And you yourself are convinced that Rebecca is *non compos,* Parson Browne?"

"I am. Colonel Browne also told me himself of the incident at Blackstone, of her tragic failure of judgment. What's more, I do not believe she's had a lucid interval for some time. I think she may be entirely distracted." He turned from the window to face Sanborn. "Would you disagree, Mr. Sanborn?"

"Not entirely, sir. But she's no nincompoop, this young lady, I assure you. Her mad freaks are an unfortunate affliction." Sanborn had not till then known whether Colonel Browne had heard of the violent reaction to Rebecca's portraits. He felt strangely relieved that the dangerous incident was no longer his, and the parson's, secret.

"You wish me to appreciate that there is a certain . . . profundity to her delirium."

"She is a young lady of fine intelligence and talents. I think it's fair to say that her rather too highly strung sensibility, however, has at times initiated her distraction, overbearing her reason."

"I would not disagree on that point, Sanborn. However, she is committed to my cure, and I am to render an account of her soul. There is an arrogance born of her gifts and in her judgment of others, her aloofness from the practical matters of living peaceably and humbly in this world, even unto her position in relation to her betters. She's still rather like a child who has never known proper discipline, who has been too much indulged. She has not learned a proper relation to this world by the example of the Brownes, the Prescotts, her own deceased parents even. And her distraction has only increased for all her refusals to countenance a civilized relation to others and to the community of Christians among whom she resides."

"You are of course right, Parson, in the main," Sanborn said. He got up out of his chair and stood beside the parson now. The two men turned to look out the front window where the business of Portsmouth in winter continued upon the snow-packed street. "Yet perhaps you, we, are too harsh in some degree. I still believe there is hope for this young woman, myself. I cannot turn from my conviction yet that, given a proper channel for their exercise, her gifts might flourish and release her from the sloughs of her melancholic distractions."

"She has not found, and I fear is not capable of finding, such a balance of humors. Everything has been tried for her, Sanborn. Yet her bodily motions would appear to remain irregular, as are the desires they continually excite in her mind."

"Everything tried? Perhaps. Or perhaps not."

"Even the sacred institution of matrimony can do nothing but breed discord, for one such as she. It is perhaps well that she has refused the suit of Mr. Buckminster and young Wentworth."

"I fear I can't quite agree with you on that point, Mr. Browne. The bonds of matrimony, if tender and flexible enough to allow a respectable pursuit of her gifts, could only release her from despair. It may simply be a matter of choosing suitors out of her own affections."

"But she does not know her own mind," the curate insisted. "Her affections are diseased."

"At this moment, perhaps. But there is always hope, sir. And there is always prayer."

"Indeed, Mr. Sanborn, there is always prayer." The curate

folded his hands as if to calm himself. "Have you a counter proposal to Colonel Browne's?"

"I'm not entirely sure. But I am searching, Parson; I am searching."

"Then I will pray for you, and for Rebecca, as well. But take care you do nothing to cross the colonel and his lady. Take care to bring them fully into the circumference of your searches and reflections. Do not allow your heart to overrule your head."

Sanborn was taken aback by the final admonition. Was the good parson insinuating Sanborn's unhealthy fascination with Rebecca? Or was Sanborn being too sensitive himself as a result of his own curious and unreasonable sense of responsibility for her? He had never been able to explain that sense—was it too much to call it an obsession?—even to himself. Once awakening in the middle of the night, after earlier expending the coarsest of his passions rather angrily upon his paramour, Gingher, he had asked himself whether he had indeed fallen in love with the other young woman. But he was unable to entertain that question for long. The growing strength of his affections made it too painful to contemplate. All he dared to consider was whether he somehow might alter Rebecca's apparently unalterable course.

It was Miss Norris who came up with an idea.

"I've been able to think of little else, sir, since seeing her for myself," she told Sanborn as they strolled along the Parade again. "Together we must present my plan to the Brownes, for trial at least."

"Agreed," he said. "I'm as desperate as you to do something, and if we can bring Colonel and Madam Browne into our plan, all the better for its efficacy and our exoneration from meddling. But you must tell me what it is!"

She smiled. "It strikes me that they have not lost all concern for Rebecca," she said, rather strangely echoing Parson Browne, "as they would not abandon her to the workhouse or lockup, but rather bear the expense of private confinement. My plan is this: We prevail upon Madam Browne to allow Rebecca to accompany you to this private madhouse. A sort of prospective visitation, you see. We then tell her we have been authorized by her guardians to offer her a clear choice, and our recommendation. She may still avoid incarceration by the expedient of marriage."

"But, Miss Norris, as you well know, she's been offered just such a choice already."

"Yes, but without a tour of the netherworld. Without encouragement from us upon the tour's completion."

"I take your point. But she has distaste of her suitors, and I don't think the Brownes will brook other suitors at this pass. It has come to be a point of honor and filial obeisance with them."

"As to suitors and husbands it makes little difference, so far as I can see, Mr. Sanborn. We must let the colonel have his way—what choice have we?—in that regard. Many a woman has made her peace with a suitor of her betters' choosing."

"You have me there, Miss Norris."

He was relieved to hear that she did not propose some variety of abduction, as she had suggested before. That was a thought he had simply not been able to entertain. He did not think her new proposal would work, or at least not readily, but he saw no alternative and refused to do nothing.

"The problem," he suggested, "is enticing her on such a tour, as you put it, enticing her to Boston."

"What would you suggest, sir?"

He thought a moment. "Well, I think she may—given her circumstances here, I mean to say—have some curiosity as to a . . . , what should I say, restful alternative. That is, if she can be assured that it will be more restful, and temporary, than frenzied. And there is, of course, the admonitory force of her guardians, if they will insist."

Miss Norris, who had stopped and turned toward him as he spoke, looked directly at him. "Go on," she prompted.

"Yes, well, something more occurs to me. As you know she has illustrated beautifully Dr. Watts. I have in the past suggested that we approach Boston printers to see what may be done. I have, in fact, a letter, in response to my earlier query, from Thomas Fleet—"

"The printer?"

"Even so, Miss Norris. And there is the bookshop of course. I would be pleased, also through Mr. Smibert, perhaps, to approach Church and Company as to the possibility of their taking on the book once printed. That would insure a much greater exposure of vendibility—to schools, country shops and traveling auction men, and the like."

"I see. What would be required?"

"I believe it's a matter of some ten or twenty pounds, to start. Fleet would have to assess the manuscript for a more exact estimate. The principal expense, no doubt, would be in the illustrations. It is all doubtless a matter finally of suitability for subscriptions, but Watts is so popular I don't see how this work can fail."

"And your idea is to increase the appeal of Boston by rejuvenating this idea in Rebecca?"

"Quite so. With success, moreover, might she not even eke out some small or partial independence from the project?"

"Anything is possible," she said, looking away now and pondering the idea. "I think it a good enticement, Mr. Sanborn."

"Good."

"Will you appeal to the Brownes for an interview with us then?"

"For both of us?"

"I think it will be better, don't you?"

"You may be right. Leave it to me, Miss Norris."

"We shall play matchmakers then," she said and smiled again.

"I think that we shall have to prepare young Paine Wentworth as well, if Rebecca relents," Sanborn said. "Her parents have kept her suitors in the dark as to her true distraction."

"It is but the English malady, sir—"

"Be that as it may, I think we may also concoct some credible story of a doubtful and inexperienced young lady whose mind has been properly awakened by the counsel of her formidable parson and her parents, as well as by the advice of her former tutor and friend."

"Not to forget the blandishments of her fine young gentleman.

Indeed, Mr. Sanborn. I see you warm to my project. That's just the thing, and we may even be able to prevail upon young Wentworth to allow her some exercise of the decorative arts, as befits an accomplished lady, including drawing and watercolors."

"Which will have to be curtailed of their more visionary nature."

"Indeed," she said. Her smile grew uncharacteristically wide. "We are of one mind, sir."

"We are, Miss Norris."

Chapter 29

Miss Norris's plan seemed to start out brilliantly; the Brownes, perhaps out of their own desperation, agreed to try it. So, that spring Sanborn returned to Boston as he had once come to Portsmouth, by coastal sloop, but Rebecca was his companion on the return journey. They stood on deck in mild weather as they left Portsmouth Harbor, where still another battery of artillery was being added to Fort William and Mary and to the point at Little Harbor. The air and adventure seemed to agree with the young woman after her confinement. Her cheeks reddened and her whole face colored. Gone was the unsanguine and sickly countenance of the lady of exquisite sensibility or the splenetic hypochondriac. Her conversation for the first time in months was occasionally punctuated with laughter. To look at her one would never have guessed their destination.

Upon approaching the harbor at Boston they passed the high stone lighthouse, or pillar rather, upon the top of which night fires would be lighted to guide ships. Their sloop moved among many islands as they approached the town, its fourteen church spires reaching high and airily above duller buildings, as if God's holy spears had been struck firmly in the earth. They passed the Castle, or fortification, bristling with thirty-two-pound guns below and more than a hundred twelve- and eighteen-pounders above. And the harbor itself was filled with scores of ships and small craft. Rebecca said she had never seen anything quite like it.

For nearly a quarter of a mile along Long Wharf sat a range of wooden warehouses, and, close by, a multitude of ships. On the wharf, they hired a chaise that took them up King Street to the Town House and out along Cornhill toward Newberry where new and elegant buildings were steadily replacing the old ones destroyed, Sanborn explained, by the fire of 1711.

"Those were bad years for many in Boston," he added. "The French War was on, and a throng of young women were made widows. Then the fire. But by that year there were also scarcities of bread. Lots of food shortages, in fact, created by the prosperous few who sold most provisions to the troops, not only to ours, but to the French as well."

"I suppose it has always been true that some will do anything for wealth," she said. "Did they get away with it?"

"Yes, or so I understood from the old men in Boston's taverns who spoke of those times when I first arrived here. They especially feared the return of hostilities. They told me that the common folk made their displeasure known finally when the next generation, still suffering from lasting shortages of all kinds, rioted and tore down the North End market house."

"Yet the city seems to have recovered," she said, looking about as they rode on.

"Most people appear to be doing well enough, now," he said. Just then they arrived at the address Colonel Browne had given them. They soon found themselves standing at Dr. Oldmixon's parsonage door, letter of introduction in hand.

He appeared to be a mild gentleman in his late sixties, and Mrs. Oldmixon appeared to be of similar age and humor. Sanborn and Rebecca were conducted to a private house beside the modest parsonage, a substantial property that, it was revealed in conversation later, the Oldmixons rented for their business.

"We accept no visitors who would come merely for their amusement," the old physic said, as he showed them into the foyer, "after the cruel pattern of the home country. Here the inmates are simply confined to their rooms, so long as they are manageable and pose no danger to themselves or others." He looked in his friendly manner at Sanborn and Rebecca. "Only the violent are restrained," he added, as if musing. "We allow daily promenades on the grounds, with the attendant, as well."

Rebecca had said nothing beyond a polite greeting since their arrival at the Oldmixons'. The color began retreating from her face once again.

"Have you any well restrained at present?" Sanborn asked, once they stood inside.

The old man turned to lock the front door behind them. "But one," he said, turning back toward them in his bent fashion. "Mr. Holt, who believes himself king of fairies, separated unjustly from his fairy queen, and sometimes steeped in a rage of sorrow and betrayal. *Ira brevis furor.*"

Rebecca glanced at Sanborn, who said, "I see. Is his madness so brief then?"

Oldmixon led them up the stairs. "Fits and starts," he said. Very little daylight penetrated the interior, but upon opening a door to a private room, daylight poured in through two undraped windows. A bed, a tiny desk, and a chair were the only furniture.

"This is our empty," he said. "I've kept it available, at Colonel Browne's request, this past fortnight. It's a very pleasant room, taking the morning sunlight till about eleven o'clock." He looked at Rebecca. "Some of our residents bring a piece or two of their own furniture."

The entire house was eerily quiet, nothing like what Sanborn had anticipated for a madhouse, just as the madhouse keeper was unexpectedly gentle. Might Rebecca be tempted to see this establishment as an acceptable retreat? Yet, he thought, looking at her, she seemed not to be tempted, and that reassured him—there was still hope for his plan.

Dr. Oldmixon encouraged them to enter the room and look

about; he insisted they take the views of the open fields and shimmering Roxbury flats from the two windows. He kept a curious eye on Rebecca. Yet he said nothing particular to persuade or dissuade her.

"You and Colonel Browne have come to agreement as to a rate," Sanborn stated.

"Yes. Thus have I held the room in his interest."

"Thirteen pounds maintenance," Sanborn said.

"And ten for physic. There's another two for warding."

Sanborn looked at the old man. "That was my understanding as well," he said, satisfied to compare figures according to the colonel's request for confirmation. He was, in fact, authorized to make a further deposit immediately.

Suddenly a heavy sound, as of something large being dropped, came from a room down the hall. Then the strange bellowing of a man's voice, as if speaking in tongues. It all amounted to gibberish, even when Sanborn could catch a word or phrase of English.

What little color remained in Rebecca's face drained away entirely.

"That would be Mr. Holt now," Oldmixon said, his face calm and expressionless.

"Silence, for the love of God, you raving lunatic!" someone else called out from behind another door.

"Mr. Snow," the old parson said. He stood silent, looking at Rebecca and Sanborn, as if no further explanation could possibly be required.

"Are any women boarding here, Dr. Oldmixon?" Sanborn asked.

"Two," he answered, nodding his white head. "Mrs. Reed, a widow of formidable spleen, and Mrs. Brixton, who suffers much from the hypp and the visions of an Enthusiast, of a devout Presbyterian sect."

Sanborn looked at Rebecca again. She looked away and turned once more to the southeast window.

"Rebecca," Sanborn said, "would you like some air?"

"Not just now," she said, without turning back toward them.

Sanborn felt encouraged that their visit was having the effect on Rebecca that he, if not the colonel, desired. "These others, do you administer treatments?"

"In some instances," Oldmixon said. "Venesection, purges, and emetics, blistering—our own special remedies. With the more antic dispositions, opium is often helpful in settling the mania."

"Depending on the particular case."

"Certainly. But most boarders require, or indeed prefer, physic of one kind or another eventually."

"I imagine they do," Sanborn said. "I wonder if we might see some of these others."

Oldmixon rubbed his jaw. "Well, I believe Mrs. Brixton wouldn't mind a visit. Let me just step 'round to see how she is this afternoon."

They waited only some few minutes before the old parson returned and ushered them into Mrs. Brixton's room. It was furnished similarly to the room they had just left, with the addition of a well-stuffed settee upon which the inmate might sit or lie as her humors took her. There was a considerable pile of books—Sanborn did not doubt of their vigorous piety—stacked on the floor beside the settee. Next to one window stood the inmate wearing a sort of night shift, ivory in color, partially overwrapped by a black brocaded dressing gown. Her hair was covered by a rust-colored turban, the only concession to fashion or public scrutiny. She was a not unattractive woman in her late thirties, Sanborn estimated, but the ravages of her soul's enthusiasm marked her dignified face, as if she spent her nights in watchfulness rather than sleep—quite alone, Sanborn imagined, with her beautiful and terrible visions.

Oldmixon introduced them to Mrs. Brixton, who bowed politely and eyed them curiously. Finally, a smile emerged from her lips and her whole demeanor brightened.

"My pleasure, sir, ma'am," she finally said. "Dr. Oldmixon informs me you have one who may join our little community."

Sanborn found himself speechless. Mrs. Brixton looked deeply into Rebecca's eyes. Rebecca returned her gaze, but also did not, or could not, speak.

The old parson broke the silence. "Indeed, there is one who may benefit from our retreat and regimen." He smiled at Mrs. Brixton. "If the lady and gentleman find our situation worthy of such a one."

"I'm sure they shall," she said, looking first at Sanborn and then at Rebecca again. "A child, I expect."

Sanborn found his voice. "A young lady, madam. A young lady who might benefit from a period of peaceful confinement and Dr. Oldmixon's care."

"You find our establishment suitable?" she asked.

"I find the good work Parson Oldmixon is doing here impressive."

"And the lady?" She turned her deep gaze on Rebecca.

Rebecca could not speak, still, and the pause grew quickly painful.

"She, Miss Wentworth, finds herself rather hyppish after our journey, I fear, and from the thought of this young lady's confinement here, or anywhere," Sanborn said. It just came out of his mouth before he thought about it, to fill the vacancy.

Mrs. Brixton smiled serenely at Rebecca. "You needn't fear for her," she said. "We live under the most scrupulous care. Dr. Oldmixon is a gentleman." She turned to smile at the parson.

"Thank you, Mrs. Brixton," he said, and made a little bow.

"You're from England, are you not, sir?" She was speaking to Sanborn now.

"Yes, some years ago," Sanborn said. "I had the pleasure of studying in London for a time."

"Then you've no doubt been to Bedlam, sir, with the droves of tourists seeking amusement."

He stumbled a bit, then said, "Indeed, madam."

"Nothing of the sort here, sir, I assure you. Nothing of the sort in all Boston."

"I'm most pleased to hear it, madam."

She returned to Rebecca. "Nothing of that sort here," she repeated. She walked over to Rebecca and offered her hand. Rebecca took it. Mrs. Brixton held up Rebecca's hand, like a fortune-teller.

"A woman of sensibility," Mrs. Brixton said. "Tell me. This young lady whom you might send here, for her repose, is she something of a seer?" She looked directly into Rebecca's eyes and smiled.

Rebecca found her voice, and Sanborn felt relief. "She is given to see things, yes," Rebecca said, "as they truly are. She thereby sometimes causes discomfort in others."

The deep fatigue seemed to leave Mrs. Brixton's face a moment. "The truth unsettles those unused to it," she said. "Yet those accustomed to it the truth makes free."

"Even in confinement," Rebecca suggested.

"Even in confinement," Mrs. Brixton said. "Even in our suffering."

"Thank you, Mrs. Brixton," Rebecca said. "Thank you for your kindness."

Still holding Rebecca's hand, Mrs. Brixton turned toward Sanborn and Parson Oldmixon, looking from one to the other.

"Does the young lady who may come here find pleasure in reading?"

"Yes," Sanborn said.

"Then she may find some of these of interest," she said, indicating by her free hand the black books piled on the floor.

Rebecca looked at the books, her face expressionless once more.

Sermons, religious treatises, books of prayer and meditation had never been her favored reading, Sanborn thought, as he looked at Rebecca's face. She seemed unable to speak again.

Mrs. Brixton looked into her eyes for some time, then gently dropped Rebecca's hand. She pulled a book off the top of one of the piles and withdrew a slip of paper, which she folded twice. This folded paper she placed in the palm of Rebecca's hand and then folded Rebecca's fingers over it. She returned to the window to stand just as she had stood when they entered her room. She looked at each of the three others in turn, smiled, and appeared determined to say no more.

"Thank you, Mrs. Brixton," the parson said, holding out an arm to indicate the doorway for Rebecca and Sanborn. Sanborn repeated a thank you, and they all turned to go.

"The truth will set us free," Mrs. Brixton called out, as if to Rebecca, one last time, as Oldmixon was closing the door.

"Would you care to look around the grounds, sir?" he said as they all descended the stairs.

Sanborn looked at Rebecca. She had opened the slip of paper and her face appeared troubled. "I think not, Parson," Sanborn said. "Perhaps a dish of tea is in order, however, if you and Mrs. Oldmixon would be so kind." He tried to indicate Rebecca without her seeing the gesture.

"I believe you are quite right, Mr. Sanborn," Dr. Oldmixon said. "I think a dish of tea would do us all some good."

Chapter 30

THEY REMAINED with the Oldmixons overnight, in the parsonage, as they had arranged before their departure from Portsmouth. The next morning Sanborn knocked gently on Rebecca's door.

She was already up and dressed.

"The return boat leaves in two hours," he reminded her.

"Am I to return then?"

"Just as we said, Rebecca."

"And such then, truly, was Colonel Browne's purpose as well?"

"Yes," Sanborn hedged. "He believed this visit would allow us to confirm whether Dr. Oldmixon's establishment might meet every requirement, as he had understood from others."

"I see. I had begun to doubt that premise, during the night."

"You did not sleep well?"

"Off and on." She handed him a neatly folded slip of paper,

which he recognized as the slip Mrs. Brixton had handed Rebecca yesterday. He opened it and read.

Oh Seeker of Truth
Dare ye look in the eye
Of the Sun at Noon?

"Gibberish," he said, folded the paper, and handed it back to her. "Of course, you are free to stay on without further delay or negotiation, or consideration." He was unable to find words to put it delicately. That, too, had been a part of the colonel's purpose.

She looked directly at him. "Mr. Sanborn, you know I am not mad."

He returned her stare. Perhaps he hesitated a moment too long. "I know, Rebecca. But, to be honest, I'm no longer certain that confinement at the Brownes' is preferable to confinement, or rather removal and rest, here."

"That is a conundrum I revolved in my own mind during the night. But, I find I prefer no confinement at all." Her eyes were defiant.

"Ah, yes. There is of course an alternative. However—"

"Blessed matrimony," she interrupted him.

"It may be blessed by comparison to this," he said, feeling equally defiant now. "Or a closed room on the second floor of the Browne manse."

"You know they do not intend to allow me to remain with them."

"They find it too vexatious. I doubt they would allow it for long now."

She turned away. There was a window in her room, west facing, and she went over to it and looked out.

"Rebecca—" Sanborn began.

"Did you hear him last night? Mr. Holt?"

"I confess I slept heavily and utterly. At what hour?"

"Near three o'clock. It didn't last long. Those strange tongues again."

"It *is* unsettling."

"Very. Even at this distance." She looked out on the parsonage garden below. "It's small," she said, apparently referring to the garden. "But quite beautiful. Mrs. Oldmixon, I take it, has a hand and eye for the flowers."

He said nothing. He could think of nothing to say.

"No," she finally said. "I'll return with you, Mr. Sanborn. I want to go home."

He had misunderstood her at first, for he did not realize she had no intention of returning by their arranged passage. She wanted to see something of Boston first, she said. They had earned it. She wanted him to pay his initial visit to Mr. Fleet with her illustrated manuscript, as they had agreed he would. There was no hurry about returning that particular day. He decided to indulge her; he was, after all, on a mission to persuade her to accommodate herself to the Brownes' proposals, and it would be necessary to humor her somewhat in order to maneuver her toward that goal. What matter a day or two more? He had been given license to do whatever necessary to bring her around. He left her at Oldmixon's and returned to the wharf to arrange passage on the next sloop for Portsmouth where passage was to be had. As it turned out, that gave them three more days.

Before he returned to Oldmixon's he stopped by the Orange Tree Tavern and put a deposit on lodging for them—half a bed in a common room for himself and a private garretlike room for Rebecca. The price of the garret was much greater than he should have expended, and the landlady had little inclination to give over the space to a single occupant. But Sanborn pleaded his "sister's" indisposition, and the woman relented once she saw the money. The lodging was near Mr. Smibert's elegant house on Queen Street, and Sanborn hoped to visit the old gentleman again with the thought that it might do Rebecca good to peruse the Colour Shop and studio in the mansion. In addition, the Orange Tree was situated near both the government (or Town House) and mercantile districts. While making these arrangements at the tavern, he hired a boy to take his card around to the old master, with a note scribbled on the back, to the effect that he would call on him the following morning well after the breakfast hour.

And then he went looking for Thomas Fleet's shop in Cornhill at the sign of the Heart and Crown. He discovered a substantial house that served as both residence and printing house with a convenient shop selling all manner of goods and notions and a front chamber for evening auctions. He entered with Rebecca's portfolio manuscript in hand.

A clerk, in a green cloth apron, who seemed as competent as he was officious, greeted him. Mr. Fleet was "not available." Sanborn explained his mission and showed his letter from Mr. Fleet. The clerk nodded ever more courteously as he read the letter.

"If you'd care to leave it with us, sir," the clerk said, "we may provide an estimate of expenses, and options available."

"May I return tomorrow then?"

The clerk hesitated, cocking his head with its small wig. "Of course," he finally said.

Sanborn hesitated to part with Rebecca's portfolio, but when the clerk carefully took the manuscript tied neatly between boards and listed it in a heavy leather-bound account book, and then turned to place the manuscript on a shelf alongside several other boxes and portfolios, he felt better about it.

"Good day, sir," he said to Sanborn and then turned to other work he'd had in hand when Sanborn had entered.

THE NEXT MORNING Smibert's nephew and assistant John Moffatt, a vigorous and efficient looking man of about forty, showed them into the Colour Shop.

"Mr. Smibert should be here shortly," Moffatt said, after introductions. "Please have a look around." Then he left them to alert his uncle to Sanborn's arrival.

Rebecca immediately began to consider the rich collections of supplies for artists and prints for patrons of the arts. She moved about as if she were in someone else's church, respectfully examining its sacred contents. On display were boxes of gold and silver leaf, every sort of painter's brush and palette knife, black lead pencils and street pencils, colors ground and mixed, cakes of pigment, all manner of papers, fans and fan mounts and brushes, gold picture frames, and a host of mezzotint prints of European and American artists—including Peter Pelham's prints of Smibert's own works, including Smibert's portraits of William Pepperrell, Samuel Waldo, and other heroes of Louisbourg. And a fine large print of Smibert's famous eight-foot-by-five-foot portrait of Peter Faneuil. There was a stack of books of ship prints, so that portrait painters might accurately depict their mercantile patrons' vessels in the background. And there were collections of the latest prints of London portraits so that New England's painters might avail themselves of the latest fashion in costume and pose.

Rebecca wrinkled her nose at the portrait prints, but Sanborn thought them all wonderful and informative. Yet they dared not speak their opinions for fear of being overheard at an embarrassing pass in conversation or disagreement. In fact, a black serving girl, whom they later heard referred to as Phyllis, suddenly appeared to assure them Mr. Smibert was on his way.

Shortly afterward the old master entered, from a door leading to other rooms of the house, wearing a dressing gown and turban cap. He was a man of some sixty years, or nearly so. His eyes were a little bleary and his handshake not as firm as Sanborn remembered it from his visits to the master some years ago. He had a weak chin running to neck folds, but an amiable face.

"Sanborn!" he said, managing a hearty smile. "Good to see you again, sir. You must tell me of your successes in Portsmouth—I've heard something of it, of course. And whom have we here?" He turned toward Rebecca, who was coming toward them now.

"Miss Rebecca Wentworth," Sanborn said. "Herself an artist of most conspicuous talent—"

"Indeed! Indeed!" the old master said, interrupting Sanborn. He took Rebecca's hand and bowed to it gracefully. "My pleasure, miss. My great pleasure. You have been perusing these wares, I see." His arm swept over the shop. "And have you found something to your taste?"

"Many things, sir," she answered. "The richest collection of colors and brushes I've ever beheld. A very heaven of colors."

He laughed. "Well, then, by all means don't allow us to detain you. Choose your heart's desire among all these." He indicated particularly the color boxes on display.

"Go ahead, Rebecca," Sanborn said. "Allow me to offer you a modest gift."

"I believe I shall, sir." She turned from them again and began to examine carefully the variety and quality of colors.

Smibert laughed in his friendly, self-effacing manner and turned back to Sanborn. "And how are things in Portsmouth, Mr. Sanborn? You have found much work to do, I hear. Portraits, lessons, what have you."

The two men talked of the Port and mutual acquaintances, eyeing Rebecca from time to time as she went about her careful, scrutinizing business. When she had finally chosen several particular colors—Sanborn could discern lake and Prussian blue among them—Smibert accepted Sanborn's payment and invited them into his studio on the floor above.

Here they witnessed an even larger collection of prints, plaster casts and busts, architectural drawings, and painterly equipment. There were also a number of his own copies of masters: *Cardinal Bentivoglio,* after Van Dyck; *The Continence of Scipio,* after Poussin; *Danae,* after Titian. And there were portraits of his own as well: *Dean George Berkeley and His Entourage* (a conversation piece, he informed them, that was painted at Berkeley's home, Whitehall, when they had all first come to America), *Grand Duke Cosimo III,* and a recent portrait of a gentleman, perhaps unfinished or drying, beside another unfinished landscape, on easels at the center of the room. Sanborn knew that Smibert was known for holding on to a finished portrait before delivering it to his most noble patrons.

"Governor Shirley?" Sanborn asked, indicating the unfinished portrait.

"A fine sitter, sir," Smibert said. "A man of patience and generosity. I had the deuce of a time with General Waldo, however. The man could not keep still, but would always be leaping up and pacing about, like the agitated and active military man he is." He shook his head.

"Very well done, sir," Sanborn said, nodding toward the Shirley.

"My powers are diminishing," Smibert said. "My eyesight weakens steadily. My hands grow less firm and sure. I've taken to landskips to refresh me. They seem now to provide repose." He pointed to the other painting upon an easel.

"Very fine as well, sir." It was a formulaic landscape but lovingly executed. Sanborn pictured him fiddling away weeks, even months, on it.

"You humor an old man."

"Not at all, sir. You are a long way from finished, or even weakened, by the look of these."

Smibert smiled and ambled over to Rebecca, who had taken the liberty to examine some prints of Italian painters mounted on both sides and above a window.

"And what do you make of these, Miss Wentworth?" he asked.

"Masterful, sir." She bordered on the impolite by continuing to examine the prints. "Masterful."

"They repay study. Much study."

"There are few enough opportunities in Portsmouth, sir, for study," Sanborn said.

Smibert turned toward him. "I expect so." He mused a moment and then changed the topic. "Robert Feke. Remember Robert Feke, Sanborn?"

"You introduced us, yes. Just before I left on the Portsmouth commission in forty-one."

"Yes. Well, Sanborn, he surpasses me now."

"I've heard no one say so, sir. And from what I had seen of his work, I can't believe it myself."

"Oh, people are too kind about such things, Sanborn. The apprentice succeeds the master, and all that, though I only offered him hints, models, and prints to observe. But he does, he succeeds me, in any case. A man whose study has repaid him well. A natural hand for the brush improved by self-teaching and study. He's due to return soon, by his correspondence to me. Perhaps this year or next, to pay me a visit and see to a commission or two."

"I should like to see him again," Sanborn said.

"Of course I don't keep up my end of the correspondence

enough. I'm a terrible one for scribbling, and never was much of a reader, to tell the truth. Ol' Berkeley used to enjoy upbraiding me on that score. But he's been a loyal one, Mr. Feke." Smibert smiled, as if musing again. "And he promises a visit."

When Sanborn didn't respond immediately, Smibert added, "And now there's John Greenwood about, capturing the best commissions."

"Rebecca has a natural genius as well, sir," Sanborn said.

"Is that so?" He turned to her again. She continued to study various prints.

"Rebecca," Sanborn said. "Would you be so kind as to depict a little something for Mr. Smibert. So he not think me fanciful, or a mere flatterer."

"A little something, Mr. Sanborn?"

"Whatever you like," Sanborn said. He had thought to alleviate her melancholy by getting her to paint again, after the dreariness of the madhouse visit. And he wanted the old master to assess her capacity, as if to confirm his own astonishment.

Rebecca pulled herself away from the print and faced them.

"I would be honored," Smibert said. He appeared genuinely curious himself now.

She curtsied and walked over to the easel with the fresh landscape. She looked at it a few minutes, saying nothing further.

"From a long-ago memory," Smibert said. "Memory is now my better eye."

"Italy?" she asked.

"Outside Florence," he said. "The ranges of hills there. You must see for yourself some day."

"If I were allowed," she said, still looking at the landscape.

The two men looked at one another. Rebecca removed her traveling cloak and smoothed her dress. "Have you an apron?" she asked. "Or a smock that might fit?" She held out her arms as if to demonstrate her proper size.

Smibert left the room and returned with an apron and an old shawl, to cover her arms and bodice somewhat more. While he was gone, she chose her brushes, palette knife, maulstick, and a comfortable palette. Then she turned to the colors assorted on one of his worktables. When her traveling dress was covered, she carefully set the master's landscape down off the easel and left it facing her against a chair leg, about five feet from her. Then without further conversation or delay, she placed a canvas on the easel and began, as was her habit, to paint from right to left a quick approximation of Smibert's Tuscan landscape. The two men took chairs behind her and observed the process. Their eyes seemed not to trouble her in the least, as if the men had ceased to occupy the room with her.

When the canvas was filled with her initial layering (which, in the past, would have served as well for a finish) she stepped back for a quick look. Then she renewed her palette and returned to the canvas again. Smibert looked at Sanborn. He was clearly affected. They did not speak. The painting now began to take on deeper, richer qualities. Details of the olive trees and the fields in the foreground were becoming suddenly discernable. A strange yet beautiful light began to suffuse the painting, and when she turned her brush upon the sky, an angelic being began to emanate from the hazy blue, as if some medieval papist were quickened through Rebecca to manipulate her brush.

Nearly two hours had passed when Smibert slowly stood up holding his back, as if he comprehended it all, finally—her rapid brushstrokes, her profluent fancy and vision, the quirky superiority of her painting compared to his own efforts to amuse himself idling in a remembered landscape. She ignored his pacing the floor behind her.

Sanborn looked carefully at the angelic being. There was no halo or Christian emblem. It was rather like a man-woman, but perfectly at home in the sky, smoothly integrated into its proper milieu. Occasionally he exchanged glances with Smibert.

Finally Smibert ceased his pacing and scrutinizing and sat down again beside Sanborn. He groaned as he adjusted his weary bones, leaned over to Sanborn, and said in a low voice, "Refreshment."

Sanborn turned to look at him.

"Refreshment," he repeated, his voice louder now. "What would you care for?" He looked toward Rebecca, too. "Cakes and cider? Or perhaps we should dine. Yes, it has passed two of the clock." He got up and went over to another worktable where he found a little bell, which he rang vigorously. Soon Phyllis appeared. Within another thirty minutes, she returned with two trays of boiled beef dinners. Through it all, Rebecca had not stopped painting.

Smibert politely insisted she partake of the meal with them. By then her landscape was well under way. She had worked it through perhaps four layers, in that new style for her, but still always moving right to left across the canvas. While they partook of the meal on the worktable, which Smibert had cleared off quickly, they considered the painting.

"The most unusual technique I've ever beheld," the old man said after consuming several large forkfuls of beef and cabbage.

"I knew you'd see it to be," Sanborn said. "I can assure you, sir, she has been most amazing from childhood." He had been anxious over whether the master would consider Rebecca's revision of his Italian landscape offensive to him. But the old man did not seem agitated.

"But how . . . ? Where did you learn, or study, my dear?" Smibert asked.

"Nowhere, sir. I had only drawing lessons of my tutor, and a bit of painting on glass, like spinet lessons. But she lent me some of her instruction booklets as to mixing and applying colors. And then Mr. Sanborn has been so kind as to offer a word now and then of advice."

"I see," he replied, taking another bite. "Extraordinary." He looked at Sanborn in an honest and disarming manner, "A wonderful prodigy, sir. Never seen anything quite like it myself." He looked at Rebecca again, still chewing. "Though the prodigious woman-child is something of a commonplace among those later known for their palette and brush. Clara Peeters, Giovanna Garzoni, Elisabetta Sirani, Louise Moillon, and Rosalba Carriera. Still, it is something to behold oneself, even in a more mature young lady like Miss Wentworth." He thought a moment. "Have you tried limning, Miss Wentworth?"

"Seldom," she said.

"I once told her," Sanborn put in, "that since she has grown to womanhood—and approaching her majority in but a few years, sir—it would be a slight matter then to prepare specimens that adapt to fashion." He of course said nothing about the riot she had caused at Blackstone. And he had said nothing to her since then about supporting herself by taking likenesses.

"Yet I'm forbidden by my guardians now to paint, or to draw."

"Forbidden?" Smibert said.

"They fear certain fancies, visions," Sanborn put in, "which Rebecca has produced on canvas and paper. They do not think such productions conducive to health of the mind and heart."

"They believe such paintings agitate a hypochondriacal mind," Rebecca said.

The old man was speechless. He looked from them to the painting. He stood and walked over to it, bending close for a good look. His attention made Sanborn very nervous.

"A most remarkable . . . angel," he said. "A very clever, if unusual, painting taken all around." He straightened up slowly and turned back to them. "Well, I've suffered for years from a bit of the hypp myself. One learns in spite of it to get on with the work at hand."

Neither Sanborn nor Rebecca spoke to explain the position they were in from Rebecca's distraction. Sanborn wondered if he might persuade the old master to take her on as a painting assistant, but that would be irregular, and it was too soon to raise such a question. Moreover, such an arrangement might come to inconvenience greatly Mr. Smibert and his family, to say nothing of subverting Colonel Browne's wishes. Rebecca had simply arrived at a desperate pass, and there was little anyone other than her guardians could do to alter her circumstances. And even though she was about to turn eighteen, he believed the Brownes would never allow her the relative liberty of a young woman either engaged to be married or in her majority at twenty-one. The case for *non compos* was too much on their side. Had he not suspected, after all, that the decision to incarcerate her at Dr. Oldmixon's was spurred on by the realization that every day she was approaching full womanhood?

A thought he had entertained twice before, and which even Miss Norris had once broached, teased his mind again: the only solution would be for him to take Rebecca well beyond New England himself. Such a ploy would set into ruin everything he had worked for and built up over the years. In the eyes of the world she would become nothing more than "the young woman whom that fellow debauched." It would be a case of wrecking his life and work to save hers. And in the end, she would be destroyed as well. It would be beyond all common sense. He would simply capitulate to . . . what? To an infatuation? A delicious infatuation? Though he had never mentioned the idea to Rebecca, he believed in her desperation now she might flee with him. Yet he could not discover the courage, or foolhardiness, to rush with her into a new and disordered life.

Rebecca excused herself, rose, and returned to the canvas. Smibert turned to watch her. The men observed her from their places at the worktable. After a half hour more watching in silence, Smibert said, "Sir, I wonder if we might retire to the parlor while Miss Wentworth continues her work."

Once seated in the parlor, the old master asked Sanborn about Rebecca's treatment at the hands of her guardians. Unable to hold in his secret any longer, Sanborn unburdened himself of the whole tale of his discovery of "her gifts and her madness."

"Good Lord, man!" Smibert finally said. "You mean to say she really is mad? Are you quite certain?"

"I now believe that she has become distracted, at intervals, yes. But I also believe her worst descents are temporary. And her tendency to distraction has been much aggravated of late. Her guardians have allowed no channel for her powers and no relief from their admonitions."

"Somehow I cannot quite believe it. She strikes me rather as a prodigy of art—as one whose soul is too large to be taken with popular prejudices." He looked at Sanborn, then down, as if he had embarrassed himself. "Still, I don't doubt your own judgment, Daniel." He looked at Sanborn again. "Her circumstances are most unsettling then."

Sanborn did not know what to say. He had seen Rebecca's largeness of soul, but he had feared—what?—her soul overmastering her reason? He felt a wave of shame that perhaps he had not acted vigorously or truly enough upon what he admired in her—the prospect of an art worthy of the New World. Had he been incapacitated by too great a respect for convention, for his training, and for his own advantage? He couldn't bear to contemplate the question any longer.

"I'm at a loss," he said instead. The thought occurred to him that even were Rebecca allowed to paint, she would never be satisfied merely producing fashionable if excellent portraits.

"So I see," Smibert was saying. "Such a fall into ruin for one of such gifts. What do you propose to do, after all?"

"In the first case, I hope to print and sell a modest book of illustrations—a new Dr. Watts—that Rebecca completed some time ago."

"It is beautifully done?"

"Quite beautiful. Thomas Fleet is considering the manuscript for an estimate of its value. I don't know whether we can negotiate a price on our account to print and a portion of the sales thereafter, or an honest purchase outright. I'd hate to let it go for under twenty pounds."

"I see. Well, that's good news. The more common's an outright purchase, of course." He thought a moment. "Fleet's one of our most prolific—and known for his children's books. Has his Negroes trained up as excellent printers, and I may say one of these fellows cuts excellent woodblocks for illustrations. You may of course require an accomplished printmaker for a project such as you describe. But Fleet will advise you as to feasibility on that score."

"And I wondered if I might ask you for an introduction at Church's, sir, to extend the likelihood of widespread sales. Either way Mr. Fleet cares to arrange it, we should be able to negotiate a better price with the interest of Mr. Church."

"I should be able to help you there."

"Thank you. But to return to the real matter of your question: I propose to do nothing more than her guardians' wishes. How can it be otherwise, sir? I'm out of my depth."

"Well, it is a kind of wisdom to recognize as much."

"A futile wisdom, nonetheless."

"You are taken with her."

Sanborn looked away. "Who would not be?" he finally said.

"Who indeed?"

"It's like having an enchanting creature about. Not quite of this world. Unpredictable. Yet lovely, intriguing, affecting. It's impossible to ignore her, or to forget her. It's impossible to hand her over to others and go about one's business."

"Even unto a madhouse," the old man said. "You will return with her to Portsmouth?"

"That's the understanding."

"You believe she *will* marry then?"

"I can't see how, given the limitations her family places upon her. And considering her state of mind now."

"Ah, I see." He considered a moment. "Therefore she dooms herself."

"So it would seem."

Smibert looked at the floor again, brooding a moment. "I think otherwise, from all you have told me, Daniel. Perhaps she will marry after all. It would be but to consent to a life among the living, even under duress of an unsuitable match, from her point of view. It is a duress many endure and surmount."

"I pray you are right, sir. But I fear the worst. She'll be given very little more time."

"You must look to the brighter possibilities, Sanborn." The old man's face began to beam. "Perhaps her husband will prove companionable to an artist. Recall Mrs. Beale—accomplished enough to attract the attention and hire of Sir Peter Lely. Her husband managed her household, two sons, and her career while she painted her heart out. He even primed her canvases and mixed colors!"

"I don't think that could conceivably be the case with the two gentlemen in question, sir," Sanborn said and shook his head. "They are quite unsuitable for a painting woman. And this is the New World, after all, not some center of Old World civilization and tradition."

The old man was quiet, as if considering Sanborn's simple realism. "Well," he finally said, "you are perhaps right, Daniel. Yes, no doubt you are. Things are not ripe, not yet, not here, for the likes of Rebecca Wentworth. Now . . ." He rubbed his hands and tried to sound jolly. "Perhaps she'd benefit from a bit of frivolity." He watched to see Sanborn's reaction. "Jervis's Public House, for example, at the Sign of the Greyhound—about four miles out of town. Mr. Moffat would be happy to conduct you. The inn's a favorite stopping place for pleasure parties driving out on horseback and chaise to rendezvous. Many of the gentry, of both sexes, make an evening's promenade. The warm spring evenings might draw some of these forth in anticipation of the season. And then there's the weekly concerts and balls, and good dancing, sir, as elegant as any I've witnessed in London. The ladies are quite free and affable at these gayer events." He winked and chuckled. "And before long, we shall have turtle feasts and frolics, picnics, fishing parties, and delicious moonlit returns."

"She has little patience for frivolity, sir."

"More's the pity, if I may say so. That is precisely what I would prescribe."

"You are no doubt right, sir. But I'm certain she'll not hear of it."

WHEN THE MEN returned to the painting room, Rebecca turned to face them.

"It would take another hour or two to polish this painting," she told them, "but it's sufficiently completed to depict my understanding of it."

The two men stepped over to the easel and examined the painting carefully.

"Very unusual," Smibert said. "You have taken my old memory and transformed it to a vision."

"I meant no disrespect, sir, but only to show my own ways, as requested."

"You have demonstrated your gifts, Miss Wentworth," he went on. "It won't meet with the general taste, of course, but I might offer it for sale in my shop. A few people of higher discrimination happen in from time to time." He looked at her.

Sanborn looked at her, too. "Why not?" he said.

She was removing her apron. "Agreed, then," she said. She folded the apron neatly and placed it on Smibert's chair.

Smibert consulted his watch, so they began to make their good-byes. Feeling sluggish, Sanborn suggested they walk. The old painter reminded Sanborn of the clangor and danger of Boston's streets—the heedless careening chariots and horsemen, carts, trucks, and tumbrels. He suggested they try the Mall on the Common, where ladies and gentlemen walked after their afternoon tea. In twenty minutes more Sanborn and Rebecca were back out in the fresh air, blinking and looking about them in the late afternoon sun.

Chapter 31

THE COMMON HAD BEEN ENCLOSED on two sides by a fence in order to protect herbage from the wear of carts and horses, and the Mall consisted of a fine green and a walkway between two rows of trees planted opposite each other. It reminded Sanborn of St. James Park in London, which served a similar pedestrian purpose. The walk ran its course along the northwest side of the Common with a beautiful view of the canal and bay.

After a turn on the Common, he directed their steps toward the Exchange at the head of King Street. He knew it was surrounded by booksellers' shops.

"My goodness!" Rebecca said as they approached the Town-house, an elegant brick building of some 125 feet in length and 40 in breadth.

"I understand from my period of residence in Boston," Sanborn told her, "that it replaces the wooden structure burned in the great fire."

When they stepped into the lower chamber of the building, Rebecca looked up at the spacious high ceiling supported by a row of wooden pillars twenty-five feet in height. She was properly awed but soon tired, she said, of looking about indoors. "I like the air better," she suggested.

Outside again, they entered the walk lined by shops where the merchants met every day at one o'clock, as Sanborn explained, "in imitation of the Exchange at London."

Rebecca couldn't resist one of the several booksellers' shops they passed, so they went in.

"There is nothing like Boston for books," he said to her as they entered. "Nothing in all the colonies. A half-dozen printing presses as well."

He insisted on buying a book for her. She lingered over Shaftsbury, Pope, Samuel Richardson, and others. Finally she chose Jonathan Richardson's *An Essay on the Theory of Painting*. They left the store, Rebecca smiling, to attend a late book auction, the notice of which they had seen posted, by one Mr. Carlile, book vendor, on the Exchange: "A valuable and curious collection of books on most subjects, just brought from Great Britain."

The young merchant was already deep in his auctioneer's patter by the time they entered. "Here must be a valuable book, ge'men," he was saying, "for it reveals everything concerning popes, cardinals, Antichrist, and the devil." There was a murmur of knowing laughter and a bottle of spirits made its way among the crowd. No one bidding immediately, he held aloft another: "And here, ge'men, we have come upon Tacitus, who gives such elegant account of good and pious Nero, who loved his kindred so well he sucked their blood." Another murmur of laughter. Hands went up; bidding took place. "I am to sell every book by an inch of this candle," Mr. Carlile called out; he smiled and motioned for the bottle to continue briskly on its rounds. These were men of heterodox tastes—snapping up Ovid's *Art of Love* with *The Marrow of Modern Divinity*,

Pamela with *Anti-Pamela*. Sanborn bid on *Joseph Andrews,* which had been highly recommended by several associates in Portsmouth but had been sold out when he had looked for it.

After purchasing Sanborn's book, they left the shop and headed down to Long Wharf, in a direct line with King's Street and out into the water and where they had landed. The sea air, like their book purchases, further improved their mood. After a lengthy turn along the wharf, they decided to have a light supper of bread and milk at Wethered's Tavern, filled with jolly merchants and shipmasters, before returning to their lodgings.

"Thank you, again, Mr. Sanborn, for the book," Rebecca said, as they were finishing their supper. "I'd like very much to go to my room now to begin it."

"I'm anxious to begin mine as well. I won't have comfortable reading arrangements in the common room, but I may be able to find a corner to ensconce myself."

Later that night, long after they should have both given up their reading for the pleasures of sleep, and once his roommates had settled into their slumbers, Sanborn rose from his mattress and made his way quietly up to Rebecca's door. He stood by listening at first, but he heard nothing. He decided to try anyway and knocked softly. He waited, hearing only the dim sounds of two or three revelers remaining below. Finally, the door opened a few inches, and she appeared in a loose white-brocade robe de chamber with silk lace around the sleeves and skirts without hoops or stays that revealed rather than enhanced her womanly shape. He was relieved to find that she was preparing for sleep; he had not awakened her.

"Mr. Sanborn?" she said.

"As you see, Rebecca," he said smiling. "I couldn't begin to fall asleep, and I wondered, if you were not asleep, whether we might have a word."

She thought a moment. "A word, sir? Now?" She looked at him, hesitating. "If you think it's important, I don't see why not." She let him in. She did not offer him a seat in the single chair, but stood there looking at him expectantly.

"I'll not fiddle-faddle around, Rebecca. It's too late for that."

She said nothing.

"After much torturous thought, I've come to believe that you must, finally, marry. There's no other hope for your liberty."

"Liberty, Mr. Sanborn?"

"Your deliverance from the path we have been set upon, by your guardians."

"Dr. Oldmixon's."

"Compared to that, you must agree, marriage—even to Mr. Wentworth—would be a deliverance."

"You would have me unfettered in one sense, only to be enthralled in another."

"You view marriage too bleakly. Your guardians only wish to ensure your security and welfare, which are delicate indeed at present, through these men of substance, who are available and willing. Comparatively, marriage, even in such circumstances, would be, rather, a disenthrallment."

"You cannot believe that, Mr. Sanborn, merely because my guardians do."

"I believe it now, Rebecca."

She refused to respond.

He stepped close to her, reaching out and placing a hand on either arm just below her shoulders. Her softness nearly startled him, and he couldn't speak at first. She looked directly at him.

"There is, perhaps, an alternative," he finally said.

"An alternative."

"Yes. You and I could leave together, this very week. We would go somewhere beyond their reach, and you would come . . . under my protection. We could open a painting room. Somewhere. We might—"

"Beyond their reach?" she interrupted him.

"And why not?"

"You underestimate their reach. They have many powerful friends and many associates in all manner of trade. I do not think there is a plantation free of their influence, the combined influence of the Wentworths and the Brownes."

"Surely some subterfuge is possible." He was suddenly at a loss for words again.

"You surprise me, Mr. Sanborn." She laughed. "With such strange, romantic notions of the world. And it is you who accuse me of willful separation from the world."

She had thrown him into confusion. Her words. Her soft female redolence. Her dishabille and loose hair. Her lucidity. What had he hoped to accomplish? His own ruin?

Then she utterly disarmed him by reaching up and placing two fingers against his cheek. "Yet I'm thankful to you. You *have* been a friend and protector to me, in spite of your own misgivings, which I understand. But what you suggest . . . think, Mr. Sanborn: Is it not impossible?"

He was hardly aware what he was doing, but the impulse to hold her to him overwhelmed him suddenly. He pulled her against him, and she did not resist. Nor did she encourage him. They just stood there against one another, helpless in a futile half-embrace.

He could not release her either. And she did not withdraw. The gentle intimacy of her body against his made him languorous. This intimacy was not what he had intended, not yet, though he could not have said what he intended. Her hands came up to his arms, as if to steady herself and, perhaps, reassure him that she shared his desperation—that in fact the desperation was more properly hers. At the same time she looked up at him, and in his continuing confusion he kissed her mouth. She offered a hint of response and he found himself suddenly aroused, an arousal driving away all sensations of languor. Yet his tenderness toward her remained.

She backed away one step, as if she sensed the depth of his arousal and did not wish to encourage his passion or awaken her own.

"Rebecca," he finally said. "I refuse to withdraw my offer, however foolish and romantic it is. I wish to be your protector, your companion. . . ." He ran out of words.

"We had better say good night, sir." She weighed his expression. "I'll consider well what you've said. Please don't think me ungrateful."

Chapter 32

"DO YOU KNOW Mrs. Johnston, in Charleston?" Sanborn asked Smibert the next morning. They were seated at a coffeehouse, enjoying their morning chocolate.

"Henrietta Dering Johnston? The Irish woman? Yes. She is wife to the rector of Saint Phillips." He pondered a moment. "What have you in mind?"

"I'm not entirely sure myself. I wondered if you might provide yet another letter of introduction." Sanborn smiled and took courage from the old master's kindly eyes. "You recall Rebecca's story, as I told you yesterday?"

"Of course."

"Well, sir, I think the best solution is for us, together you see, to remove ourselves entirely from New England. I find I wish to protect her from the destruction her guardians are contemplating—nay, winging to its conclusion."

"I see." He thought a moment. "You are deeply ensnared, Sanborn. But it is understandable, and, considering the risks, you are magnanimous."

"That is not for me to say. But as an accomplished face painter herself, Mrs. Johnston is one who ought to countenance Rebecca. Charleston, Antigua—who knows where we may end up? Far away, is all. I'm sure we shall have to remove farther than Charleston. I wondered if Mrs. Johnston would put us up for a day or two, upon making our escape, as it were, from Boston as soon as possible. We'll need to collect ourselves to make necessary arrangements. Her guardians expect us, or me at the least, by week's end. In Portsmouth. We would need some initial, secret destination, you see. And Charleston would put us out of immediate reach."

"Not for long, I'd wager. But would you ask me to incriminate myself in this . . . decampment, or even, surely in their view, abduction?"

"I beg your pardon, sir. We would be able to keep you out of it if I were to approach Mrs. Johnston myself, merely traveling as friends of yours who have asked for advice and assistance. After all, no one knows that I enlightened you as to Rebecca's case." He assessed Smibert's mood. "I would not for anything ask you to place yourself at risk. We have a confidence between us, and I give you my word it shall go no further."

"The post ship returns in two or three days, I believe, but you'd require something more immediate." Smibert thought a moment. "I think the only hope for you, Sanborn, is to book passage and go, if you are so determined. What I will do is provide you a letter of introduction. Then you can appeal to her yourself. As travelers, bound for the Indies, or whatever story you wish. I can't imagine she wouldn't show you a proper hospitality. After all, she need know nothing more than that you are conducting Miss Wentworth to some place of her merchant father's interests. Or what have you."

"Thank you, sir. I can ask no more of you. I had better purchase some final things from your shop, as well," Sanborn said. "Rebecca has some colors now, and I've carried some minimal equipment with me, but not enough to make our way for long."

They returned to Smibert's Colour Shop where, pleading his financial instability for the moment, Sanborn bargained with some effect.

Rebecca considered his proposal during the night. She told him that it was a tempting offer, but she was full of foreboding. "I leap from the lip of one abyss only to throw myself into another," she had said just before departure. Yet neither could she formulate any other plan to put them beyond the powerful reach of Colonel Browne. All she could say was that once having chosen flight they must flee utterly. Their planning and committing to throw their lives together, furthermore, had the effect of bringing them closer still, into a kind of mutual dependency and absorption, as if, for the moment, the world around them were receding, becoming ever more distant or dreamlike.

He booked passage for them on the next boat for Charleston, South Carolina, and Rebecca and Sanborn soon found themselves in fair weather aboard ship. The plans they had made during their final hours in Boston were to work their way south to the Indies. The more he thought about it, the more Sanborn liked the prospects of the West Indies—living and painting among the wealthy planters, government officials, and shipmasters.

He was particularly interested in assessing Antigua, for he knew the family of an old school friend who had settled on the island, and he supposed he might be introduced to the better sort of patrons. There were, however, two difficulties: Would they be more secure by assuming other identities, avoiding all potential connections with their past? And then there was the question of money. There had been no time, nor would there have been an inconspicuous method, to turn over some of his assets in Portsmouth and elsewhere in New Hampshire. The Brownes and the Wentworths, among others, surely would have learned of his fiscal preparations for flight.

Moreover, the indifferent world kept sending little shock waves in their direction. After booking their passage, Sanborn began to understand fully how low their funds had become. Since there was no time to secure a commission in Boston, he placed his hopes on the merciful kindness of Mrs. Johnston, in South Carolina. Sanborn could not allow himself to contemplate the less amiable turns of Fate, for that would have thrown him into a paralysis of indecision and inaction. So it became necessary, in the very face of uncertainty, for Rebecca and Sanborn to turn ever more to one another.

The night before their departure, Sanborn returned to her room rather than to his bed. He found her under the covers brooding, he assumed, upon their imminent and no doubt irreversible flight. She made as if to rise and greet him more properly, but he asked her to remain as she was.

"I'm staying but a moment," he said, not entirely sure he meant it. "I wanted to confirm your state of mind, Rebecca. To see whether your resolution is as firm as my own."

She looked up at him, seeming to compose herself under the bedclothes. "I see no alternative, as we have spoken. I'm determined to remain resolute."

He moved to stand beside her. Her face, her eyes particularly, appeared determined. He felt encouraged himself.

She placed one arm outside the covers and then reached her hand toward him. He took her hand and bent over the bed, his other hand stabilizing his leaning body on the bedpost. He looked directly at her and said calmly, more calm than he felt, "Are you quite sure, Rebecca?"

"I am resolved, Mr. Sanborn. But if I do not act soon on my resolution, I fear delay and failure of my liberty. The time for dithering is past. I'm prepared to leave on the morrow."

"I mean to give you your liberty, Rebecca. And perhaps my own into the bargain."

She looked at him, as if unsure how he meant it. He did not stop to explain himself for he was uncertain of the full implications of his own words. She squeezed his hand as if to indicate the bond of their headlong gamble. He would later recall the moment: the sensation of dreaming, of fanciful helplessness mingled with desire, as he let himself go slowly toward her until her hand came up, as if to guide him, and he found himself lying full length beside her. Then they were holding one another, without passion yet, but with assurance for the desperate trust they were placing in one another, a trust assured by the very proximity of their bodies and by gestures of fully awakened tenderness.

Neither one fell asleep completely. Sometime in the night Sanborn arose, removed his clothing—save his shirt—and slid under the covers, as if, he thought almost to his amusement, they were two bumpkins tarrying for a night of courtly bundling. She greeted him warmly, easily, her hands immediately under his shirt and along his waist and back, relying, perhaps, on sheer virginal instinct to guide her touch.

Then, finally, she caressed him into an urgency he could no

longer restrain. He flung wide the bed covers and threw up the skirts of her linen nightgown, exposing secret blonde curls that moistened as he dallied along Astarte's bud and stem. She began to move in a slow rhythm against his circular touch—light at first, growing steadily firmer.

"Oh," she said. But it was not really "Oh." It was some other word he had never heard her say before, close to Oh but becoming part of her breathing—a slow synchronous rhythm of her body and breath, and the sound like Oh but not Oh repeated and repeated on the out-breath.

Somehow he restrained himself just long enough to be certain she was ready, and then entered her tentatively while her breathing sound still rose with her body. She uttered a sharp little cry and bit into his shoulder.

But like some schoolboy stricken helpless by his sudden good fortune, he was soon unable to check himself against all the familiar aches and tugs and pulls accelerating madly and he called out to her against her own breathing and lifting and released without any further possibility whatsoever of self-control.

Her own movement continued awhile longer, emptying him now with sweet, delicious constrictions. But she soon subsided as well and they merely embraced one another, saying nothing for a long time, until he pulled away and sat up on the bed to hold his head in his hands. She watched him for several minutes. He couldn't imagine what she was thinking.

"It is the wrong time, Daniel, our time of desperation." She forced him to look at her to be sure he was really listening. "But after all this time we're fully together now all the same."

He didn't know how to respond. All he could think to say was precisely what he was thinking. "I'm sure, yes, we have sealed our doom. Still, we have sealed it with love."

"Do you believe it is really so, Daniel?"

"I've loved you, I suppose, for years—"

"I had thought, once or twice, you might have." She waited for him to respond but he didn't. "Then 'tis sweet to doom oneself after all," she added, almost as if she were speaking to herself in the room alone.

He stood up to dress. She watched him, again with a hint of playfulness in her eyes that unaccountably disturbed him.

"We may be doomed, Rebecca, but we are fully together nonetheless. You are right about that. Maybe we can strike out and gain a week's, a month's, a year's 'liberty,' as you put it."

"I'm glad it's so." She pulled the covers back over her.

He looked toward the single window in her chamber. "A hint of daylight, if I'm not mistaken. You better rise and prepare yourself as well. The captain awaits us on the tide. The hour is near."

He left her to wash and pack a few final things in her bag. He went to his common room and picked up his own bag, and then quietly made his way out and down into the kitchen where the host's table stood. A single serving girl was stoking the fire back to life, as if in her sleep, and arranging pots and kettles on a trammel.

She did not seem interested in acknowledging him in any way at that hour. So as he waited for Rebecca to descend, he glumly recalled the contents of an epistle he had written and then torn up.

My Dearest Gingher,

It has become necessary for me to extend my sojourn in Boston with travel by sea on business—a wonderful opportunity for fine commissions. I cannot say when I might return, but I have arranged in a separate missive to my old business associate Mr. Hart to see to your financial welfare out of the proceeds of certain investments. His understanding is that you are a particular longtime companion whose security I am most anxious to insure. As a man of the world, he understands such things— which are, after all, sufficiently commonplace—and I have no apprehension as to his friendship and loyalty to me. He should be calling on you soon, and as he is a man of discretion and independent wealth, you need fear nothing as to his reliability in executing my request.

My intention is to return to you as soon as practicable, but please don't trouble yourself with any watchfulness or concern over the dangers of sea voyage. You shall be looked after, and know that you travel in my heart wherever these prospects of patronage may carry me.

God willing, we shall renew our lessons some day. Yet as I have said, you progress so well that surely you will improve on your own for the time being. Please know that you hold my deepest affections and fondest memories. I shall write when I can. But for now, I bid you adieu, even as I seek my greater fortune, a beneficence you, too, I promise, shall one day enjoy.

It wouldn't work. He would expose himself and Rebecca and their desperate plans for flight. It wasn't that he didn't trust Mr. Hart's goodwill and friendship, but when a powerful man's stepdaughter did not return he could not count on an associate's silence. Browne and Hart were old friends and had waged mercantile war together over the years against their mutual enemies. No more could he count on silence had he asked for Hart to turn some of his, Sanborn's, assets over to cash and send the money along to a future address in Charleston or New York. It was tempting, but after much thought and internal debate, he decided such pleas would place them in too much jeopardy.

He felt rotten over all the necessities—the duplicities and betrayals—to which he now found himself enslaved, but there was no help for it. He put the letter out of his mind and began to count the money left in his pocketbook. It shamed him. He would have to find work in Charleston, or somewhere, even to clear passage to the Indies. Perhaps now he and Rebecca could work together, exercising their individual gifts to mutual profit. But she would have to learn a new, tasteful manner of painting, one ambitious patrons would approve and desire.

And there was, of course, no time now to reap any fruit from Rebecca's Dr. Watts. Mr. Fleet, on Sanborn's return, had given a range of options, from his own woodcuts to local engravers and printmakers. Sanborn and Fleet had agreed to put the illustrative matter out to bid to see what would be required. Fleet opined that they might expect 500 to 800 copies to be subscribed for initially, if he could control the costs. But all that would take more time than Sanborn now had: time for bids to come in, for preparation and distribution of the publisher's prospectus, and longer still for subscribers to respond and for the production process to run its course. There was to be no relief from Dr. Watts, not yet anyway.

He heard footsteps on the stairs—Rebecca, no doubt. He decided to tell her nothing about the sorry contents of his pocketbook.

Chapter 33

THEIR SEA PASSAGE, however, was not propitious. Doubts started after an elderly man in rather disorderly dress approached them.

"How seems the weather to you, sir?" he inquired of Sanborn, and then added, with the offering of his hand, "Doctor Benjamin Warren, of Philadelphia."

"Fine enough," Sanborn said. "Does it not seem so to you, Dr. Warren?"

"To the eye, perhaps," the old man said in a flat voice and shook his head doubtfully. His head indeed was comical despite the gravity of his countenance. He wore two conspicuous carbuncles upon his face and, from beneath his well-worn hat, a wig that had become all straightened and yellowish at the extremities, exposed, no doubt, to years of sun, moon, and rain. "I overheard the captain saying to his mate that there was no remedy for it but he had failed to procure a conjurer."

"That is but sailorly superstition, sir, surely."

"Nonetheless, even to men of investment and science, to sail without a horoscope of the journey is foolhardy."

"You believe so?"

"Every waterman in Britain and the colonies believes so, sir. But I fear our captain capitulates to expediency."

"Perhaps this once," Sanborn said. He looked about at the sky again. "It seems a pleasant enough day for sailing, nonetheless, Dr. Warren."

"We have little choice but to cast our lots with what seems."

"There would be time still to disembark, sir, if that would set your mind at ease."

The old doctor looked at him. "There is time. Yes—time." He turned away and they did not cross his path again on deck.

A day out of Boston, storm clouds began to appear on the southeastern horizon, as if a great deluge were blowing up out of the tropics. The captain warned the few passengers to prepare for a treacherous gale, and then began ordering his seamen about. Sanborn and Rebecca left the still-sunny deck and secured themselves below, choosing her own tiny quarters in which to ride out the storm together. From below, in an apparent calm, they were unaware of the storm's development, and its full force hit them suddenly. They held one another in the sickening motion and in the clamor of furious waters against the hull and bulwark.

So, Sanborn thought, this was how it would end after all. He felt a frightening inevitability about their doom, as he had called it, though the doom he had referred to was not likely to have been going straight to the bottom in a gale.

It was a long second day, riding on an angry sea in the hold of a ship. When the fury abated, sometime before dawn the following morning, the captain called everyone on the still-wind-battered deck and announced that they had taken on water from some undetermined damage, perhaps more extensive than they knew. They had been blown east and then southeast out to sea. They were now limping back to the coast, he said, and the safest harbor in their approach would be New York. They would be putting in for an indefinite period of time for inspection and repairs.

The passage to port seemed to take forever, but the ship finally limped into Turtle Bay with the tide and began searching for a proper mooring where the captain might arrange for repairs. Everyone was relieved just to have come through alive, but the captain had managed to hint darkly that it would not be possible for passengers to remain aboard while extensive work was done to the vessel. How, Sanborn wondered, would he and Rebecca afford lodging for perhaps several days, even before they would have to pay for lodging in Charleston while they earned their passage to the Indies? Might a commission be garnered quickly? That did not seem likely. Were they to starve, finally, on the streets of New York where Chance had for some reason planted them? He would have to explain now to Rebecca the full measure of their insecurity. He had, he saw now much too clearly, been a great fool. And now he would have to reveal himself a fool to Rebecca.

There were about a half dozen passengers the first mate gathered together to disembark. The passengers were to be lodged at a fair price, the mate explained, at Mrs. Hog's, a clean establishment with dining aid and a number of other dining rooms within a short walk. While they were below decks gathering their things, Sanborn described their frail estate to Rebecca.

"I wondered if we might be near the end," she said and looked away.

He finished putting his things into his portmanteau and hurried the two of them up to the deck where the other passengers awaited them.

As the mate conducted the passengers to Mrs. Hog's, Dr. Warren appeared and fell in with Rebecca and Sanborn. "Sailing without a horoscope always tempts Fate," he said. "I thought I'd die even before we sank. I was sure we were to sink!"

Sanborn now noticed that if his attire was weather-beaten and old-fashioned, it was once of considerable expense. Dr. Warren explained that he had sojourned in New York on many occasions. He vouched for Mrs. and Mr. Hog's at the corner of Broad and William Streets, recommended two other establishments to dine or to sup—in particular one Robert Todd's establishment, which served as the start of the Boston Post Road. Then he began his inquiry into the nature of Sanborn and "your pretty wife's" travels. Sanborn concocted a story of travels for his wife's health to visit relatives in Charleston, which seemed to satisfy his curiosity. He then launched into a lecture on the people and habits of New York, where they might hear as much Dutch as English.

"These people are of good cheer with strangers," he advised, "being all, or most, good topers, but if ye cannot join them in their revelries they think nothing of standing aloof. E'en the gov'nor himself, Mr. Clinton, was a jolly one before illness plagued him. He exemplifies their knack for bawdy punning and wit. The government is under English law, y'see, but the chief men are Dutch — mayor, recorder, aldermen, and assemblymen." He glanced at Rebecca, who had remained silent, and then winked at Sanborn. "And unlike Philadelphia ye'll see plenty of handsome women here riding out in light chairs or walking the streets of an afternoon under their umbrellas painted prettily and all befeathered."

"Never been to Philadelphia, sir," Sanborn said.

The old man looked at him with a sort of pity for the untraveled. "Indeed," he went on, "some were celebrated for beauty and intellectual accomplishment before they were eclipsed by their excellent marriages: Admiral Warren's Susanna DeLancy and her captivating sister Ann. And Mrs. Clinton of course, whose ambition, clear intellect, and strength of will some say are still greater than her august husband's."

That very afternoon, Dr. Warren took them to dine at Todd's, where there was a mixed company, and where Rebecca and Sanborn found they had to excuse themselves soon after an enormous dinner of bacon, chicken, veal, and green peas, as the company around had settled in for bumpers to take them, perhaps, till supper. Rebecca soon found she preferred to excuse herself from all but the necessary mealtimes, thereby avoiding rather rowdy and eccentric company, while on occasion Sanborn stayed on for drinks and conversation, or such as passed for conversation among men in their cups and laden with food.

At the Hogs' table one evening, when Rebecca avoided supper, Mrs. Hog inquired after her health. Sanborn replied that his wife suffered from occasional attacks of vapors and melancholy, and at times found herself indisposed for table. Mr. Hog lifted his glass of charged punch and winked, as if vouchsafing a bit of wisdom from an older man to a younger. "There's nothing to cure it for the ladies, then, sir," he said, "but a vigorous and regular mowing." Sanborn was taken back by such lewd wit in public, but he recovered momentarily. He had heard such language frequently since arriving in New York, but he now saw that his host's wife and daughters thought nothing of it from husband and father.

Rebecca tended to stay indoors, reading or sketching or conversing with Sanborn after he returned to their connubial room from the Exchange or the Merchants' Coffee House and a few hits of backgammon or a game of chess. He had been meeting sundry persons and putting about that he could paint likenesses; he even entered a small advertisement in the *Gazette*. But within the first three days no patrons called.

On the third evening when he returned to their room, she had locked the door and refused to let him in. After her refusal, she no longer spoke to him from behind the door. He shook the door, spoke to her earnestly but quietly from the other side, and rattled the handle, but he soon thought better of all that for fear he might disturb the house and be thrown out.

He descended to the common room and began to drink with others he found there, well into their cups. At some point late that night, he ascended to their room once more, but still she would not let him in. He ended up sleeping in a corner, head on table, after the other tipplers left for their own dwellings or beds. Mr. Hog chuckled when he found him there upon closing the rooms.

"Ah, sir," he said, "'tis nothing unusual, these falling-outs with the ladies." He laughed outright. "They need their privacy now and again. But they always come 'round in the end."

Sanborn barely heard him. It was as if someone were speaking to him from a dream as he lay half-awake. He felt the man place a blanket over his shoulders at some point later, and then all was silence.

Late the next morning the innkeeper, keys in hand, helped Sanborn up the stairs. He was about to turn the key in the lock when the door opened. Rebecca was in bed, still asleep in the darkened room. They were careful not to disturb her.

Mr. Hog left and Sanborn lay down on the floor to nurse his hangover a while longer. He plumped some of Rebecca's clothes that had been flung on the floor into a pillow. The room finally stopped spinning. His eyes and head ached, but he could sleep no more. Drowsing, waking, turning, he finally noticed for the first time that the room was covered with sketches and drawings and a painting or two tacked to the walls.

So that's what she's been up to, he thought. What in the world could she have been thinking, excluding him and spending the last two days, perhaps longer, secretly, manically making these images?

He lay there looking about. The room was not well lighted because the blinds were drawn. Some of the productions appeared quite strange, others less so, but it took him another hour still before he was ready to rise off the floor, soak his head from the pitcher of water, and scrutinize them in better light.

As he opened the blinds somewhat and began to examine them, he heard Rebecca stirring beneath the bedclothes. He glanced over to her, but her eyes were still closed and she did not appear fully awake. The paintings were of the sort he would not wish anyone here to see. Among the drawings, less mystic, as he put it to himself, were many studies of heads and torsos of the Hog family, some of their fellow guests from the ship, and regular customers to Mr. and Mrs. Hog's board and bar. Her depiction of Dr. Warren was quite comical, the others more somber. She had done them all from memory, and despite all he knew of her, the feat astonished him still. But even as he looked at the comparatively innocuous drawings, he knew that they would be unacceptable. They were perhaps less objectionable than the paintings she had done at Blackstone. Still, they penetrated the character of their subjects in a manner too unconventional, too truthful, to hazard a disagreeable response. Could she have possibly imagined she might sell these? Was that her object in producing them?

"What do you think, Daniel?" Her voice from behind startled him.

"As ever, these are exceptional."

"I had to do something!"

"Yes, I see you did. But of course these as they are, Rebecca, cannot be shown, can they?"

"Shown? I had hoped to sell them. What else would I have done them for with our precious materials? And there was little enough time left to us." She got out of bed and began to pin up her hair as she stepped over to the wash table.

"My dear. . . ." He hesitated, trying to think how to begin. "My dear, do you not see these excellent depictions might cause offense if taken wrongly?"

"Offense?" She was washing herself quickly. "How are they offensive? I drew these people precisely, without pretext or satire—"

"Rebecca! Have you forgotten the effect of your portraits the last time you assumed no offense? Would you have us on the streets?" Perhaps he was being too insistent. These drawings seemed, after all, less . . . he searched for a word, *revealing* than the Blackstone portraits.

"Do you begrudge me earning our subsistence, Daniel?"

"Don't be ridiculous. I'm at the point, we are, to accept, to take joy in, anything that might contribute to our security. How can you doubt that?"

She stood straight, wiping her face. She came toward him, looking at the drawings particularly. "I see no insinuations here," she said. "Are you saying there is too much truth?"

"Call it what you will, my dear; there is more of it than these common folk might bear."

She stood there in her nightgown, towel in hand, looking at them all again. Then, calmly at first, she began to tear them off the wall, crush them into balls, and throw them on the floor. The more she did so, the more agitated she became. As he stood helpless in his surprise, watching, she continued her destruction of the drawings and moved to the paintings. When she ripped the first canvas off the wall, he ran over and grabbed her arm to turn her toward him. Her other arm came around, as if unconsciously but vehemently, and struck him on the shoulder with the painting. Then she dropped the painting and her hand reached for his face, but somehow he managed to grab the hand first and, holding both arms now, arrest her thrashing movement completely.

She writhed in anger and frustration for some moments while he held her. All the time she said nothing more, weeping silently, only her tears betraying the depth of her wound. Then almost as suddenly as the outburst had begun, it subsided. He released her. She would not look him in the eye. She returned to the bed, wiped her eyes, and put on her dressing gown. He dared not speak further.

She then walked over to a small chest of drawers and pulled out a little sack with a drawstring. She pulled open the drawstring, reached into the sack, and drew forth a large silver ring with several bright stones in it. "Left to me by my mother," she said, "upon her demise. It's the only thing of value left to me in the world. It was the only thing of value she could claim of her own by then." She did not explain her meaning, or the final circumstances of her father and mother. Her eyes were clear now; she had fully regained her lucidity. She looked down at the ring and the little sack. "You have found no work here. We are out of time and money."

He stared at the ring and Rebecca.

"What's left to us now, Daniel?" she said. "Debtors' prison? Starvation as a final resort, once we are thrown into the street?"

He hesitated. "We've already incurred debt beyond our means."

"Then it's dire necessity." She thrust the ring toward him. "Sell it."

"I'm not sure we can continue to the Indies. Perhaps Charleston, perhaps our luck will turn there."

"Only if you sell the ring. But this is no time to be fooling ourselves. Charleston is no sanctuary from my guardians."

He took the ring she held out to him and looked at it. It was beautifully done and possibly quite valuable. She was right, of course. She had careened from her frenzy to a clear-headedness that discomposed him, but she was now, suddenly, right. Desperate, angry, she was forcing him to admit what they already knew.

On the advice of Mrs. Hog, he avoided the pawnbroker and found an honest buyer of jewelry in the city.

Afterward, as he was returning to their inn, he felt ashamed. Instead of presenting him with a ring as a priceless token of her affection, she had been forced to sell it as a memorial to their desperation. He entered the tavern and thanked Mrs. Hog again. He turned to go up to report to Rebecca, and caught sight of himself in the tavern's great looking glass. He started and stared a moment.

His face had changed. What was it? The face of a failure? The face of a seducer?

THE NEXT DAY they paid their debts. But they would now be reduced to watching the very last of their funds begin to dwindle, a circumstance that would soon trap them in the Dutch city with no means of further travel south or return travel home.

Rebecca had no intention of another voyage by water. He doubted he could soon get aboard ship again himself. Upon inquiry, Sanborn learned that they had enough left to purchase overland travel on the post road to Boston. When Rebecca heard this, she grew very calm. She seemed to be quietly examining all the alternatives, like a mathematician eliminating variables. He did not see how he might return to Portsmouth. And despite the likely prospect of losing Rebecca, he could not help thinking that he might lose Gingher now as well. He would be alone, uncertain whether it would be safe to return even to an outlying town like Greenland.

Rebecca, on the other hand, had little more to lose. Perhaps she would be able to offer a convincing case for having been delayed some weeks in Boston while Sanborn was persuading her into the incarceration her guardians desired. Even if she could be convincing, she would have no choice but to accept the madhouse or return home utterly pliable. Rebecca's choices they turned over together and singly, waking and sleeping.

In the end, while there was still money sufficient for their passage, they set out for Boston. He was to remain there, while she, after sending for the expenses of her final passage, went on to Portsmouth. Upon her return she would write to him of her disposition and his own prospects for return, if any remained. Further, as men who resided in the province of New Hampshire were currently being enlisted and impressed into a great army preparing to join the king's forces for a final attack and reduction of Canada, Sanborn thought it better to remain in Massachusetts. He would be seen as a mere passer through, while the battle frenzy everywhere played itself out. It was all very simple suddenly; it was the simplicity of capitulating to powers much greater than oneself.

. . .

EVEN AS they journeyed to Boston, Sanborn was plagued with doubts: about the strength of their bond, about Rebecca's circumstances upon her return to Portsmouth. He was unused to such misgivings, to dreary thoughts of any kind.

"There is still your Watts to consider," he said against Rebecca's silence, once their fellow passenger had fallen asleep.

She looked up at him. "Watts? I don't think that would be a good idea."

"It might mean, at the least, a modest return."

"It's too late for that. And they would look at it quite differently now—my name, the family associations, my depictions of the doctor's meditations on the more bitter of life's potions and disparities."

"They did not seem to before."

"That was beforetimes, when they considered the piety only and made no comparisons to my illustrations that have frightened them. There's a settled, well, a repugnance now. Successful publication would only open their wounds."

"Perhaps a pseudonym—"

"It would be all the same to them," she interrupted him and looked away. "How should that fool them now?"

He had, of course, no answer to her question. In her lucidity she saw clearly anything that might provide foundation to their further persecutions. He would not go against her wishes after all they had suffered together, after his headlong folly. He would withdraw the manuscript.

She looked out the coach window and said nothing more. It was clear she did not have it in her heart to speak further.

As the post rattled over the long miles and they maintained hours of silence together, he realized how often in her presence he had felt his own dullness in comparison with her agile mind and brush. At times this sense of dullness left him in a sort of self-induced stupor. She had been deeply appreciative of the efforts and risks he had taken on her behalf; she had had absolutely no one else to turn to. He had tempted her to become his lover. But he began to doubt her love for him now as they rode north in defeat.

Chapter 34

Thursday, July 10, 1746

Mr. Daniel Sanborn, Orange Street Tavern,
Boston in Massachusetts.
Dear Mr. Sanborn,

I have been charged by Rebecca to inform you of matters since her return to Portsmouth. So far as her guardians are concerned, she has accommodated herself to their wishes and protection.

She is to be married to Mr. Paine Wentworth, who was easily led to assume the young lady had come to her senses finally, as she really wished to all along, that he might soon be taking his rightful place beside her as lord and master. Colonel Browne, in relief one imagines, promised an ample portion and by all accounts the settlement is to be equally generous in turn, including, as I understand it, a handsome jointure of lands. Upon the third Sunday's reading of the banns, Mr. Paine's father, Jared Wentworth, Esq., pledged to build the bride and groom a fine house on family property in Kittery, and work has begun even some months before the marriage date. Among the Brownes and their closest circle, you, sir, would readily believe the atmosphere was tending toward the celebratory, if yet cautiously so.

I make bold to suggest that you and I might finally exhibit a degree of comfort and complacency, if we would only avoid fatuousness, over our ultimate success in unraveling the puzzles and dilemmas of Rebecca Wentworth—and steering her toward the safe harbor of matrimony, a situation that will provide comfort and fashion, for herself and her heirs, all their days.

As to your own reputation, Miss Wentworth wishes me to assure you that nothing has been tarnished. You are rather famously touted as the hero of an insoluble family drama, ever tending to tragedy, who has by singular efforts cut a Gordian knot.

I do think, if I may be permitted a personal suggestion, that you would do better to remain in Boston until all is quite settled and Rebecca fully enamored of her prospects for a new life. At that time, I will ask her to send for you, and you may return in proper, if wisely subdued, triumph.

> *Your respectful servant,*
> *Adeline Norris*

Sanborn began to see, as he suspected Miss Norris must have, visions of epithalamic revels in his head—organ music, flower petals, toasts and dancing, jovial (even florid) relations and friends. The only thing that unsettled him was a subsequent letter from Rebecca summoning him to Portsmouth sooner than he had hoped.

Monday, August 4, 1746
My Dear Mr. Sanborn,

Our wedding plans, previously expostulated by Miss Norris in her letter to you, have been moved forward considerably. No one but Mr. Wentworth, his father, and my guardians know, but I am with child, so this is the only course to take. I have made up my mind fully to this marriage. Mr. Wentworth believes the child his own, and I have not found it necessary even to assure him that such is the case. Would you please do us the honor of attending our celebrations, beginning the twelfth of next month, in Queen's Chapel and at the home of Colonel and Mrs. Browne?

The letter went on for two pages, but he read it all without comprehension. For God's sake, a child. What had he, her lover, expected? *Mr. Wentworth believes the child his own, and I have not found it necessary even to assure him that such is the case!* So they, too, had become lovers. She must have done so to seal this marriage, while absolving herself (and Sanborn into the bargain) of the early fruits of their reckless passion. She must have sensed her pregnancy early on.

And what could he do about this whole turn of events that would not be futile, or worse? Rush in and dishonor her while making a fool and a knave of himself in the process? "The young man who corrupted Rebecca Wentworth." He could hear them now. "A scandalous young bawd." And so on. She would be utterly lost. And he? He, the source of her "corruption" in their eyes, would be ostracized.

His actions had also assured, he saw now, that in another sense she would be lost to herself—she was to be a *femme covert,* utterly subject to her husband. Surely Rebecca had seen all this and had acted out of a sort of womanly courage and fatalism that would forever separate him from her. Everything had been settled and sealed, and there was nothing to be done but accept her choice and save his skin, just as she had saved her own.

1748

The Bill for ye more effectively preventing Cursing & swearing having been read three times, Voted unanimously, That it pass to be enacted. . . . Mr. Secretary bro't down ye above mentioned Bill & said Council were of opinion that said Bill ought to be perpetual.

> —*Journal* of the House of Representatives under the administration of Governor Benning Wentworth, Thursday, June 18, 1747

I hope no reader imagines me so weak to stand up in defense of real Christianity, such as used in primitive times . . . to have an influence upon men's belief and actions: to offer at the restoring of that would indeed be a wild project . . . and would be full as absurd as the proposal of Horace, where he advises the Romans all in a body to leave their city and seek a new seat in some remote part of the world by way of cure for the corruption of their manners.

Therefore I think this caution was in itself altogether unnecessary . . . since every candid reader will easily understand my discourse to be intended only in defense of nominal *Christianity; the other having been for some time wholly laid aside by general consent, as utterly inconsistent with our present schemes of wealth and power.*

> —Jonathan Swift, *An Argument against Abolishing Christianity*

Chapter 35

SANBORN PULLED UP in his chaise before Hawkshead Hall, home of Squire Paine and Madam Rebecca Wentworth. He had been commissioned to paint a mother-and-child, the heir apparent, who was now approximately two years of age. He expected three or four sittings, given their specifications, and had made arrangements to stay over at the Hall until completion. There had been a second child as well, a girl named Seafair of some six months now, but she was not yet of an age that her parents wished a portrait. However, as he turned his horse over to livery and walked up the cobbled walkway to the main door, Sanborn had every expectation of future commissions of the daughter and the squire himself.

The great house struck him as an odd affair, cultivating a rather too-refined European taste, perhaps. The roof of the edifice was surmounted by a balustrade, as if to form a high terrace from which to observe the grounds and the greensward leading down to the magnificent river. He could see extensive gardens and graveled walks bordered with box.

He was shown in to a conservatory of plants, an extension immediate to the house, the servant telling him that his mistress wished that the gentleman observe the room.

Sanborn looked about him. It was high autumn, but the large-windowed room was warm, despite two partially open sashes, and unnaturally late blossoms nodded from branches and stems. He thought that it would be like Rebecca to shun the conventions of background and request a painting in situ and detailed from life. He expected she would ask the same as to garmenture and attribute. It did not please him to do so, but he was being paid well and the lady required a certain amount of indulgence.

Feeling someone was watching him, he turned toward the doorway he had come in, and there stood Rebecca in a rich silk brocade dress of light blue, her abundant hair caught in the light and done up high on her head, looking every bit the lady of the manor. She rather stunned him, by both her beauty and the suddenness of her appearance, like some creature emanating from a better world.

"You've come then," she said and walked toward him with her arms extended.

"Did you for a moment doubt I would?" He took her offered hands.

"There were days, I fear, I was burdensome."

"If that were ever so, they are long past, madam." He made a little bow. "A beautiful room," he added, looking about.

"A little too English an indulgence, as my husband said when I proposed it, but, yes, it is, barring winter, my favorite place. My private bower."

"I noticed the comfortable chairs, the reading couch," he said, still looking around.

"Even in the depths of winter, this can be the warmest room in the house, if only the sun shines." She smiled and he was charmed all over again, as he had been years ago, in another bower, by a child in white.

If only, he thought. The previous winter snow had begun on November twenty-seventh, and held for twenty-six days. The deep snows lasted till the end of March, no men or horses able to break a way before that time. This room must have been miserable enough all winter, even with the heat of charcoal fires. And then after a brutal winter, the summer had brought a great drought, and many fires far off in the woods.

"That is well planned then indeed," he said, "if you have even a week or two in here between a November and April like the last." He smiled. "When I was shown in I had the feeling that you would

prefer the portrait to be taken here and to fully reflect the actual setting. Was I right, Mrs. Wentworth?"

"How did you know?" She offered a modest laugh.

"Our long acquaintance."

"Do you accept?"

"I'm here at your service."

"Then you've quite learned to expunge painterly formulas and
convention, after all," she said. She smiled playfully, as if to be sure
he recalled their long-ago discussions, as if she knew he had ex-
punged no such thing. She knew as well as he that every portrait
was an advertisement.

"Shall we agree on a precise site and background?" He extended
his arm for her to lead him.

She chose the couch, before a stand on which a pot of exotic
white blossoms he could not identify had somehow been forced
into late bloom. They discussed the angle of view, her and her son's
posture, the extent of background to be included, attributes for
mother and child, and several other incidentals. She then called for
a servant; a man appeared and was told to have the governess bring
in her son, Giles. While they were waiting Sanborn began to set up
his easel, canvas, and colors. Rebecca tried several postures for comfort and endurance of sitting.

When the child arrived, dressed in a darker blue petticoat that
complemented his mother's skirts, Sanborn was introduced to the
youngster, who was quiet with the stranger. They made some childish banter, the boy grew more relaxed, and they decided on a final
arrangement for the sitting.

He was extremely curious about the child, of course, but he
tried not to be obtrusive. He felt a certain affinity toward Giles,
perhaps merely an affinity he was all too prepared to feel since
Rebecca's letter two years ago announcing her new marriage date.
He noticed, as well, the boy's already abundant brown hair, hazel
eyes, and ears lying close to his head. He was reminded of a
drawing of himself Rebecca had executed years ago. She had
joked that he had the intense, narrow eyes of a demon. "Women
like them," he had replied. And they had laughed. Now the boy

had those burning, clear eyes. The child and mother seemed at their ease together.

AFTER THE first hour of the sitting, Sanborn changed the direction of their innocuous conversation. "Have you found you are able to draw and paint, Mrs. Wentworth?" he asked. He hoped to drop the colder formality he had observed upon first meeting her in the conservatory.

"Alas, Daniel, little more than an occasional watercolor, an acceptable glass painting perhaps. I find my duties here rather consume me."

He was not sure he believed her. "But you appear so . . . settled in these elegant circumstances, so at ease. You must have found being mistress of a grand house, and family, sufficient occupation and pleasure."

"It's true, I'm fully occupied. And I've come to love this place." She hugged her boy to her. "And my children." The boy looked up and smiled at his mother. He was being remarkably docile for a second hour of sitting. But he was a winsome child, and he basked in her attention.

"And where, may I ask, is Seafair?"

"Oh, with the wet nurse, who cares for her at such times as well."

Had she really given over her visions and illustrations, Sanborn wondered, so that she might finally live at peace with the world, share in its benefactions? He found that perfectly understandable— and preferable. Moreover, she had grown into full womanhood, he assured himself, and the authority and dignity of her position had matured her. Anyway, to accommodate the prick of skepticism now would distract him from his task.

His task was to embody her current serenity, the expression of this woman she had become. Mistress of a grand house, amiable hostess among the quality of town, beneficent young mother whose fruitfulness, like her full white bosom, adorned her, lover of flowers and clothing and furniture—these were the characteristics he wanted his painting to depict, the attributes his patron had hired him to display.

After the second hour he suggested they stop for the day. She did not ask to observe the painting's progress, and he was thankful for that. He would carry on some time longer to put the final touches on the first day's work, but he did not want to tire them, or become tiresome. He wanted, moreover, a freshness about the work, a freshness Rebecca deserved. He would try to please them both—Mr. Wentworth and Rebecca. Her portrait would display his lady to advantage in every conventional sense, yet he would try to suggest something of her extraordinary mind and spirit, or at least some individuality of face. He didn't know whether he could accomplish both goals, and if he found it was beyond him, he would have to suppress the individual in the conventional. But he was going to try for both, for something closer to Rebecca herself— not merely Mrs. Paine Wentworth.

Within another hour he had completed the first day's work. Then a servant showed him to his room where his bag had been placed and where he settled in for the next couple of days.

Later, before the supper hour, he met Rebecca in the garden for a tour, as he had requested. Being outside the confines of a city's house lots, the grounds and garden were extensive. They sloped down toward the mighty river—a series of paths and plantings and views that someone had labored to design and install.

She knew all the names of shrubs, trees, and autumn flowers, as if they were her particular charges. Servants had been cleaning up the beds against the arrival of deeper autumn. The areas of lawn were still green and half the trees still clothed in brilliant leaves. It was the cusp of seasons—looking toward that dreary time of ever-shortening days, drizzle, and snows yet to come. And the early evening light was pleasurable, the air bracing and pure. He felt a sharp flicker of old love at his heart, but he struggled to send it away. He tried to tell himself that he had not come here to be hurt. He had come to execute a fine commission, to exercise his own powers and talents, to embody a lovely woman and child in an enduring portrait. He had never been painting better, and his practice flourished. Portraits of the Paine Wentworths were but one more trophy to bolster his claim to be an English painter of the first order in the New World.

"The boy is remarkably well behaved, for one so young," he said, tiring a little of their conversation of the vegetable kingdom.

"He is sweet. He's never given his mother, or the servants, a hint of trouble."

"There seems a mildness to his nature."

"Just so," she said and smiled.

"And your baby daughter, is she much the same?"

"She's very young, of course. But she's a good baby. Mr. Wentworth believes she'll prove to be rather headstrong, and he may be right."

"It's very early."

She laughed a little. "She'll show us soon enough who she is."

"Her mother has been known for her headstrong trait."

She laughed again, more openly now. "As you well know, Mr. Sanborn."

"But even the headstrong grow to adulthood and find means to accommodate themselves to things as they are."

"It was ever so."

"And you are quite . . . content now? Here?"

She looked at him as they continued walking. "Who would not be, Daniel? There is a security here in our remoteness from Portsmouth as well, which I was glad to discover when the smallpox troubled town last year."

"I left town myself," he said. "I was one of several acquaintances who left." He did not tell her that he had escaped to Boston that June and July.

"The whole legislature nearly adjourned to another town for the duration," she said, "but they thought better of it, as if it would signal the Port were cursed, as some put it. Finally they believed such a move would be bad for commerce. So they stayed on."

"I heard something of that—"

"Nonetheless," she interrupted, "I don't know how I could live, now, without my children. They sustain me. And you see how pleasant it is here, in this removal from town." Her arm swept around the garden.

"There is a joy to life it is madness to avoid," he said. He looked at the river as they approached the grassy bank, boats and ships plying the tidal waters. Church spires lifted above Portsmouth on the opposite bank a half mile or more in the distance. Everything appeared well ordered and fitting at just that moment. He understood how she must feel, walking here in the sunshine on fine days, perhaps with her son, or her husband of two years. Save the sudden bludgeons of disease or domestic tragedy or war, one might come to see how well—yes, how beautifully—ordered things are. One might embrace life no matter what one had endured. Perhaps that, he thought, was her final accommodation, the flower of her maturity.

"I'm often uneasy close to the river," she said, as they continued their downward progress toward the bank.

"But it's radiant, and even more so in the full sunlight of an afternoon."

"Radiant, yes." They drew close to the bank. "But you see how dangerous it is as well. The currents, whirlpools, tidal surges and undertows."

"Of course," he said, as if placating her. "One must take care. A pilot is necessary. And it's no place for the casual bather."

"My aunt died in this river," she said, apropos of nothing in particular, so far as he could tell.

"Your aunt?"

"Colonel Browne's younger sister. She was not literally my aunt, but Browne elder-women relatives are by tradition called 'aunt' by all the children. She took her own life."

"Really? My goodness, Rebecca." He recalled Miss Norris's tale of family woes. "Why did she do it? Does anyone know?"

"She went mad in the middle of her life. Who knows the whys and wherefores of such things? They are more often a mystery than a puzzle with a solution, are they not?"

"I suppose you're right."

"Moreover, his grandmother, Elizabeth Browne, took her life as well. Nearly in the same spot—at the beginning of the old Indian wars."

He stopped and turned toward her. "Miss Norris told me of her. She said nothing of the particular sister, however. Does Squire

Browne then believe there's some family . . .—what would one say?—curse, or something?"

"Wouldn't that be understandable?"

"Yes, that there might be some familial . . . disorder, perhaps."

He did not say that such a legacy helped to explain her guardian's oppressive attitude toward Rebecca in the past. The point was plain enough.

She halted ten feet from the bank, almost as if she had been warned to avoid close proximity to the currents. They continued parallel to the stream. He avoided the darker subject now, as did she. It was better to feel the late sun, the salt air, the dry autumnal breeze. It was better to imagine oneself a proper heir to the richness of sun and garden, luxury and elegance.

They bantered as they returned to the manse. Neither of them seemed to have the heart to dwell upon old wounds or old difficulties. Rebecca, her son, and daughter too, were, above all, safe now. They had come to anchor in the placid harbor of Wentworthian largesse.

THAT NIGHT, however, his dreams were troubled. There was something of a woman in white beneath the waters of the great turbid river. He rose from his bed and went to the window. First light, duller than moon glow, swept the grounds beneath his second-story window. An edge of the river was just visible, the current a swift torrent of dark tidal flow. He turned from the window and began to pace. Why was he troubled? Why wakened? Over the past two years he had first learned to live with and overcome the pain of her absence from his immediate life, and he had felt gratified knowing of Rebecca's safety, of her elegance, poise, and beauty. She had entered life here. He had no idea what she had come to feel for her husband, but she loved her children—he was sure of that. But now, now: Was the pain he had long buried within him to be awakened all over again?

He returned to the window, to the dull light in the garden and the deep river below. Suddenly a ghostly figure stepped from the cover of a tree by the water's edge. A white cape and hood, almost the whiteness of ermine from this distance. A woman? The shade of the aunt, of the great-grandmother?

A small dog appeared suddenly beside her. The dog ran tireless circles tangential to her mistress's ankles. There was the appearance of a predawn ritual, together. The dog and the woman connected by affection, by familiarity and custom. Two creatures of the gray hour, the hour of crows, the hour of rebellion and quietude.

He ran downstairs in his bare feet, a fool who did not consider the proprieties. He ran to her out in the light fog on the grass between the walkways and ample planting beds.

"Rebecca! Rebecca! Is that you?" He did not know even what he said, or why, as he ran toward her. "What in the world are you doing?"

"Mr. Sanborn!" She looked at him in his nightshirt and flannel cap. He must have been, he thought later, an absurdly comical figure.

"The river!" He was inchoate and strangely inconsolable. He ran to her and held her, as if he were protecting her from the hungry river, as if he needed to feel the surety of her corporal existence. In her astonishment, in the entanglements of the small dog barking and growling now, in her sudden confusion, it was clear to him that she did not know what he wanted or what he was doing.

He held her. He kissed her brow and cheek. She was alive. He was sure of that now, as if that was all he needed to be sure of.

"You had been terribly close to the river." He couldn't ask her the question in his mind.

She pulled away and gave him a curious look. "I can walk close at this hour, with Misty here. She keeps me landed." She laughed a little. "She's my little protector. Together we can face the river, tread along its closest margins, and rejoin the rising day."

He held her still, at arm's length. "My dear lady."

"You were frightened for me," she said, without surprise or question in her voice.

"The river," he said again, as if that explained everything.

She stepped away and looked at him. "Yes. The river and I are like old friends at this hour."

He followed her, stepping in beside her as she continued up the incline toward the great house. They remained speechless for a time and watched Misty, once again settled into her revolutions about her mistress's feet.

"Is ten o'clock all right?" she finally asked.

"Ten o'clock?" he said, his mind still foggy. "Yes. For the sitting? Yes. Ten would be fine."

She looked at him, amused. For the first time he was painfully aware of the ridiculous figure he cut on the cold morning grass. He began to shiver; he folded his arms about him and let out a laugh.

Chapter 36

DURING THE SECOND SITTING, the little boy charmed him. Giles came out of the restraints of shyness from the first sitting. He began to talk in snatches, in phrases, and to get down from his mother's lap. He tottered around and gave rein to his curiosity about Sanborn's painting equipage.

The autumnal river fog had lifted and the morning was bright. Sunlight poured into the conservatory. Rebecca resumed the dress she had worn yesterday and her dress and hair seemed to glow in the light. Little Giles, however, was dressed less formally now. He seemed to act appropriately, as if considering his liberty of clothes. Rebecca indulged him rather more than most mothers indulged their children, but the boy was always well enough behaved, or at least in Sanborn's eyes. He had seen children who were raised under a strict regime, yet who were nonetheless downright feral in habit and demeanor. Somehow her milder presence restrained the boy. He would point at some piece of equipment or bladder of color and blurt out a sort of question: "That?" or "This?" Or some less recognizable interrogative. But he never grabbed or flung himself at physical objects that gathered his energetic interest. His wondering hazel eyes looked up directly at Sanborn for answers and assurances. His hands and fingers would reach out but refrain from touching, unless Sanborn handed him some harmless trinket. Then the child would take it, perhaps taste it, assess its solidity and reality and possible functions. Rebecca found these interchanges amusing. Sanborn's heart lightened in turn.

But the progress of the painting slowed over these domestic pleasures. He knew his ultimate patron, Squire Paine Wentworth, would want to see and approve the portrait before full payment, and out of the courtesy of a viewing, so Sanborn forced himself back to work.

"If you wish, Rebecca," he said, "you can have the boy out from under. I've got enough of him for now, probably for the finish as well. He may prefer other amusements anyway, a little less painterly tedium."

She called the governess, and the child was removed after a kiss from his mother. Sanborn could not tell whether Rebecca felt a strange, even awkward intimacy, as he suddenly did, being left alone in the room together. He had yet to see her husband, who had been away on some errand or another of commerce. They had barely spoken of him, or of Rebecca's life with the squire. There was only the abundant material evidence of polish, comfort, and gentility. And Wentworth had indulged her eccentric wish for an impractical room such as this. They must, he assumed, be on good terms, despite her original misgivings over his extraordinary unsuitability. To Sanborn's mind there was a mystery here. Had she seemed unhappy or disgruntled or under distasteful restraint, he would have understood better her reluctant accommodations to grinding necessity.

His only doubt was what appeared to him as both her fear and love of the river. For a brief moment he saw the Piscataqua River looming in her life like a great stream of ambivalence in the deeper currents of herself, an ambivalence she must have managed to suppress or ignore. Or, and here was that more comforting thought again, she had simply changed, "grown up," as people say, and found her proper place in life. What need one with visions when one had all this?

Such thoughts, as he worked on the painting with Rebecca looking at him, were not coherent. They were mere random flashes of intuition and musing, like fish spooked in their garden pool.

"He's a good little boy," Sanborn finally said, to stop the rattling voice in his own head. "You've done a wonderful job with him." He chuckled.

She said nothing at first, but only continued to observe him, as if merely watching him work entertained her. He was busy with a point of difficulty in the coloring of flesh tones, so he was able to avoid returning her gaze.

"Yes" she said. "He's a comfort to me, as I am to him." She laughed a little herself. "Mr. Wentworth loves him, also, of course. But the lad seems to ingratiate himself with his elders readily. He never demands much of us, and he has that easy and hesitant way about him, as you've seen for yourself."

"I see that, yes. He's a child easy to have about."

"And he loves to draw. Just silly things. Or just splashes of watercolor. I purchased a set for him."

"Is that so? Well, he comes by that honestly."

She hesitated again. "I've not discouraged him, though as he grows older I doubt his father shall want him pottering about with colors and canvases. Mr. Wentworth has already contracted a tutor for Greek and Latin, and mathematics, when the boy turns four or five. He's very ambitious for his son. I don't look forward to the days when, as a young man, he will be apart from me—in Boston and Cambridge, in London no doubt, even in Portsmouth still too busy to see his aging mother. So I make the most of it now while he is still mine." She smiled. "And my little girl will be with me somewhat longer. That comforts me."

"He will certainly have every advantage. It's a better life than, well, than some other. He shall never want." He looked at her. No, he thought, Giles will enjoy power and prestige, live an interesting life, and raise privileged children of his own. (Unless the boy foolishly were to cross his patrimony to pursue a life in painting.) What could he, Sanborn, have offered him in comparison? The greatest turn he could do the little boy—that he could do both of them—would be to keep his distance and let Giles's life run its admirable course. He lifted his brush, continuing to look at her. "And you are his true benefactress."

She gave him a curious look.

"Because," he added, "you chose all this."

"Well, yes, I suppose in a sense you are right, Daniel. But without the squire there would be nothing of all this for him."

"Of course." He smiled at her. "I mean to take nothing away from your husband, Rebecca. His good fortune is yours, and your son's."

Chapter 37

HE HAD BUT ONE MORE DAY with them. When the painting was finished, Rebecca looked at it curiously. "Ah, I see," she said. "I see what you were after now." She continued to study the portrait.

"After?" he said. "And have I succeeded then?"

"Certainly, Daniel."

"You used to chide me for painting within the proprieties. You find this one so still?"

"As you would wish, a necessary propriety." She moved around the painting to see how the light changed it. "But there is some new strength in your work, in your use of the brush certainly, I had not noticed before."

"Thank you. It has pleased my patrons as well."

"Then you are blessed," she said. He did not doubt her sincerity, but he could not keep himself from doubting that she wholly approved: she who had once told him that she believed only the truth of the inner eye, that very "truth" of an overbearing imagination that had run her afoul of the world.

The following day the squire was due home to express his own approval or disapproval. While they awaited Paine Wentworth, they took a turn in the garden before midday dinner, Misty making her revolutions about their feet. They spoke pleasantries and about the future of young Giles. Neither of them broached the issue of his provenance. It was as if no query were necessary. It was as if to speak of such things might curse them all. It was as if it would be far better to accept in silence the way everything turned out for all three of them.

THE HOUR of her husband's arrival set the whole household on edge. A hubbub among the servants announced that Squire Wentworth had arrived by the front door. Sanborn stepped into a room adjoining the conservatory so that he might peer around the corner of a window. A great silver-trimmed coach, emblazoned with family arms, had pulled up before the portico. A young servant in a blue coat, yellow cape and cuffs, and yellow velvet buttons was holding the four, large, beautiful gray horses to stabilize the coach. The coach door opened and another servant in similar livery helped the occupant out and down onto the drive. Without watching long enough to really observe Paine Wentworth, Sanborn ducked back into the conservatory. Suddenly he recalled Miss Norris's long-ago words: "Not only are such men unworthy of her, they will never understand her and therefore soon tire of her. She will live abandoned in her marriage." Still, Miss Norris, too, had finally come to her own accommodation—that Mr. Paine Wentworth was far preferable to a madhouse. And then Miss Norris herself had married the much older Abidiah Sherburne, her employer, within six months of his wife's death, much to the scandal of Sherburne's clan and circle.

Sanborn remained in the conservatory with the portrait, hoping he was not about to suffer an impertinent fop, while Rebecca and her children appeared at the door to greet the master.

Within minutes Rebecca and Paine Wentworth entered the conservatory. Sanborn stood and bowed round with the most polite and affable address he could manage. The squire made a little bow in turn, and Sanborn went up to him to invite him to view the portrait. All three moved toward the painting and then stood in silence while the squire took its measure.

"The painting is remarkable, sir," Wentworth said. "It looks to set a new standard."

"You're too kind, sir. I only wished, and bent every effort, to do justice to the character of Mrs. Wentworth and your son. Their beauty is their own."

"But you have caught them precisely, Mr. Sanborn. I haven't seen a portrait in Portsmouth or Boston quite like it." He stood back to observe the painting and slowly removed his gloves.

Sanborn knew he hadn't fully caught her extraordinary mind and spirit: That achievement was beyond him, and perhaps would have been dangerous to his trade in any case. "As long as it doesn't disappoint, sir," he said. "Then my task is executed to satisfaction."

"Quite, Mr. Sanborn. Quite."

Sanborn, who had seen Wentworth about town, believed him to be perhaps twenty-three or -four years old, about seven years his junior. He recognized in Wentworth that aggressive energy mingled with the optimism of a young man who devoted every vital hour to the accumulation of wealth. Yet he paid Sanborn—hired artist and guest—every courtesy due his position.

"You no doubt know Mr. Steele's view of English portraiture, Mr. Sanborn," he said.

"I believe I've heard it, sir. That we excel all others in the art of face painting."

"Precisely. 'Tis Italy for history painting, Holland for Drolls, and France for jaunty fluttering pictures, but England for portraits!"

"Indeed, Sir, my own training was in London—"

"So I understand, Sanborn. It shows here in the mother and child before us."

Here was a young man, Sanborn thought, who had already mastered the art of being at once aloof and at ease.

With a sweep of his arm and a hint of a bow, Wentworth led them into the dining room. The table was set in delicate china on a fine damask cloth. A glass of fine old sherry, pale gold and dry, awaited each diner—the squire, Rebecca, and Sanborn.

During the meal, the conversation turned mostly upon London, where the squire was due to return next month on business, even as he had but four months ago returned to Kittery from London.

"As the Congress of Aix-la-Chapelle is finally to bear fruit," he explained, "there are certain pressing matters of trade . . ." He broke off a moment. "I have been asked to represent Governor Wentworth, the trade interests of Portsmouth, as matters develop with France. Once we are assured hostilities have indeed ceased."

"You believe they really shall cease?" Sanborn asked.

"One cannot see the future, Mr. Sanborn. I fear the vagueness, the lack of stipulation that is, of certain boundaries in the treaty as proposed. But all Europe is exhausted with these wars, I really do think."

"For now, perhaps," Sanborn agreed.

"Indeed, sir. Only a fool casts his skepticism aside in matters of war."

"But for now, trade may be advantageous abroad."

"Neither I nor my father has ever visited London without some profit for our troubles. You yourself, Sanborn. Will you return some day?"

"I had once thought so. I'm not so sure anymore. Yet it's ever a delight to hear news of my old city."

"Ask away then, Mr. Sanborn. I may know something of your former associates."

"And the latest in painterly rivalries and fashion?"

"I'll do my best, sir."

They all laughed.

When the meal was over, the table cleared away, the cloth removed, and a bottle of canary and three glasses brought in, the squire offered a toast to "my charming wife, Mrs. Wentworth." Then he toasted Sanborn and his "most remarkable portrait." In his turn, Sanborn offered toasts to his "patient sitters" and to his "generous patron." He had been paid immediately and in solid guineas the agreed-upon sum, with a guinea extra in appreciation. Finally, Rebecca toasted the men. Bowing gently to her, they returned the conversation to London.

Yes, Wentworth assured Sanborn, his old acquaintance Allan Ramsay, the younger, was still fashionable and well employed. And, yes, old Hogarth, upon entering his fifth decade and about to set out on some latter-day Grand Tour, was, according to the best witnesses, still in full command of his overweening self-assurance and self-promotion.

"I was surprised to see him a man of small physical stature—I doubt he bumps five feet. I thought, seeing him at some distance, that he must rather have adopted the effrontery of his pencil and his tongue in defiance of the diminutive figure he cut in the world, than out of any more noble satiric motive." Wentworth laughed pleasantly over his wine.

"Well, sir, it's good to hear Ramsay's still employed upon faces," Sanborn said.

"Indeed. With, as I understand it, Hudson's Vanaken now much in assistance on the remainder of the canvas."

"I recall," Sanborn said, "when Mr. Ramsay suddenly became the new thing, about 'thirty-nine or 'forty. After Dr. Mead took up his cause. He had a way of laying in faces to make the flesh clear, transparent. I've never been able to replicate it. Said he learned it in Italy from Luti and Titian. His practice was to begin with a red mask and then build up the flesh with a toner of lake and vermilion—in a half-dozen layers, apparently."

"He is still known for his flesh," Wentworth said.

All three of them laughed.

"I would be pleased to carry any letters you wish to the city," Wentworth offered. "And a list of colors and supplies to Emerton's for shipment to you."

"It would not be an inconvenience to you, sir?"

"Not at all. Carrying lists for merchants is for me a commonplace."

Perhaps he had misjudged the man, Sanborn thought. Perhaps

Rebecca, too, had found him more than bearable. There was a certain charm about him, a worldliness and serenity about the justice of his place in the world that leavened the natural haughtiness of his clan. And, of course, he had won his prize, the beautiful Rebecca—the most exotic blossom in all Portsmouth.

The remainder of the day Sanborn spent in cleaning and packing his equipage and clothing. He walked out and took the early evening air. The Wentworths had doubtless connubial matters to catch up on, and he was relieved to find himself alone and at his leisure about the manse and its grounds. After a late tea, he withdrew to his chamber with a book from the library, an amusing collection of Addison's essays.

He read for a while but his mind began to wander from the page. Was she truly in danger from herself? The thought began to plague him. And could she really give up, essentially, her painting and drawing, and the visions that inspired them?

He would not allow himself to believe she had presented him merely with a mask. He had to believe everything he witnessed that indicated she was engaged in this life here, reconciled to reap the bounty of its beneficence.

But for how long? Are bounty and luxury and elegance enough? For perhaps one in ten thousand they are not. Or for one in a hundred thousand, not enough. Surely, however, for the whole general run of mankind they were enough: the only ideal worth achieving or, if necessary, cozening. But for Rebecca?

He recalled what Smibert had said. "Things are not ripe, not yet, not here, for the likes of Rebecca Wentworth!" Would there ever be a place here, as in the Old World, for a Mrs. Beale, a Clara Peeters, a Rosalba Carriera, for the others? Even the Old World had nourished few enough such women, and their lives, he seemed to recall, were the result of strange and fortuitous convergences—in addition to their prodigies and talents: as if the rarest strands of Fate had been woven to produce lives of passion and beauty and accomplishment. Yet who among the women Smibert had named would anyone call, as Miss Norris once had called Rebecca, "a dear little visionary"? A dear little prodigy perhaps, at most, had these others been called. Rebecca in her distraction had drawn and painted work that was beyond even these fortunate women.

And what had she become now? The doubts kept returning: Was she truly content, or was she merely resigned? Was she secretly afflicted still? Was she, in sum, a danger to herself? He had to believe—he must believe—in her reconciliation. Just as he had of necessity come to believe in his own narrowing reconciliation to his loss of her.

BY THE FOLLOWING morning, the sun rising into cerulean heavens, he convinced himself that she was no longer in danger. At breakfast, Paine Wentworth was again absent on urgent business. Sanborn had last evening properly taken his leave of the squire.

He dawdled some moments in the dining room before Rebecca arrived. For the first time he looked closely at a watercolor on the wall. Bright flowers, an unusual canvas but perfectly executed, the kind of incidental and innocuous painting Rebecca referred to earlier as what she might do on occasion. He looked more closely. The painting was a decorative confection, as if executed by some elegant mechanism. He could hardly credit the work to Rebecca.

She arrived at the table in a pastel yellow silk gown. They found it difficult to speak now in the hour before his departure.

There had been no mention of subsequent commissions, as he had hoped for, once satisfaction was secured. But he was not discouraged. There was time enough for commissions.

"That rather sweet watercolor behind me," he finally said. "Where did that come from?"

"Oh," she said, and laughed. "A product of some odd moment of leisure." She waved her hand as if to dismiss it.

"Yours?" He stood up and turned around to look at the painting again.

"Yes."

"It's well done, and surprisingly bright. And as to the flowers . . . accurate enough—"

"But it doesn't look like mine," she said. Her voice was composed.

"That's what I'd say." He returned to the table.

"Mr. Wentworth is pleased with one such as this, now and again."

"He would appreciate the elegance." Well, he thought, isn't dull elegance better than a madhouse?

She changed the subject to the coming season, their preparations, her worries over extremes of weather. They bantered through the rest of the breakfast hour. And then it was time for him to leave.

She accompanied him to the end of the front walk after the attendant announced that his chaise and portmanteau awaited him. She offered her hand. He bowed nicely and took it. When he could no longer hold her gaze he looked down and put her hand to his lips. Then he climbed into the seat and took up the reins.

"It does my heart good, Madam Wentworth, to see you settled and happy amidst your domestic duties and amusements."

"I'm settled, Daniel, yes," she said and smiled, as if to eschew the formality he had taken up again.

"It is a shame to flee the world."

"Perhaps you are right, after all, Daniel."

"That was a hard thing for a girl I used to know to admit."

She laughed. "It was a hard enough thing." She placed her hand on his arm. "Thank you, Daniel. I shall never forget your help, and your courage." He reached toward her and took both her hands. She smiled; her face lit up and understanding filled her eyes. There was so much still unsaid that he would speak. But he felt himself choke up. He feared tears would give him away. He turned from her and said merely, "Good-bye then, Rebecca." He snapped the reins and the horse jerked the chair into motion. As he hurried down the long carriage drive that wound from the house to the road, he glanced back once. She stood in her doorway now with more than a trace of sorrow on her face.

He loved her still, that was plain enough. But there had never been any hope for them, and he expected by now she considered that a blessing. If she would not stray too close to the river, there was nothing to fear for her any longer, and that for him was a blessing. Still, he felt sorrow and loss. But why should he? By now he was a confirmed bachelor anyway. His commissions were only from the very best people. He had his friends and amusements, his clubs and gatherings. And he had Gingher. There was nothing more to wish for, save continued health and commissions. He told himself several times, as he made his way to the ferry, "I will not despair. I will not despair over her. As she has the courage not to despair over herself."

He forced his mind away from Rebecca. He calculated that subtracting his fares for ferry and horse and chaise, he would clear—well, minus materials, of course—approximately twelve guineas from this handsome commission alone.

Still, this tack could not occupy his mind for long. He examined the nature of her world at Hawkshead Hall again and again as he rode on. Had she been destroyed as an artist to be saved as a woman? Had Smibert, the kindly old fox, tried to tell him that here, that now, it must be so? And if the incandescent artist had been tamed, what role had he, Sanborn himself, played in the long, tortuous way of her defeat? These were the gall and wormwood of thoughts he simply could not endure. These were doubts about her, about himself, he had no choice now but to suppress and deny.

Ultimately, he assured himself, he must conceive of her only as one who had come through, as one who had succeeded in life. Only a cynic would disagree, and he was not cynical.

He could see the ferry moored at its dock, the cattle aboard already lowing for the sense of merely wood and water beneath their hooves while the carts and chairs rattled aboard. He snapped his reins.

Across the river from the ferry he saw Portsmouth now, its streets and spires rising in the midday sunlight, the masts of ships swaying and flickering in the silver light rising off the water. He had never tried to paint the flashing masts of Portsmouth, as he had once long ago thought he might. If Rebecca had, he had never seen the painting. And now, of course, he had come to believe that she never would.

Marrying well had saved her, he thought. It was as simple as that. And it was time to let her go now and return to the prosperous life he had forged out of nothing, really, beyond his own talent and labor over the past seven years.

"It's time to let Rebecca go—and Giles, into the bargain," he repeated aloud as his chaise rumbled over the dock to approach the ferry waiting on the bright wide river. "It's time to let them go."

Reading Group Guide

Questions for Discussion

1. How is your experience of the story shaped by the fact that it is told from Daniel Sanborn's point of view? How would your experience of the story be different if it were told from Rebecca's point of view?

2. When first confronted with examples of Rebecca's paintings, Sanborn concludes that she is "alarmingly gifted in some incomprehensible way." How do you respond to this description? What expectations does it establish?

3. When Rebecca critiques Sanborn's painting of her, she describes it as "a necessary imitation of the best models," while he counters that it is "rather a kind of quotation." What expectations does this early exchange establish about their relationship and their respective attitudes toward art?

4. What do you make of Rebecca's more visionary paintings? How do they seem to be in keeping or at odds with her character? What do you make of the repeated assertion that Rebecca "paints what she sees"? What do you make of her question "How can there be light without darkness?"

5. How do Sanborn and Rebecca differ in their understanding of the economic value of the activity of painting? Rebecca is not averse to making money from her paintings—she attempts several times to do so. Why does she fail? Why does Sanborn succeed?

6. In what ways are Rebecca and Sanborn defined by class or social standing? What implications does this have for their behavior?

7. What do you make of Sanborn's obsession with Rebecca? How does the character of his obsession change over time? How does Sanborn's response to her paintings differ from those of others? How does John Smibert's response to her talents differ from Sanborn's?

8. What do you make of Sanborn's relationship with Gingher? Why does he take such an interest in her? Of his relationship with Miss Norris? How do the changes in Sanborn's own status affect his relations with these women?

9. How do the episodes in Blackstone affect your understanding of the period and the circumstances of the characters? How do you feel about Sanborn's return to Portsmouth with Rebecca? Was it a rescue or an abduction? Or both?

10. Do you believe that Rebecca has successfully accommodated herself to her circumstances at the end of the novel? Does Sanborn believe that she has?

11. Is there considerable irony, perhaps, in the conventional happy-ending elements of the resolution? If so, how does that irony fit the novel's themes of art, business, and individual freedom and self-definition?

An Interview with Robert J. Begiebing

Rebecca Wentworth's Distraction completes a trilogy that also includes *The Strange Death of Mistress Coffin* and *The Adventures of Allegra Fullerton*. Did you plan these books as a trilogy?

No. Only while working on novel number three in the early stages did I realize I could tie the two previously published novels together with this one, the "middle narrative" of an historical trilogy set from roughly the 1630s to 1850. From that point on, I was working within a degree of restriction, in the same sense almost that one is limited while working within a particular genre or poetic form. But often the restrictions, the demands of the form, or the series, or in this case a trilogy, challenge you in a new way. These demands might even result in a better, tighter book. I hope that's the case here. The reader will have to judge. I've wondered myself how many rather daunting series were started with the whole series in mind: Anthony Powell's twelve-part A Dance to the Music of Time? Faulkner's Yoknapatawpha novels? Trollope's Barsetshire series? And so on. And, of course, Cooper's Leather-Stocking Tales were not planned as a series or published in order. Finally, in 1850, Cooper published a new edition of the five novels, in chronological order this time.

Did you gain any new perspectives on the earlier two books by writing this one?

Well, this new one confirmed that I had to keep returning to the past to serve my muse, and that I had to keep returning to certain themes to serve myself. I guess I proved myself to be as monomaniacal as many of the authors I admire. I did gain a new sense of how the themes that interest me sweep broadly across early American history, and for the most part resonate for us still today. I think I also learned something about the flexibility of "historical fiction." I was able to employ (and enjoyed employing) a number of different genres along the way within the larger genre of historical fiction—mystery and crime novel, artist novel, epistolary novel, coming-of-age novel, business novel, the picaresque novel, the quest tale, and so on.

Though each of these novels is set in New England, they are set in different centuries, and you have described the process of writing about each era as "living in it." What insights did you gain about New England by "living" in these three different periods? What continuities or discontinuities did you discover?

I can only write about the past by immersing myself in the period I am writing about—largely through continual reading and thinking and fantasizing about the place and time and characters. This is a process that takes years (usually three to five) for each narrative. The insights I gained are, I hope, explicit in the texts, and to list them here would probably seem reductive or a little too pat. What one discovers most, I think, is the deep and lasting foundations (the continuity) of human nature over time—our foibles and our accomplishments; our folly and our intelligence; our greed, lust, and spiritual hunger. Maybe everything changes around us, but I believe more than ever that we don't change much in our deepest selves. Nor in our secret selves.

I did come to appreciate (not so much an insight) the sheer difficulty of survival with all the natural forces arrayed against one before industrialized humanity developed the technologies (and the culture of convenience) most of us take for granted today. That seems an obvious point, but only by living vicariously as I did in these former times could I really begin to appreciate it, or should I say "feel it." What I came to feel is something like the hovering presence of death that we all sort of know about but that these earlier generations lived with very differently and immediately. "In life we are in the midst of death" had absolute, real meaning once upon a time; it was not just one saying among many in a perfunctory religious service.

You say in the autobiographical profile that at one time the eighteenth century left your imagination "a little cold." Was there something specific about that period that left you feeling this way? What changed your perspective? What surprised you about the era when you did begin to read and write about it?

I think my problem was that I came to the eighteenth century through my literary training, mostly. I was young when I studied the eighteenth century in Britain and seemed to find the literature a bit chilly and dry, with a few exceptions like Stern, Swift, or Fielding. I came to know it as a time of conventionalized forms and rules and "neoclassicism." Those endless couplets, for example, as if some demonic machine were cranking them out. Of course neo-anything is going to be a lame spin-off of the original. And then there's that Age of Reason brag—the perhaps arrogant foundations of modern science, technology, capitalism, and so on. I had a prejudice, in short. But slowly I became aware of countercurrents in the century itself—the radical foundations of Western democratic revolutions, the visionary artists like Blake and Smart, the challenges to the old, essentially feudalistic, order from young Wordsworth and Thelwall, to name a couple. But America, for all our desperate aping of the British gentry among our rising classes, was another world indeed. Pre-Revolutionary America had its own Age of Reason, to be sure, but it was also here, across the pond, a time and place of romantic richness, irrational behavior and violence, wild-man capitalism and adventurism, religious enthusiasms, and almost continual warfare on the seas and in the wilderness, a time (like all times) filled with drunkards, politicians, prostitutes, and other obstreperous folk.

You have conducted extensive research for each of your novels. What characterized your research for *Rebecca Wentworth's Distraction*? What sources did you find particularly useful? In what ways was the experience of researching this novel different from the earlier books?

Researching this novel was faster than researching the previous two in the series. I think I'm getting better at it, more efficient, and I'm learning as I go along. I've developed my immersion process and refined it. I'm better now at picking out essential sources and telling details than I was when I started the trilogy. To name even the most useful books and articles would be a tedious exercise for me and for the reader, but there were some highlights I might point out. The archives of the Portsmouth Athenaeum, the Strawbery Banke Museum, the American Antiquarian Society, and the University of New Hampshire's Special Collections Department were indispensable. Mostly, these resources provided original sources of the period (published and unpublished) and a few data-based studies by modern experts. Diaries and journals are very helpful, such as those of James Birket, Andrew Burnaby, Alexander Hamilton, and Timothy Walker, who all saw eighteenth-century New England and Portsmouth and gave us glimpses of them. If I had to pick a single most-helpful source it would probably be the New Hampshire Provincial Papers for the 1740s—a published version of the court/legislative activity, day by day. This is a remarkable window into the doings and concerns, large and small, of the people and leaders of coastal New Hampshire and the immediate interior communities. But I also had to research the costume, the art, the military and militia, the taverns and byways, the business practices, and the religious beliefs and frenzies of our forebears. The research is, literally, endless, but one finally stops when the narrative is itself apparently "done." Or at least that's the way I work. I write the story while I'm researching the story, and the research doesn't stop until the story (much revised) feels "finished" to me.

Was Portsmouth a significant city in the colonies at that time?

Portsmouth was a significant commercial colonial seaport and the provincial capital with its first royal governor during the 1740s and 1750s. It was in the network of Europe's vast Atlantic trade circle at the time—fish, timber, rum, slaves, etc. During the decade my story covers the town had roughly 3,000 residents, growing up to 5,000 residents, and a considerable transient population beyond that, as did all seaports. (Compare Boston, which had economic troubles during this decade, at nearly 20,000 residents.) But Portsmouth was intimately connected by economics and politics to all the surrounding towns—a huge population base.

Your story makes evocative use not only of prosperous and settled Portsmouth, but also of the rather more volatile interior frontier. Was this juxtaposition inspiring to you as a writer?

Well, the frontier and its juxtaposition to the urban center was inspiring because the two ways of life demonstrate the reality of the colonies as they evolved from a "wilderness" filled with natural resources toward a nation of great power in the world. But more to the point, the frontier seemed to suit my tale of love, art, betrayal, and ambition. The newer (but by the 1740s not really "primitive") settlements to the west (those still east of the Merrimac River) became the locale for my exiled child-artist, the place of her maturing, the dangerous zone of the Indian wars, the area that even then was being so thoroughly exploited for financial return that my "little visionary," Rebecca, could hardly not remark on the destruction in a few of her paintings.

Once again you have incorporated some historical figures into your story as characters. Which are based on real people and why did you choose them?

I try to avoid having the more famous historical figures be main characters in my novels. It sets one up for having pasteboard characters pop up mouthing famous words, as if in a bad Masterpiece Theatre costume drama. But I do use the famous and obscure from history as supporting characters and as minor characters. In this instance there are just a couple out front, so to speak: John Smibert, the major Boston painter who came with Bishop Berkeley from England, and Arthur Browne, minister to the Anglican church in Portsmouth. These two were not only in fact there at the time, but my protagonists (Sanborn and Rebecca) could hardly have avoided them, given my story. In both cases I decided to use them because we have diaries and biographies of these men and a lot is known about them. This might increase the authenticity of the novel—of the imagined characters and action happening at that time and place. The "real" characters also give an important point of view on the conflicts and dangers the main characters face. I try to keep their consciousness and words true to what I've learned about them. Numerous other real people are referred to in varying degrees, or their family names used: Robert Feke, William Pepperrell, Governor Wentworth, Reverend Gilman, and so on. But my central characters are imagined, often from composites of people uncovered in my research. One example of a middling character's provenance: Captain Carlyle is in part modeled upon (or initially inspired by) one Captain John McNeil of Hillsborough—a six-foot, six-inch powerhouse who tossed a rival tavernkeeper through a window.

This novel shares an interest with *Allegra Fullerton* in painters and painting. Have you always been interested in painting? Are you particularly interested in American art? Do you have some favorite

paintings? What is the significance for you as a writer to tell a story about painters?

The painters in my stories are more or less stand-ins for individuals laboring in any of the arts. They just happen to be painters. We probably don't need another novel about a writer. Still, think about it: Can any person be stranger than that creature the artist? What is this desire to create art, to create it against all the forces of a culture that doesn't reward it or even want it? And this seems especially true in America where our artists—in nearly all media— have been and are now more than ever oddballs out. That's what jazz saxophonist Gerry Mulligan meant when he was asked in an interview why so many jazz musicians left America for Paris, or Rome, or Copenhagen, or wherever: In Europe, they love art and esteem the artist, he explained. In America, it is the businessman and the sports/entertainment celebrity we esteem. Mulligan spoke of how an Italian man came up to him one night and asked why this was so. It was a question the musician couldn't answer, beyond to say it just was so. For these and other reasons, artists of all kinds interest me, and not only because I'm a frustrated musician myself. And I've always sort of seen the artist as a stand-in for anybody who feels at odds with his or her culture. Some days I wonder if that might not be most of us. But then another day something happens and I get cynical again and figure we're by now a nation of robots programmed to consume.

I've grown more interested in the visual arts as I grow older. My daughters studied painting and drawing, and that caught my attention. I took a course in American art preparing for Allegra Fullerton. I research art history for my novels. I go to art museums now and feel moved by what I see in ways I never did before: if the art is good, if the art is an expression of something other than the artist's ego or some dry-but-hip theory about art or politics. I don't have any favorites, really. But I gravitate toward beauty, evidence of real dedication, and great skill. That means I often spend time, once again, with artifacts previous to the twentieth century. But from the period I'm writing about in this novel, in America in the eighteenth century, I doubt anybody outdid Copley.

Allegra and Rebecca are both individuals, women, struggling against the roles set for them in their time and place, their cultures. Mistress Coffin was also a woman out of her time and place, and perhaps that is why she was murdered; she made herself vulnerable by her boldness and difference, so to speak. I guess it's time for me to stop writing about women, though. I don't want to become a one-note novelist.

Were there actually portrait painters in Portsmouth in the eighteenth century?

Yes. There's been a considerable amount of work done on early portrait painters, even in Portsmouth, but many are still nameless to us. Most of the "names" came later: like Copley and Joseph Blackburn (who made it to Portsmouth). Joseph Badger was about in the 1740s but his work is notoriously naïve and literal. John Greenwood was in America between 1745 and 1752. And Robert Feke, an American rather than a Brit, was active very much during the time of Sanborn's Portsmouth adventures, but he never made it this far north, apparently. More specifically, Carolyn Singer's work on Portsmouth painters, if I have these numbers right, shows about fourteen surviving portraits from 1701–1725 in Portsmouth, mostly of merchants and their families. Clergymen, military officers, and physicians figure in also. Men and women were painted roughly in equal numbers. Thirty-six Portsmouth portraits from 1726–1750 survive. Blackburn signed his later, but most are unsigned. After 1750 the itinerant amateurs increased (for the more middle-class patrons), Karen Calvert's research reports. When I started, I had Blackburn in mind as my rough model, but I made Sanborn younger and got him into the busy port nearly a decade earlier. Such is the license of a fiction writer.

Why did you choose Daniel Sanborn as the point-of-view character? Was the story always told from his perspective? Mistress Coffin is told from two viewpoints, while Allegra Fullerton is narrated in the first person. What are the challenges and benefits of various point-of-view strategies?

I vary points of view among novels, and sometimes within novels, for a number of reasons. First, I like the variety; anything that makes a long process (like writing a trilogy over a decade) less tedious and more fun is good. The next issue then is what point of view (or points of view) is best for the tale—both overall and at a particular narrative moment? Once you ask that question, the writer's desire for variety begins to serve the story. These are always judgment calls and only the readers (and reviewers) know whether you've succeeded, made the right choices for them, too. Now we get to this particular book. Sanborn. Why him? Well, I wanted Rebecca to remain as mysterious as she could be (without getting melodramatic, that is), so, seeing her from the outside contributes to retaining her mystery and strangeness. Then, Sanborn is also an artist, a particular kind of accomplished, schooled, commercial artist. As such, he is something of Rebecca's opposite. He is a little too dull, too conventional (to say the least), and perhaps represents most of us when we are confronted by visionaries, geniuses, prodigies, or true artists and their work. He feels a degree of confusion, destabilization; his comfortable attitudes and mind-set have been challenged; he is a little threatened, yet fascinated. In short, he becomes rather unhinged by Rebecca, and it doesn't help that he is also, ultimately, falling in love. His voice and viewpoint were the point of view I found, mercifully, from the very start of the first draft. Sometimes you get lucky. Every now and then a little gift.

You mention in the autobiographical profile some of the themes that you feel tie these three novels together: the circumstances of women, the role of class, the dangers of religious fanaticism, etc. Why do these particular themes resonate for you as a writer, and as a person?

That's a hard one. "Only his shrink knows for sure"? I may be the last to know. But there is something, I suppose, to the saying, "It's a historical novel about the present." First of all, the themes have to resonate for me and for readers, I hope, because the issues they raise are with us today—in different forms, different degrees, different guises, perhaps, but still with us. Then, I have my obsessions. How does one escape them? I hope my readers share a few of them, at least. I hope readers think some of my own obsessions are still important to us all. If readers see no relevance to themselves and their world, I expect they won't read for long. On the other hand, I bank on readers' continuing interest in the foreign country of the past. Like all travel, there is a great deal of pleasure to be had in discovery, in difference, in the beauties and adventures of someplace new.

You have said that you enjoy writing historical fiction because you find the research involved stimulating. Now that you have completed

this trilogy, do you think that you will continue to work in an historical mode?

I don't know. Since finishing this novel I've been fooling around with some short pieces. And I've been working on and off since 1993 on a novel set in post–World War II America, largely in the Berkshires, but I haven't been able to make that one work yet. Maybe I can't write about the twentieth century. Wouldn't that be a ridiculous handicap for a writer? I do know that I don't want to write about contemporary suburbanites or urbanites up to their nostrils in angst. I just get bored with it. History, particularly New England history, for some reason, still interests me. So maybe I will return to the past. It's actually kind of pleasant, having just spent more than a decade on a trilogy, not to have a big new project under way at the moment. But I've never gone for long without an idea for a new book.

I wrote *Rebecca Wentworth's Distraction* to complete a New England historical trilogy that began with *The Strange Death of Mistress Coffin*, set in seventeenth-century New Hampshire, and *The Adventures of Allegra Fullerton*, set in nineteenth-century New England and Italy. When I was looking for my next novel project, I realized that there was not only a similar New England setting in my two previous novels, there were recurring themes. The historical circumstances of women, the enormous influence of social and economic hierarchies on people's lives, the conflict between the desire for self-expression and the pressures of conformity, the perils of religious fanaticism, the overwhelming yet confining temptations of material wealth (the American Dream?), and so on, all seemed to gather my interest. These themes, I realized, were essential to understanding our formative, early American experience between 1648 and 1850. But I had yet to fill in a huge gap: pre-Revolutionary America during that most revolutionary eighteenth century.

The eighteenth century had always left my overheated imagination a little cold, at least in comparison to the seventeenth and nineteenth centuries. But I was aware of a deficiency in my understanding and in my New England narratives. Then, by good fortune, I happened to attend, with my wife and in-laws, a series of summer lectures at the Wentworth-Coolidge Mansion and the Portsmouth Historical Society. The people of the colonial province of New Hampshire, beginning in 1741, started to fascinate me, and it is people (characters), finally, who make a novel. Thus began my two years of research into the people of eighteenth-century Portsmouth and New Hampshire—their houses and accoutrements; their reports and maps; the records of their wars, governing bodies, and personal joys and fears. And there were others to enlighten me—early travelers to the province and later historians.

I gradually began to see that I could, with a third novel, tie the two previous novels together through common themes, genealogical and economic lineages, and the historical settings. More than that, I could develop another central thread introduced in *Allegra Fullerton*: the complex, ambiguous role of the artist in the New World. The more I thought about it, the more it seemed to me that this mysterious creature, the artist—in her desire for independence, for creative fulfillment in conflict with the imperatives of social and aesthetic orthodoxies—is a metaphor for us all, for our secret, innermost, rebellious selves. Once I found my way to Rebecca Wentworth (my artful American prodigy) and Daniel Sanborn (my academy-trained British portraitist), I was off once again on yet another journey into the useable past.